THE LUCKY MAN:
AN ACT OF MALICE

Dear Reader,
Thanks so much
for spending time
with my book
All my best
Monika.

THE LUCKY MAN:

An Act of Malice

A novel

by

MONIKA R. MARTYN

BOOKS

Adelaide Books
New York / Lisbon
2021

THE LUCKY MAN:
AN ACT OF MALICE
A novel
By Monika R. Martyn

Published by Adelaide Books, New York / Lisbon
adelaidebooks.org

Editor-in-Chief
Stevan V. Nikolic

For any information, please address Adelaide Books
at info@adelaidebooks.org
or write to:
Adelaide Books
244 Fifth Ave. Suite D27
New York, NY, 10001

ISBN: 978-1-954351-97-4
Printed in the United States of America

Coming to this page of a novel is a milestone for any aspiring author. The end of a journey and a new beginning. While writing is often solitary, we never arrive here alone. For my husband, Kevin, who believed in this story and my talent. Love you always.

To the memory of my Mama and Papa, you remain the light in my eyes. Forever.

My siblings, Gerti, Maria, Lini, Fredi, Roswitha, Gundi, and Anita, I love you all, and Marlo Ackerblade for her input on my cover design.

Barb Martyn and Rick McAskill for their unwavering love and belief in me.

And, for the beached whale in Mexico that inspired this novel.

Contents

PART 1
AN ACT OF MALICE

Chapter 1

Malice

When Jack awoke, it was already too late. While adrift in his self-inflicted state, he was comfortable enough until he lifted his head and opened his eyes, then he thought, no—no, this can't be happening. While fighting for clarity, images played out like a foreign movie he couldn't understand. In this predicament, Jack was the star of the show, but the boring details of what was real and what he couldn't put his finger on intruded on his reality. Who were those people? Despite trying, he couldn't make sense of them.

"Wanna go for a ride, Jackie?"

It was a sinister question. Jack consented because it was best to get away from the two menacing faces. Besides, he wasn't in any condition to answer reasonably. Jack remembered the jolt, the motion of being shoved off, a weightless sensation of being adrift on the water.

"I need to get back to my hotel room." He mumbled. Instinctively, his arm shielded his face. The stench of cigarette smoke blown into his face milked the saliva in his mouth and he was close to vomiting.

"Sure, Jackie. Soon."

Jack kept his eyes on them as their faces moved away. Only it wasn't they who were moving away. It was him. Drifting on the open water, he watched the shoreline. Lit only by a sliver of a pale moon, their silhouettes faded, and the dark shore blended away to nothing in the darkness. It was his fault. He had crossed the border of being drunk to inebriated hours earlier. He had only a sparse recollection of how he got to the beach and into the canoe. Although a few reminders explained part of the story. The pain in his toe throbbed, and Jack remembered stumbling on something painfully hard on the beach. It turned out to be a harmless coconut, and he was barefoot.

"Don't mess with local girls, Jackie. Or else!"

The threat surprised Jack. He'd been having fun since he arrived at the resort three days ago. Images of the beautiful women who flirted with him flashed at intervals. But the goon wasn't referring to them. He was referring to the beautiful woman Jack met on the stairway. The beauty, whom he left abandoned in his hotel room, triggered a series of questions. What was her name again? Kelsey, Elsie, Chelsie. She might have been Hawaiian, but that didn't come up in conversation. There had been so much more to their intimate dialog.

"Okay," Jack remembered consenting. Nodding wildly made him dizzier than he already was—to play along was his only choice. They didn't look like the type of men who listened to reason. And Jack wasn't in the mood to explain that the woman had made the first move. She seduced him; the temptation was more than the lure of her smile.

An image of his last conquest broadcast behind Jack's closed eyes. She'd been descending the stairs. She wore a dress which made her look like a mermaid rising from the deep sea, and she bewitched everyone.

But Jack knew she had chosen him because he had his own set of magic skills that didn't need translating. After leading her to the dance floor, they engaged in risqué dancing that somehow moved them out onto the terrace. A storm that came out of nowhere put an end to her undulating rhythm. He ran with her down the corridor and snagged a bottle of champagne on the way. She had an enchanting laugh, and they ended up in his room. Jack couldn't decipher how those two goons fit into the equation. He had never seen them before. But he had felt their presence when he came out for fresh air. As if they'd been waiting for him.

Because of them, he slipped beneath the rope that cordoned off the cliff. He knew from an earlier excursion this stretch of beach was treacherous and off-limits to guests. But they followed him. He smelled their cigarettes, and their menacing voices loomed closer. The whole time, he didn't understand their insinuated threats. He had taken off his expensive ostrich leather shoes; he needed them for the wedding. And they were too slippery on the rough-hewn steps leading to the beach. It wasn't a conclusion he came to until after his feet slid out from under him. He clung to the rocks without falling all the way down. The storm and sea spray waxed the lava rocks, and he skated downward, scraping his knee and elbow. He was sure of the bruises, blood was a possibility, but he hadn't time to assess his injuries. They kept coming closer.

"What's the hurry? Jackeeeee."

No one called him Jackie. Not even his mother. They cornered him on the slice of the beach the tide was busy reclaiming. Jack stumbled not only on the coconut but on his own feet. And then the lone outrigger canoe became his only refuge. Wading knee-deep in the foaming water, he hoped the distance and incoming tide would save him. He wobbled when the retreating waves sucked the sand out from beneath his feet. Even the goons struggled in the strong surge. To free his hands, Jack set his shoes on the canoe, but regardless, he was outnumbered.

"Nice shoes, Jackie."

If they wanted the shoes, so be it. The uncomfortable shoes pinched mercilessly in the toe, and Jack never liked them anyway, but Tessa insisted all the groomsmen buy them. He shouldn't have worn them dancing or on the beach; he couldn't save them now. And Jack had nothing on him worth bartering. He left his wallet, phone, Rolex, and gold chain on the dresser in his room.

"Have a seat." The lanky one offered, and he meant the canoe.

Jack obeyed. Blinking and straining to focus, their faces swam in the soup of his confusion. He'd been drunk before, but this sensation was entirely different. Had someone slipped something into his last drink? No. Who would have done something like that in a classy place like this grand hotel? Jack saw the flick of a lighter. They lit another cigarette; the glow of the light made their faces more sinister. It was best to play along.

"I'm being nice to you. Normally, I'm not this kind to tourists who fuck around with what doesn't belong to them. Lucky, you caught me in a good mood."

Confused, Jack thought he meant the canoe. He couldn't possibly mean the lovely woman who spent the last four hours in his company of her own free will. He learned long ago that certain women would never consort with men like this threatening creep. And it could be a case of mistaken identity. Earlier, he overheard them whisper, "you sure that's him?" "Sure. Same sissy-boy haircut, that fancy suit."

So, they saw him as an easy target. But he wasn't a sissy. His job required an impeccable appearance. He chose the haircut from a trendy magazine, and the Armani suit, well, it was a birthday present from his sister. He looked good wearing it.

Jack tried to clench his fists and brace himself, but his arms and legs tingled as if some spell cast them in bronze. Did he smack his head on the way down? A strange numbness spread to all parts of his body, even his lips. A sharp shove sent him adrift. He knew the feeling; the canoe rocked beneath him on the current. When he opened his eyes, he saw the lights of the hotel, the solar lamps that lit up the garden, and the beach shimmer in the distance. He consoled himself. If he could keep his eyes on the lights, he'd be fine. But getting away was his safest choice. A question carried on the current floated toward him, "you sure he'll float back?"

In the stillness, Jack waited for the answer.

Jack awoke in the fine weave of his own making and a nest of solitude. During his fitful sleep, his body retaliated from the abuse it endured, and crippling pangs forced him to vomit. He mustered enough strength to hoist himself over the lip of the canoe. Bent over, he deposited a small offering onto the eager waves. It was payback.

Since arriving in Hawaii, he'd indulged in liquids but few solids. The options on his menu had been a tempting assortment of delicious babes. He spent hours rubbing lotion onto their lithe bodies marked by interesting tan-lines. An efficient set of waiters served him fluids with the slightest wave of his armband and supplied never-ending drinks, served in hulled-out coconuts, pineapples, and fancy, long-stemmed glasses. He was simply following the advice; to stay hydrated. But this was no ordinary hangover. He knew from experience that a trip to oblivion left its mark but not a death grip. Somehow, he had ingested something far worse than too much booze. His body ached, thirst crippled him, and he moved as if he were a marionette, and someone else was pulling invisible strings. Even his eyelids seemed alien, and all he saw was the waking of shades of blue.

Before opening his eyes fully, Jack listened to make sure he was alone. Or had he imagined them all along? The singsong of the ocean next to him confirmed his suspicions. He was still in the canoe. He hadn't dreamed that part. But the stench of their cigarettes and the lingering odor of halitosis no longer afflicted his nostrils. It was time to float back, crawl into his bed, order room service to settle his stomach. Hopefully, the lovely woman kept his bed warm.

When he moved again, pain exploded in his body. A tear split his silk slacks at the knee, and his big toe throbbed, swollen and purple. When he tried to sit up, his elbow gave out. Crammed, as he was into the small compartment of the canoe, explained the pain. The space between the two benches wasn't large enough and even under normal circumstances his long limbs would have trouble fitting.

Inventory. Jack needed to make a list of what, where, how, and when. If only thinking didn't hurt as much as it did. Fighting through the fog, he floated in a confusing void between the reality behind his closed eyes and the mist of make-believe. Instinctively, Jack knew the truth, and he raised himself to stand to confirm his suspicion.

There was no mistaking what the shades of blue on blue meant. "I'm fucked." Jack realized the futility of his predicament. Hawaii and the entire world had vanished. As far as he could see, there was nothing but rippling waves heaving the canoe softly as twilight teetered on the horizon. Jack wiggled his toes; even his shoes had disappeared. He was utterly alone.

Chapter 2

Gone Fishing

Kai's belt clanged on the floor when he slipped from his standard uniform. He kept a set of modest clothing in his locker; it was all about keeping up appearances and on many occasions, hotel guests paid him to go fishing. They craved that authentic feeling of being on the open water just as he did. The freedom of drifting in his outrigger canoe with nothing but the vast sky as a witness bridged gaps. And reeling in the freshest catch was something to brag about. Though most of the guests preferred the luxury of fishing from a hired sportfishing boat; expensive boats he couldn't compete with. But even the wealthy wanted to experience nature. It happened often enough and supplemented his income.

"Anything I need to know about?" His replacement asked.

"I guess we had a storm. Nothing out of the ordinary."

But that was a lie. After one o'clock, Kai fell asleep. Creases from his shirt sleeves still marked his face. He missed the storm that unleashed the gale-force winds and sideways rain. Based on the weather report, it pegged the gale making landfall at around two o'clock in the morning. He slept through the storm, unleashing its misery on the beach, and it didn't spare the garden either. However, seasonable weather was part of the routine. A trained ground crew would sweep any detritus away; the guests would never see the ugly side of things.

He was on his way to the hotel kitchen. When he woke, it was to a craving for a bold batch of coffee. Not the diluted stuff they served to guests in giant vats, but the real coffee brewed from ground Kona beans. Even a whiff of the aroma was reviving enough. He stifled a yawn into his sleeve, swerved among the trolleys, and waiters dressed in impeccable uniforms on his way to the kitchen. Despite sleeping for almost three hours on his shift, he couldn't shed the exhaustion and sleeping on the job wasn't ideal either, pangs of guilt shadowed him. As the manager of security, he should lead by example, but no one needed to know.

"What a storm!" The cook said from behind a large tray of steaming frittatas.

"Seen worse." Kai grinned. There was no reason to broadcast.

"Want some breakfast?" She winked.

Being on good terms with the morning staff came with edible benefits. Cook fed as many of her friends as she could. It was a shame how much food they tossed in the trash each day, and she knew Kai, just as she was, had a tough time making ends meet. It wasn't a secret that locals scrimped on every dollar. A free meal might seem trivial to the fat-cat hotel guests, but to Kai, it meant making ends meet at the end of the month. Everyone Kai knew worked side jobs or had other means of making a few indiscreet dollars. Kai preferred fishing. Cook had a way with her hips when she slipped into a grass skirt and swayed to the rhythm of the Pahu drums.

"To go, please." Kai winked back. He filled his empty bottle with ice water. Being management had other perks too. But this morning, a free meal might appease his rumbling stomach. He needed something to settle the churning acid in his gut. Like everyone else, he had bills he couldn't keep pace with. It was akin to running a Marathon in bare feet and never seeing the finish line. For that reason he couldn't afford to linger in the kitchen and chit-chat either. He had swung a deal with a new fusion restaurant, and he had promised to supply a variety of fresh fish seven days a week. Kai fought hard to land that lucrative gig, and it meant a pocketful of silent money he didn't need to declare. Even in the quiet morning, above the clatter in the kitchen, he could hear his father's medical bills screech like a child having a tantrum. As if he could ever forget about the demands on him.

Cook loaded an assortment of meats, fresh bread, fruit, and eggs into containers for Kai. At the front desk, he asked if anyone requested a fishing adventure, as he did every morning, but because of the weddings, the guests were fickle. They preferred the leisure of lounging by the pool and engaged in other, tamer, adventures. The backdoor closed with a soft thud and he filled his lined backpack at the grumbling ice machine. He slunk around the back of the building unobtrusively, as if he belonged there. Being on the security staff meant he knew precisely which corner was on camera and learned which frangipani shielded a person from the roving eye of the rotating lens. He set up the system to his advantage, but he wouldn't take the amenities for granted either. Everyone bent the rules a little; it was about survival. The trick hinged in allowing the rules to snap into their proper place unobserved.

He walked through the garden, inhaled the scent of flowers, and was eager to set out. Broken branches, tender limbs, and leaves lay scattered on the ground. It was worse than he suspected, but cleaning wasn't on his duty roster. He whistled while walking, and his gear rattled, keeping pace with his brisk stride. Cool against his back, he felt the weight of the ice. The collapsible rods strapped over his shoulder jiggled. If this fishing gig panned out, then he and his family would be out of debt in ten years. He prayed silently as if it had the power to forbid more unforeseeable circumstances. As it was, the financial burden of managing his household, and that of his father was a strain. But it was a family matter. His father's circumstances were an unfortunate accident, leaving him encumbered with partial paralysis. It had been the company's fault. But who were the Hales to battle a conglomerate and win? Such cases only ever won in the court of Hollywood, and the Hales didn't have a suave leading man to steal the show. Instead, his father's finances broke the piggy bank. The price of his medication crippled him as much as the accident and infected the whole family.

In the garden, Kai spotted two new hires. He'd have to have a word. They were workers who had the enviable talent of hiding among the foliage and vanish. But it was more complicated than that.

He stood hidden among the palms and watched, to have anyone fired meant keeping tabs on them before making a move. The ugly, lanky one had already trespassed onto the hotel's sacred ground and swam in the pool after hours as if being entitled. And last night, Kai spotted them on camera when it panned the dance club. "Who let them in?" Mingling with guests was a no-no.

Kai looked over his shoulder to ensure no one was following him. He was essentially breaking the rules too. And the two creeps he had spotted smoking in the garden would use it to their advantage. They weren't the sort to butt out because of a sign. With little effort, he ducked beneath the stretchable rope. He found it interesting that guests complied with the warning sign, but trespassing onto the dangerous terrain wasn't on their agenda. The stern warnings worked, and it scared anyone foolish enough to consider ducking under the thin rope. One look over the edge made descending the stairs leading to a secluded beach below hazardous. Kai should know. He knew the beach like the back of his hand, and he read the tide schedule as if it were his bible. On the first rugged step, he hoisted the backpack and settled his rods against his back. With his right hand, he felt his way down. Not that the wall would save him, because one slip could mean the long and uncomfortable trip down. The wall was for balance. Spreading out before him was the morning sun. It was stretching its limber arms across the ocean; igniting the waves with diamond-studded capes. Kai loved the sea, but at high tide, it could be especially dangerous. Beyond the stone wall that served as his safety net was another beach. From above, when the tide retreated, it looked idyllic. But at high tide, it had the suction power of a vacuum and would grind anyone dumb enough to try into a fine powder. It was foolish to tempt fate and climb into the abyss. He'd been on that secluded beach only once. It was a lesson in who wielded power. The ocean took its gold medal and delivered its warning.

By the rights of the moon's passage, the tide had vacated the small beach but was predestined to return. Kai had minutes to retrieve the outrigger canoe, which, according to tradition, passed the heirloom from father to son. A beloved third-generation ritual. Christened Kilo by his grandfather, its meaning had roots in the phrase to observe. Or at least that was the explanation he handed out to the paying clients he took fishing. Ironically, only those who were observant asked about the meaning. The romantic version of Kilo meant Stargazer. And for as long as Kai could remember, Kilo had been an integral part of his life. He had learned how to swim and dive before reading and writing. Walking and talking came sometime between.

At the inception of the hotel, which traced its lineage back to 1929, there had been a small pier for wealthy guests to moor their yachts and sailboats. But this stretch of beach had other ideas. It shirked the dock, the luxury boats, and imported planks on the very first storm that breached the seawall. Now only one post stood like a sentinel against the endless circle. And this morning, it dumbfounded Kai. He spun in the sand and did a full three-sixty. The post was solid, but his canoe was missing.

"What the…?"

Thoughts of the two goons on the landscape crew reared. Kilo had survived hundreds of storms and inclement weather. The nylon rope was brand new, and Kai could trust his cleat hitch. There wasn't a storm that could untie it. He reached for the rope and confirmed his suspicion. Someone had untied it. But doubt also made him second guess, and he scanned the waves for a sign of his beloved canoe. His wife, Cindy, often teased him; he loved the canoe as much as her. Which was ridiculous but also a little true.

"Kilo!" Kai scanned the waves. He dug around the low-growing shrubs that climbed up the sandy slope, and his oar was where he had buried it. So whoever took the canoe, if that happened, was up the creek without the proverbial paddle.

"What the hell!" Kai reached for his forehead and scratched. He moored Kilo to this post for fifteen years; for as long as he worked at the hotel. He hid his backpack next to the oar; his decrepit old cooler vanished with the canoe. There was no question about the rods, he had to take them with him. The damn things were an investment he couldn't leave behind.

By the time he reached the top again, the sun had spread its arms across the entire ocean, and he was sweating. He'd stink

THE LUCKY MAN: AN ACT OF MALICE

in less than an hour. On a mission to get his canoe back, he stomped through the garden. His flip-flops slapped the soles of his feet with each step. He approached the smaller man first and grabbed his shirt collar. As creepy as the goon was, Kai could be just as menacing when he allowed his barrel body to do the talking.

"Seen my canoe?" His face dived close, but he regretted it instantly. The guy reeked, and his breath was in dire need of mint candy, a wad of gum, or, better yet, a dentist.

"What the fuck! What canoe?"

There was no way to prove it, but the guy was guilty. He had expected Kai's assault and the question. As if he had rehearsed for it.

"Don't play dumb. Where is it?" He tightened his grip.

"How the fuck would I know? Am I your boat keep?"

"What about your greasy friend?" Kai inflated himself to his maximum height.

"Ask him!"

Kai let go of his collar, but the wrinkle his fist made in the cloth remained puckered. He glared for a few seconds to stand behind his threat, then swung east toward the orchid garden. That is where he suspected goon number two was wasting his time. Sure enough, the lankier one was leaning against the trunk of an ancient koa tree, plumes of smoke gave him away. Shaking his head to the rhythm of grunge music, he didn't hear Kai's approach.

"You seen my canoe?" Kai took a softer tone.

"What if I have?" He didn't bother removing the cigarette dangling from his mouth. A hint of malice slunk across his eyes.

"Please." It was as cordial as Kai could muster. He'd swallow his tongue alongside his pride if it meant getting his canoe back.

"I didn't say I did. I just wanted to know what it was worth to you."

Cat and mouse. Kai was being played. He considered his options before making his move. For starters, he could reprimand him for being in the pool and the club. That would take care of strike one and strike two. But players like this one understood the loopholes. Under no circumstances would Kai offer up a ransom because the river of greed would never dry up. He needed to barter.

"What will it cost me?" The direct approach was the only way out. That way, he wouldn't offer something too costly.

"How about a good word with the boss? Ya know, about moving me off the push mower and onto the riding mower? Getting too old for sweating the heavy stuff."

"Consider it done."

"Fine. Not that I have anything solid, but I saw some tourist jerk around down there last night. Sometime after the storm."

"You saw him with my canoe? Can you describe him?"

"Not really. Tall and skinny. Definitely a tourist."

"Nothing else?"

"He was drunk."

"Did you see him take my canoe?"

"Not exactly. Just putting one and two together. Saw someone go in that direction," he pointed toward the forbidden beach, "and now, like magic, your canoe is gone. Them tourists are forever takin' what's not theirs."

"Was that the only time you saw this guy?"

"Think so. You know them haoles all look alike."

"No. Not all mainlanders look alike."

Kai stormed off. If by some chance a hotel guest took the canoe, it improved his chances of recovering what belonged to him. In his fifteen years of working at the hotel, most guests behaved well enough. Sure they indulged, but he couldn't imagine any of them taking his canoe. It was old. Decrepit even. Besides, the hotel offered access to sailboats, Seadoos, catamarans, yachts. Kilo was out of their league. But he wanted to explore one more option. Regardless of the canoe's vanishing act, Kai had to keep to a schedule and catch a few fish for his client. He needed to have a word with the paragliding crew. If anyone could spot a vagrant Kilo, it was them. Kai needed to keep a level head. He had already made a series of errors this morning. When he reached the beach crew, they were in the middle of their routine safety checks.

"Hey, Skipper. Got a minute?"

"Sure, what's up big kahuna."

"My canoe's missing."

The skipper dropped the parachute lines and motioned for one of his staff to take over. He led Kai toward the shade of the tiki hut.

"What happened? You think the storm took her?"

"Not likely. Heard a rumor that some tourist was messing around with it. Not sure I'm buying. Have some bad ones on the garden crew."

"Seen 'em. Bad apples them boys."

"If you could keep an eye out. Please."

"You bet. I'll remind everyone. It'll turn up. No worries."

Kai wanted to believe him, but for now, he had worries. Time was wasting away, and he had nothing to show for his efforts. His slippers had difficulty keeping pace with his stride, and the soft sand impeded his speed. By the time he reached his truck, a pattern of sweat streaked his shirt. He was miserable.

Chapter 3

Aloha

Myra craned her neck to get a better view. In less than half an hour, she'd be landing. The voice of the pilot came through the garbled microphone. Introducing himself again, he announced that they were within an hour of landing. For a second, she didn't think she could stand it. And he rambled on about the local temperature, that they were chasing the tail end of a storm, but sunny skies were included in the price of any Hawaiian hotel. He laughed at his own joke, but Myra didn't care about the weather. She cared about getting there and seeing her son.

Below her, the ocean did its best to tame her restlessness. The dramatic topography shifted; cobalt blues merged with emerald greens as if someone had spilled buckets of paint. The turbulent surf ran across the palette, skipping across the whitecaps. At the approaching altitude, she could see a pod of dolphins. Agile, they broke the surface and sliced through the water. Beside her, John finally closed his laptop and unplugged his earbuds.

"See anything?" he asked, leaning toward her.

"Only beautiful water and there, just there, are dolphins." She pointed on the glass.

"Beautiful." He checked the large face on his watch.

Time meant everything to her husband. Time that he didn't have to spare, time meant money and business. It still surprised Myra that he had agreed to come to the wedding. But then Brody was almost like a son, and he'd been a part of the family since Jack and Brody met in playschool. And if it hadn't been for Dr. Hibbert's advice to take a break, she doubted he would have made the concession. He took her hand and wrapped his paw-sized hand over it.

"Are you excited?" He asked.

"Aren't you? We haven't seen Jack for months." Verbalizing Jack's name made her smile.

"Has it been that long already? Maybe we can convince him to move back. You could use your persuasive powers and talk sense into him. It's harder to say no in person." John squeezed her fingers.

"Haven't I tried everything? I'm still not sure what happened. Something we aren't privy to. I bet Tessa had something to do with it."

"Now, don't go down that road. Tessa makes Brody very happy. And Jack is right; he needed to find out about the world. We've always sheltered the children too much."

"Well, Jack isn't a child anymore. He's a grown man. I hope you're right about Tessa."

Myra closed her mouth and ended the discussion of Tessa. She had a feeling, but John traded heavily in reason, and she liked to run away on the heels of instinct. When Tessa first arrived on the scene, Myra recognized something unfamiliar in her son; something she hadn't seen before. It was innocent fun between college friends at first, and none of Jack's girlfriends ever tempted him into something tangible. Tessa, however innocently she played it, changed the game. Myra noticed how Jack's eyes zeroed in on her. A whole script of an unspoken dialog lurked behind his big eyes and full mouth. Jack was keeping something vital from everyone. When Tessa's intentions radically shifted focus and chose Brody, Myra breathed a sigh of relief. Fate spared Jack until he made another even more startling announcement. Without anyone knowing, Jack found a job on the other end of the country. The news rattled the entire family.

John sensed both Myra's pulsing joy and dread. Something about Tessa bothered his wife. As a man, he saw Tessa from a different angle. She had attributes and the gumption to use them to her advantage. He couldn't deny that he was glad too, that Tessa had set her sights on Brody. When the news became common knowledge, Myra breathed again and gushed. She couldn't do enough to ensure the couple's happiness. Myra never said it was a narrow escape, but he had seen the look in Tessa's eyes often enough too. She hungered for Jack and hid behind Brody. And as close as they were as a family when Jack moved away, John knew something was amiss.

"It's too bad Michael and Stacy couldn't come."

"Well, the timing is bad. I need Michael for the merger, and Stacy, well babies, have a way of changing everyone's flight path. We're going to be grandparents in a few weeks."

"I'm so glad you took the advice to take time off. I rarely get to have you to myself. But, I promised, I won't harp. Let's enjoy Hawaii and each other. And time with Jack."

Below them, the topography continued to change. The string of islands came into view and gave away their secrets. Volcanoes and cliffs dipped their feet in the water while pristine strips of sand frolicked in the foaming waves running to make landfall. Anchored sailboats, yachts, and catamarans plotted a sporadic pattern in the crystal clear water. The plane continued dropping altitude. Myra's ears popped, and the pressure eased. Mansions and homes sprung to life. They could discern people going about their business.

"In less than half an hour, we'll be at the hotel. Have you heard from Jack this morning?"

"Not yet. You know Jack, he's never been a morning person. It's kind of cruel to arrive at this hour."

"Do him good."

Myra gripped the armrest when the plane landed and skidded to a halt. They had arrived.

Myra couldn't stop herself from twitching in the back seat of the car. Despite the flight landing on schedule, everything took too long. Even the hired shuttle, as it sped through the quiet streets, moved too slow. At the hotel, she was out of the car in an instant. She sailed through the revolving doors of the hotel with a singular thought. Jack. Where is my Jack? Coming in behind her, John managed the luggage, the monotony of the check-in, while she scanned the lobby.

Anxious, despite the uneventful trip, Myra stood in the grand entrance. She didn't expect Jack to be pacing with impatience; she knew him better than that. Instead, she expected him half-asleep, lounging on a rattan chair, barely able to keep his eyes open. Tessa had done her homework when she chose this grand hotel for her wedding venue. A stunning woman dressed in a tropical sarong greeted Myra with a frangipani lei. The custom was charming. Myra scanned the lobby and gazed at the stunning staircase. In each direction, the architects had seen that the view was a drawing card. But Jack disappointed her. That he should oversleep on their arrival was unexpected. She texted him, "we're in the lobby. XO."

"He must be on his way down." She smiled when John joined her. The porter would meet them on the eighth floor with their luggage. Myra stared at the screen waiting for Jack's reply.

"Do you have his room number?" John put his hand on the small of her back, guiding her toward the bank of elevators.

"He's two doors down from our room."

"We'll knock and wake him. He probably had a late night."

"Probably." Myra tried to take it in stride and cover her disappointment.

"Look!" John pointed toward the vast terraces and infinity pools drifting toward the beach. But the star was the calm ocean lollygagging sideways on the blond strand.

"Gorgeous."

The porter thanked John for his tip. He left them on their own after suggesting they call on him should they need anything at all. A maid had tentatively knocked on their door and offered her help in unpacking. She did so with quiet efficiency. John led Myra to the balcony. The view was as stunning as the brochure proclaimed. But Myra had a hard time keeping her disappointment in check.

"Room service? Or the terrace?" John slipped off his jacket and folded the cuff of his shirt halfway up his arm. He wasn't a fan of the lethal combination of heat and humidity.

"Should we call his room?" Myra unfolded herself from the delicate pashmina scarf.

"Myra. He's a grown man."

"I know. But ..." Despite being downcast, she tried to tease a smile on her mouth. "I'll change into something more suitable. The terrace, I should think. Not that I expect anyone from the wedding party to be up this early."

"Good. Ready in ten."

John pulled Myra toward the long bend of his body. He could easily have tucked her under his armpit and kept her there, but he had seen the storm cloud set in his wife's eyes. It was best to allow her to fight for composure unseen. After thirty-five years together, he knew the tricks. The tricks were a simple balancing act. What he understood was this: nothing stood in the way of her children. Ever since the nurse laid Jack into her arms, Myra became the lioness of the pride. He often watched her shower Jack with kisses when he was little. On those long nights when both mother and child should have been sleeping. Myra exuded a fierceness of protective love that he could never match or claim for himself. Two years later, when Stacy arrived, Myra blossomed with a gentler love. Michael rounded out the foursome, and John knew when he met his match. And despite denying that she loved one child more than the other, he had seen it. It was always Jack. Jack resembled his mother not just physically but also in temperament. Stacy and Michael were replicas of the Spencer side of heritage. But Jack inherited something from his father too. A gift for numbers.

"Ready." Myra stood in the doorway wearing a pale pink sheath-dress.

John whistled when he saw her, and Myra understood that John had never loved another woman as he did her. There had been some minor infractions. She was never blind to the insignificant markers of lipstick on the collar of his shirt. She wasn't faithful to his love either. If push came to shove, she knew she'd choose the children over John. Not that she'd ever be forced to make such a choice. John had all the qualifications of a good husband and provider. Because of John's drive, they were wealthy. But wealth also came with a price tag.

"I'm surprised you're not tired," John said.

"I slept on the plane," Myra picked up the keycard and handed John a blue bracelet he was to wear around the hotel. It was the ticket to paradise, and every wish would be at his command. They had given her a pink one.

The door clicked behind them, and Myra led them toward Jack's room. She knocked louder and waited, holding her breath. Her sandal skimmed over the carpet woven in an impossible pattern of blues, olives, and rust. No answer. John didn't bother to point out that Jack might very well be asleep in the bed of a conquest. Jack's prowess wasn't a secret, and his son was a bit of a player, and even Myra wasn't blind to her son having a way with women.

"Hungry?" John offered Myra his elbow.

They took the elevator to the terrace floor. Set on a stunning terrace, a cornucopia of breakfast dishes arranged in crystal bowls, chafing dishes, and tiered plates whetted their appetites. As soon as they were seated, the aroma of warm bacon tempted John. Despite being on a restrictive diet, he'd treat himself. Myra most often settled for a plate of fruit, and cheeses.

Then she'd eat nothing again until noon. She had discipline in spades.

Most of the tables were vacant. Their waiter, as he served them coffee, explained that eight-thirty was the magic number. He mentioned that the hotel had booked two weddings back to back; they were bursting to capacity. Myra buttered John's toast with jam. She ate little but pretended to enjoy the sweet pineapple and mango.

"I guess I should thank Tessa and Brody for dragging me away. Absolutely stunning."

Over the clatter of dishes and cutlery, the hum of voices, the ocean still had the lead in the show. Lazy waves dragged away pieces of the morning. Myra inhaled deeply. The ions supercharged the air, and she reluctantly allowed herself to relax into its draw.

"Beautiful setting for a wedding. I wonder what Tessa's connection is to Hawaii? Did she ever mention anything to you?" Myra took a small bite of cheese.

"No. Frankly, I thought she'd jump at our offer of the beach house in St. Kitts."

"I did too. I felt as if she were trying to snub us. Choosing Hawaii is a long-haul trip for many of us."

"Maybe she thought St. Kitts was too small." John defended Tessa.

Myra shrugged her shoulders and bit her tongue. Tessa. But John was right. That their home on St. Kitts wasn't good enough was insulting, and Myra believed intentional.

"Oh, look! There's Brody." John rose.

Chapter 4

Tap out

Under the intense glare of the morning sun, Jack splayed his fingers and gingerly peeled the layer of silk from the gash on his knee. The saltwater softened the scab, but it didn't make it any less painful. He had done a number on himself. Wincing in pain, he remembered something else from the foolish episode that sent him sliding down the path. He shouldn't have been there.

Not that it mattered now, but the fall ruined his slacks. He pictured his sister admonishing him, then she'd wrap him in a hug. Even drifting on the ocean thousands of miles away, he could envision his sister and her emerging belly. Within a few weeks, he'd be Uncle Jack.

Pulling on the last corner of the fabric, he winced again. The spray of saltwater wasn't exactly pleasant on open sores. His elbow throbbed whenever he moved his arm and was already a horrendous shade of purple. He couldn't extend it for the swelling. For the moment, paddling was out of the question, and he didn't have an oar. Is this where the phrase stemmed from? The irony wasn't lost on him. Although it was impossible to tell time, he figured his parents had arrived at the hotel. His mother would make an entrance, she always did, and he hated being the one to disappoint her.

"Mom. Come find me." He said into the breeze that skimmed over him.

In the canoe, he was vulnerable, but without it, he'd be fucked. He had already taken the drawstring from his slacks and unbraided it. At first, he thought he'd tie his hand or ankle to the canoe in case a wave swept him overboard. But he had to think that through. Out on the open water, every decision mattered. He already regretted tossing the plastic bottle. That was epic as far as stupid went. Not that he knew how to make a still to purify water, but everything on the canoe was a tool. And the three inches of liquid in the bottle was the best he ever tasted. Now he understood that on the brink of desperation, he'd drink rainwater from a puddle. He wouldn't be choosy.

For the last hour, he tried to piece the vestiges of the night before together. From what he could recall, he pretended to have fun. That was until Brody elbowed him. They were ordering a tray of shooters at the bar when she appeared on the upper landing. Gracing the stairway, she scanned the crowd below. Suddenly, her exotic eyes, like a giant jet, her gaze landed on him. He excused himself. Brody whispered, and gave him a shove, "go for it, Buddy." Had she singled him out as a target? The possibility was there, but why? To be fair, there were several good-looking men in the bar and on the dance floor. But it seemed she had zoomed in on him. Jack didn't question his skill with women, yet he had to concede it was possible.

"I'm Jack Spencer." He had offered her his hand. Over the loud music, he thought he heard her reply, "Kelsey." But it might have been Chelsie or Elsie. She took his hand, and never letting go of his eyes allowed him to lead. As if she didn't want him to see anything but her.

"Champagne." She said when he asked her about a drink. And so it began. She wasn't into small talk, and, instead, they communed via body language on the dance floor. Risqué is what he would have called her lithe and fluid movements. Somewhere along the way, she had danced as a professional. His friends gave him the thumbs up whenever their girlfriends weren't looking. Tessa sent him a look too, one that didn't need decoding.

Tessa. She was the reason he had indulged in more alcohol than usual. They'd had a blow-out in the corridor. It took all his resolve not to warn Brody off. His suspicion that she wasn't all she claimed held true. But Tessa wasn't a fool. She also held a trump card, and without flinching, she'd use it to her advantage. But did Tessa have something to do with his predicament? Was it possible?

"You say one word to Brody, and I'll show him the pictures."

Tessa didn't raise her voice when she threatened him in the corridor. Instead, she hissed with the lethal accuracy of ice. Confessing to Brody had occurred to him, but the price and the consequences were enormous. He couldn't risk it or wound his best friend as the truth would.

Groaning, Jack extended his leg over the bench seat. His body was seizing up. Not knowing how he got into this predicament wasn't the biggest quandary he had to battle. Thirst nearly made him lick the waves that spilled over the rim of the canoe. And he lived on the high note of expectation. Any second now, he'd hear a plane, spot a helicopter, or see the stern or bow of a ship coming to rescue him. As it was, not even the sky produced anything interesting. Cloud production was at a standstill.

He had wiggled himself out of his briefs and was wearing them as a hat. Even the early sun had the power of a death ray. Not that he couldn't handle heat or sun, he played tennis for hours in the unforgiving heat of a court. But this was different. There was no escaping. He buried his feet under the spare vest and put the other one on for safety. He had tied the thin rope around the life jacket he was wearing and fastened it to the canoe's metal ring.

"You don't like Tessa, do you?" His sister asked him again as if she hadn't asked it before. Seeing his sister on camera, while she patted her bump, swelled Jack with pride. It made the distance more bearable.

"Of course, I do. She's marrying my best friend. It's best I don't like her too much." He stretched his mouth into a charming smile. But Stacy was like a hound.

"Well, I don't. Something about Tessa gets under my skin. I can't deny she's gorgeous. I've always said that. But! There it is. It's not that I don't want Brody to be happy, I love him like a brother, but I still think it's a mistake."

Stacy and Brody had a fling once. They kept it a secret, albeit everyone suspected something. Then Tessa arrived and put an end to things. He understood Stacy's resentment.

"Well, you know I want nothing but the best for Brody. He's been my best friend since we were four. Despite our misgivings, which I might say are completely biased, Brody is utterly and completely in love with Tessa."

"Yeah. He can't see past her boobs."

"Stacy!" Jack knew what she meant. Tessa had it in spades. She oozed with exotic sexuality that made men adore her, and women hate her.

"Besides. Do we know anything about the fantabulous Tessa? Where did she come from? Her family history."

"Does it matter?" Jack defended Tessa, which surprised him. Tessa had no history. She came out of nowhere. For that reason, he hired a private investigator when Brody announced their engagement. False step number two on Jack's part.

To appease his rumbling gut, Jack feasted on his thumb-nail. He had already tried to scoop a handful of fish, little darting silver bullets, out of the water without so much as touching one. Jack was glad he didn't bring his watch; it would be cruel to watch the minutes eek by. A change in the weather made the water too rough to stand, and he felt too weak. Whenever Jack exerted himself, his muscles burned from lack of fluids and calories. "Any minute now," he told himself to appease the dread spreading from his gut upward. He hedged his hope on his mother. They were undoubtedly wondering where he was. Jack was hoping his mother would panic when he didn't show. Brody would have told them about the woman he met. But then again, the entire wedding party retired long before he and his date did. They were still on the dance floor when the storm hit. Then, another fact smacked Jack's memory into running backward. When he needed to step out for a breath of fresh air, he delivered his dance partner into the safekeeping of Brody's brother. The transac-tion took less than a minute, and he knew she was in good hands. Although she turned her lips into a sultry pout when he left, she complied. Outside, leaning up against the wall were two shadows. They were smoking. Were those the same guys on the beach? He overheard the word haole. He knew it as a derogatory term for tourists when used with the word fucking. That they were there, on the fringes of his memory, startled him. He didn't think a luxury hotel like The Grand would allow locals to loiter either. Mistakenly, he assumed they were off-duty staff, there to mingle with guests. But that night, he didn't care about such details. He needed to clear his head, and he suspected that his dance partner was a local girl too. He remembered concentrating his thoughts on the sliver of the moon. Clouds zoomed past it as if they were in a hurry to get where they were going. Someone mentioned a storm, and on the horizon, he saw lightning split the sky.

Back inside, somewhat clearer from the fresh air, he took over on the dance floor again. It was the last time he saw anyone from the wedding party. There were half a dozen other couples left in the club, and the skeleton staff was busy collecting glasses and wiping the tables and gleaming bar. When the thunder cracked, it surprised everyone, and it didn't arrive alone. The wind unleashed its fury. It took care of the deck furniture and umbrellas, chairs, and plants slid across the tile floor, seeking shelter up against the glass. A few minutes later, the power went out, and he, with his date in tow, ran. On the way, someone handed him the bottle of champagne. A faceless waiter. That's how that happened.

Jack, nestled into the spare vest, buried his face in his hands. Frustration got the best of him. He had three suspects that he could lay the blame on. Tessa. The two creeps who sent him adrift. And he couldn't rule out the pretty woman: coincidence or fate? It was simply too confusing a riddle to solve. Exhausted from overthinking, he dozed; there was no telling how long. He drifted on the memories that trespassed and confirmed his suspicions that the two men outside the dance club and on the beach were the same. But why had they had it in for him? He had never met them before. Since arriving on the island, he hadn't so much as had the smallest interaction with any strangers. Not true, he retracted. Strange men. He hung out with the wedding party and met three pretty women by the pool. He had a few words with the bartender, a friendly chap who was the beneficiary of his generous tip.

"Who the fuck?" He asked himself. The utter frustration of his situation, the unsolved riddle, brought tears to his eyes. He bit down hard on his teeth. There was no fucking way he would tap out of life this way. If he couldn't paddle, he would swim.

Chapter 5

In Your Shoes

There was always a kick to his senses whenever Bruce unlocked the door to his room. Stale cigarettes, the lingering skunk odor of his dope, dirty laundry, and sweaty bedding assaulted his nose. But Bruce didn't give a fuck. It was his room and his to do with as he pleased. He set his sports bag on the layer of dirty clothing carpeting the floor. He gave the door a swift kick, then bolted the latch. He didn't need an audience barging in on him. And worse, he didn't need to hear his mother harping at him from the ratty Lazy Boy chair on the lanai.

He peeled his sweaty uniform off and flung it toward the hamper. Without shame or turning away from Wayne, he stepped into the nearest pair of surf shorts he found on the floor.

"You think he floated back?"

Bruce knew the question had plagued Wayne all morning. At least, he had the brains not to ask the stupid question in public. Besides, Wayne was a coward and only good for one thing. A steady supply of smokes and beer.

"I don't give a fuck! And it's the last fucking time we're talkin' about it."

"I just think we should…"

Spurned by the provocation, Bruce sailed across the room like a clipper in a storm. He slammed Wayne against the wall. The violent shove surprised Wayne, and his head ricocheted off the wall. Bruce invaded with all his height, and the pressure he applied on Wayne's throat did the talking. The sharp glint in his eyes seconded the motion that the debate was over.

"What did you score?" Bruce asked, removing his hand.

"An iPhone, earrings, a watch. You?" Wayne coughed and instinctively massaged his throat. He rummaged in the lining of his jacket and pulled out the goods.

"Let's see." Bruce lowered his voice.

"Gotta keep an eye on that security twat. Kai or whatever the fuck his name is. Thinks he's some sort of cop, fucking lolo." Wayne was desperate to regain Bruce's favor.

"Good stuff. That's an X. Nice haul." Bruce flattered Wayne.

"Cufflinks, a bracelet, not worth much, a wad of twenties." He unzipped his bag to show off his share. What he didn't show Wayne was the stashed at the bottom of the bag.

Working a side job was getting harder. Most hotels had a Big Brother system on every floor, every aspect, and every corner. A surveillance camera filmed guests and staff alike; monitoring each movement and keeping a record on film, like a movie shot on location. Filming twenty-four hours a day wasn't easy to work around. A person had to have quick fingers and finesse. Wayne had that gift. He might even concede that Wayne was a better thief, but he would never say those words aloud.

"Hey, mind running the fence. Mother's been barking at me."

Asking Wayne to fence the goods conveyed confidence and was a better compliment than words. One Wayne would understand. Bruce unfolded the bundle and counted out the bills.

"Twenty, forty, sixty, eighty, one-hundred, one-twenty." Despite knowing exactly how much he had scored; he made a show of it. The fruits of labor but not harvested entirely from one hit. He had taken some money from the bar last night at the end of the shift when the staff was too tired and eager to get home. It was one of those opportunities. Take a little, it will go unnoticed. Take a lot, and the game is up.

"Two-hundred and forty." He took one bundle and gave the other to Wayne.

"Nothing better than instant cash." Wayne kissed his share. Wayne was sentimental and more so now that he had a kid. He was forever contemplating shit and asking him for an opinion on life's biggest questions.

"See ya!" Bruce unlocked the door. "I got shit to do."

He slapped Wayne on the shoulder and ushered him to the front door. Bruce hadn't been lying when he said his mother had been harping about getting stuff done around the house. But first, Bruce had one more thing to take care of.

Alone in his room, he peeled off his sweaty tube socks. They stank. Wiggling his toes, he made a mental note to get a sharp knife and trim his toenails. He listened for footsteps in the hall before unzipping his bag. Crammed beneath an extra set of dirty clothing were the shoes. He'd never seen shoes like those before and couldn't stop himself from caressing the bumps on the leather. He'd lied to Wayne and said he had thrown them in the dumpster. But the smell of warm leather hooked him. That jerk had worn them on the beach. Idiot. Running his nose over the leather, he inhaled. A gold Gucci emblem shone in the light sliding in through the slats. He slipped his feet into the cool loafers, and they fit like Cinderella's glass slippers. For the first time in his life, Bruce understood the worn-out cliché: fit like a glove.

Chapter 6

Ruled by Instinct

The chair scraped the tiled floor when Myra rose for the embrace. She laid her napkin on the table; she was bursting with a million questions. But John hadn't stopped pumping Brody's arm long enough to allow him an escape until now. She had a soft spot for Brody too. He was like an adopted son, and as children, Jack and Brody were inseparable. It wasn't until Tessa arrived that their friendship made the inevitable detour. As it should.

"Brody. Tomorrow's the big day." Myra kissed him.

"I can't believe it's finally happening. But to be honest, I can't wait for it to be over."

"Stress. I'm sure. How's the bride?"

"A ball of nerves. All I can say is that the sunset better complies." Brody rolled his eyes. "I'm not even married yet, and I'm already in the doghouse." He pointed to the tan line his sunglasses left. His tan also enhanced the whiteness of a brilliant smile.

"A bit of makeup will cover that. I have just the shade. It won't show in the pictures." Myra was dying to ask about Jack.

"Will you join us?" John asked.

"Maybe for a quick coffee. I still have a list of things to take care of. Where's Jack? Sleeping it off?"

"Haven't seen him yet. We knocked on his door."

"We had a fun night. I'm not surprised. Last I saw Jack was in the arms of one exquisite woman. I've never seen Jack so taken."

"Really? Tell us more so we can tease him." Myra elbowed Brody and pretended to care about the woman who could steal Jack's attention away.

"We were having fun on the dance floor when she came out of nowhere. Like an angel. No, let me rephrase that. A mermaid. As the groom, I'm supposed to be blind to such things, but that woman would make a dead man take notice."

"Wow. She must have been special. Any other details. Where is she from? Her name?"

"I told you all I know. I never spoke to Jack again."

"Well, that explains his absence." John tried to console Myra.

"Is there anything we can do to help with your list of duties?"

"I wish. But there isn't. But please, I want you to relax and enjoy the day and the island. If I don't see you again, but I'm sure I will, I'm in room 1010. Tessa's in the penthouse suite."

Minutes later, they were alone again. Brody heeded the call of duty. While they were talking, his phone vibrated every few minutes, which could only mean the demanding Tessa. John stabbed the last few pieces of juicy pineapple on his plate. He considered getting another bowl full. Myra glanced around the tables and evaluated every woman. There were no candidates that matched her idea of what Brody was describing. She knew Brody's exaggerated description was merely that: exaggerated. Like a mermaid. As if? She shook it off, and, lost for words, waded into silence.

"How about a walk on the beach? Before it gets too hot." John suggested.

"I'd like that."

She took John's hand, and they wound their way along the terrace leading to the half-moon beach glistening in the sun. While walking, she expected to hear Jack call out to them, "Mom! Dad!" She could picture it happening at any moment and holding her breath, she anticipated Jack running toward them, they had so much catching up to do.

They followed the flagstones to the beach. Small crabs scurried sideways, creating an intricate pattern on the sand, and the sandpipers chased the rhythm of running waves. It was beautiful. But Myra sorted what she heard from Brody, all the while smiling into John's eyes and pretending that she was okay. She couldn't make sense of the information. Would Jack trade her in for a woman he had just met? Never. As a doting mother, she wanted nothing more than to see her children well married, loved, and planning a future with someone special. It had been an absolute joy to watch Stacy fall in love, get married, and explore parenthood with a man who adored every complicated nuance within her. Michael, well, she was sure that that special woman waited around the corner. And Jack, it would take an extraordinary woman to ensnare Jack. She'd have to be adventurous, good-natured, and fun. Beautiful was an option. Although it wouldn't surprise her if Jack brought home a woman whose smarts were the appeal. If only she could see him and ask about the woman who kept him away.

On the soft sand, Myra slipped off her sandals. She made exact replicas of her feet as she walked on the edge of the running waves. As quick as she could make her prints, the waves erased them. As if she had never existed at all. John was busy watching the paragliders skim across the blue sky. He was deathly afraid of heights. On the plane, he took a mild sedative. But for John, it had more to do with not having the floor beneath his feet. At his height and weight, he was a foot-ball-player-sized man. During his college years, he had toyed with playing as a professional. But business sense won out over desire. An excellent choice, Myra always thought.

"You okay?" John asked, squeezing her hand.

"Fine. Just surprised is all."

"Me too. But as Brody said, they'd been partying pretty hard for days. It was bound to catch up with them."

He didn't want to repeat that Brody had said Jack was leaning on the wind. That he had consumed every tropical booze concoction served to him since his arrival. Drinking wasn't unusual for Jack. But Brody's casual remark made it sound like a problem they'd been avoiding. He could see the admission landed like a lawn dart on Myra's heart. She had a habit of twirling her diamond bracelet when she was biting her tongue.

"I know. It's just that when I last talked to Jack, he sounded so happy, so full of joy at seeing us. He said he had a surprise in store for us. I'm disappointed that some woman would, you know, take precedence over us. It's not like Jack, regardless of how pretty a woman tempted him last night."

Their shadows walked ahead of them on the sand. The dark silhouettes signifying the difference in stature. Myra kept her words in check. There'd been many women who cruised past Jack's life. He never offered them a place to park their hearts. He said he wasn't in love.

"Don't read anything into it. You know, boys having fun." John squeezed her fingers.

When they looked over their shoulders, they realized they had walked at least half a mile. An outcropping of rocks stopped their walk. A dangerous riptide flung the waves against the cold lava deposited centuries earlier and gushed like a geyser. A spray of water burst into the air.

"We better turn around."

"Looks dangerous. How quick the water changes."

A phone call interrupted. John slipped the phone from his trouser's pocket and mouthed, Michael.

"What's up, son?"

"Yes, gorgeous. Yes, your mother has her sandals off?"

"What's that? Sorry, bad reception on the beach."

"We will. No, we haven't seen Jack yet. But Brody is jumpy as if his feet were on fire."

"Yes, to be expected."

"Michael? I'll call you back when we get to the hotel."

"Bye. Your mother says hi."

Business always invaded their lives at the most inopportune moments. Another minor glitch in the merger that couldn't wait but relaxing with Myra was his priority at the moment.

"Look at that. What a view?" Myra gestured toward the hotel. It reminded her of the Taj Mahal. A palace built for love. One minor infraction: Jack was missing from the view.

Chapter 7

Reeling

Sliding into the bench seat of his truck, Kai grunted. He reached for the air-conditioner dial and set it on high. On full blast, the arctic air-cooled him enough while he took the familiar route to the marina. It was late, but there was time enough to catch some fish, providing he could find a suitable boat or canoe to borrow.

He sprinted down the swaying dock, most of the small boats had already set off. Holding his breath and betting on hope, he breathed a sigh of relief. He spotted the old outboard that some haole left abandoned years ago swaying on the swell. She wasn't much to look at, but she was trustworthy. Agile as he was, Kai jumped from the dock into her hull and checked the gas. A shimmering rainbow sloshed in the full gas tank.

"Thank God."

He gave the outboard a quick tug, and it responded with a willing purr. Only he had forgotten the most elemental gear. Without an ice-chest, ice, bait, and a net, it was pointless to set out. He killed the engine. Exhausted, he swung his legs up and ran toward the bait shop.

"Woody?" He poked his head into the dark shop.

"Here," the old man was comfortable swinging in the hammock, "what' cha need?"

"Some supplies. Mind if I borrow a few things?"

"You know the drill. Return what you borrow. And Kai? Take some of that cake and coffee with you. Ice and water are in the cooler." He pointed to the counter. The old man never asked questions. They shared a relationship based on trust. The transaction to refuel his supplies took less than two minutes, and Kai was off. He hadn't realized how thirsty he was until he took a long draft of water. While skimming over the waves, and plunging into the troughs, Kai kept a steady eye on his surroundings. Reading the ocean was something he learned from his father. This morning the signs spelled *good fishing, beyond the break. Over there.* Albatross and frigate birds marked the spot with a giant X.

But Kai swung the boat toward the coastline of the hotel. If Kilo were drifting, he'd find it. Along the way, the tin outboard met a coconut floating on the current going about its merry trip, following the trunk of a palm that the storm uprooted. He also came across plastic bags floating like jellyfish; bloated in the water. Beverage bottles supplied by countless manufacturers were as common as day and night. Under normal circumstances, he would have slowed the boat and fished out the trash. But this morning, he didn't have the luxury.

Riding at full torque, Kai did three laps across the shoreline. Zigzagging and transparently hoping on the next pass, he'd find his canoe. Close to shore, docile waves played on the beach, and only one or two people were enjoying the water. Squinting into the glare, he made out a couple walking along the beach.

Disappointed, he swung the boat toward his favorite fishing spot. Kai didn't dare think it would be easy to find his canoe. The ocean was endless. He understood the rules the ocean set, and in a game of hide-and-seek, the infinite body of water reigned as the champion.

Calming himself, he cast off, an albatross perched on the bow flapped its wings and was talking gibberish to Kai. The birds didn't mind his proximity, and this bird seemed to remember his generosity from before. Kai shared his catch when he could. A jealous frigate bird dived into the water, squawking in protest. While waiting for a fish to bite, Kai dialed on his phone.

"Hey, Sam. It's me. Kai. My canoe is missing."

"Yeah, I know. No, not the storm. Please keep an eye out and pass the message on."

"Hey, Bobby. Kai. My canoe is missing.

"No. Maybe some tourists. Thanks."

"Hey, Ty. No. No, it's okay. Yeah, for sure, I appreciate the offer."

"No. No. I haven't had a chance to tell dad."

"Hey, Ben. Yeah. You heard. Oh. I'd appreciate it. Call me if you do."

Between casting and reeling, Kai called his cousins. They were a tight-knit weave, and he could count on the brotherhood to keep an eye out. They all dropped their tone when they asked if he had told his father yet.

After an hour, Kai had three beautiful mahi-mahis on ice. Despite their admirable fight, this morning, it was easy pickings. He even came up with two snappers. With the fish on ice, he spun the boat back toward the marina. He was cutting it close timewise and still needed to gut and trim the fish before making his delivery. While he fished, he formed a conclusion. Someone took his canoe. Whether it was an act of malice against him, or some dumb person taking a chance, he couldn't decide. If he took the advice from his gut, then he could easily pronounce the two goons as guilty, but he had no evidence. If it was a tourist, then so be it. He'd deal with that via the video surveillance, which he planned to scrutinize as soon as he got back to the office. If Cindy bought into his little lie, then he'd leave half an hour early. There was no point in admitting to her or his father yet that he lost the canoe. Sometimes things worked out. He had to have some faith.

"Thanks, Woody." He laid two twenties on the counter for the gas he used.

"Anytime. I heard from Sam. I put a poster up on the board, and we'll find your canoe. No worries. Send me a picture if you have one."

A ball of tears welled in Kai's throat. If anyone knew about lost hope, it was Woody. There was no doubt, each time the door swung open, the old man looked up. He clung to the belief that his son would return from riding the last wave in that fantastic tournament ten years ago. Kai reached and patted the sea-worn hand.

When Kai pulled up at his house, he realized he had made a mistake. He hadn't called Cindy. She'd have been worried. All he could do now was to send her a quick text. He'd explain later. Relieved to have the house to himself, Kai immediately set to preparing the fish. Most of his friends and cousins envied him for his knife skills. Pound for pound, he always saved more meat than anyone else.

"There you are." His father snuck upon him.

"Dad! You scared me."

"We worried. You didn't call."

"I know. Trouble at work, and then things sort of fell apart on me."

"I'll let you to it."

His father shuffled toward the door, leaving Kai alone at the cement sink in the yard. Despite disinfecting it, the residual odor of fish permeated the corner next to the shed. Flies didn't mind.

There were many painful things about watching his father shuffle away like that. The most vicious of them was that before the accident, he had been so fit and healthy. Considering his age, he once had the body of someone much younger. But in the careless blink of an eye, all that changed and maimed his father. Now he looked worn out because the cruel hands of time had tightened their grip. A limp slowed him, and an uncontrollable rivulet of drool embarrassed him to the point of being a recluse. Hindered by physical limitations, his father couldn't climb into Kilo any longer. But he loved listening to Kai's stories about fishing from the heirloom. It would be torture to explain.

"Have you had lunch?" He asked his father while sluicing his hands at the kitchen sink.

"Yes. Cindy made pork laulau. And her delicious pineapple cake."

His father didn't bother to turn his attention away from the television. Game shows had become his one indulgence, and the Price is Right dominated.

"I stink." Kai pointed toward the bathroom. "Then, I need to make a run. Need anything?"

His father shook his head. Since the accident, his father had a hard time accepting anything. Even small gifts at Christmas made him uncomfortable. While the spray of the shower refreshed Kai, he came up with a plan to delay telling his father. Besides, there was a good chance his father would fall asleep before he returned. That had become a ritual to set a clock by.

Before leaving, Kai shoved an entire wedge of cake into his mouth. He didn't think he could ever get sick of pineapple or cake. He also rehearsed the lie he'd tell Cindy about going into work earlier. There simply weren't enough reasons yet to let her in on the bad news.

An hour later, when Kai returned, his father dozed on the overstuffed chair. A sense of relief washed over Kai, and, suddenly, he wanted nothing more than to shut his eyes for a minute too. Kai laid down on the rattan bench and listened to contestants' shriek with excitement. He fell asleep to the bells and whistles going off when someone won a car. If only life were that simple was his final thought.

Kai woke to a kiss on his mouth, and the sequence of his confusing dreams interrupted. They were about Kilo.

"Time to wake up." Cindy said while her long strands of hair brushed against his nose. Her kiss tasted of cola and cake.

"What time is it?" He raised himself up and instinctively looked for his father, who had vacated the chair.

"Five. You slept like a baby. Everything alright?"

"Fine. Ah! Tired. Sorry for not calling. Something came up at work and then went south from there."

"I worried." Cindy shot him an X-ray look. She didn't believe him for a second. But she'd allow him the time to sort through the complexities he faced. She set a warm plate of laulau at the table and added ice to a glass of juice.

"Two weddings. It's hectic. I should head in early to make sure everything is ready for tomorrow. You know, all the extra staff. Orchestrating a sunset wedding is a challenge."

"Sunset? Sounds romantic."

"I hope the sky and sun comply. Rumor has it, she is a Bridezilla." Kai looked to the ground, hoping to sound convincing.

Before he took his lunch box and keys off the counter, he kissed Cindy on the back of her head and smacked her tush. She didn't even turn around to reprimand him. But why poke a sleeping bear? That had always been her wise advice.

When Kai arrived, the ambiance at the hotel was in full swing. Although their clients were always a more upscale crowd, every corner and terrace were a buzz. He made his way down the garden path as inconspicuous as possible. Ducking this branch and sidestepping the concealed cameras, he descended the hazardous pathway. He had every hope of finding his canoe returned. He could visualize Kilo drifting on a few inches of incoming tidewater.

But it wasn't to be. He tried to mask his disappointment behind firmly set lips. He retrieved his backpack, and while he strode through the garden, he pasted a fake grin on his mouth. Neither guests nor staff needed to see him frown.

Chapter 8

Piece by Piece

Before Kai could reach the entrance to the hotel, a guest approached him.

"Excuse me. Can I have a minute?"

Kai slowed and waited for the man to come closer. He smiled. "What can I do for you?"

The man was enormous. A heritage built Kai like a warrior too. He had short legs, a powerful upper body that made him adept at swimming and freediving, and if he had to, he could fight. But this man should have worn a helmet and a football jersey. He eclipsed the afternoon sun.

"I'm wondering if you can help me locate my son. He arrived four days ago, and we've heard he's been enjoying himself. But we haven't heard from him. Last night, at around two o'clock, was the last time his friends saw him. It's not like him."

"Tell me his name again?"

"Jack Spencer. He's in room number 810."

"And your name?"

"John Spencer."

"And who was he with? I need all the details."

"His friends. They're the ones dubbed the Sunset Wedding Crew."

"Oh, yes. The terrace venue. And where did you say your son was last seen?"

Kai recorded the information and made his assumptions. It wasn't difficult to add one plus one. The sunset wedding team had already broken the record for the amount spent on drinks. He heard the menu for the wedding was astronomical. Because of Mr. Spencer's bulk, Kai had to look up, but he didn't need to shield his eyes. The sun had met her match.

"The dance club. His friends mentioned he met a beautiful woman. But no one knows who she is or where she came from." John had pried the information from Brody and confirmed it with the others.

"Follow me. I'll see what I can find out."

"John Spencer." He reached and shook Kai's hand and bestowed all his trust with him.

"Kai Hale. No worries. These things happen frequently. It's a big resort, and we're booked to capacity."

John followed. He had read the name Kai Hale on the brassy name tag. He could tell from the shined shoes and the impeccable uniform that Kai took his job seriously. The man whom he had quizzed this morning hadn't instilled any confidence in him. Myra was beside herself with worry.

Out of sun and heat, John relaxed enough to slow his pace. Kai hustled to keep up. In the air-conditioned corridor, John allowed Kai to lead the way.

"Have a seat. I'm sorry, but the security office is off-limits. I'll do a quick search and see where that leads." Kai pointed to a row of plush chairs in the outer foyer. He smiled with the warmth of the typical Hawaiian attitude, but a missing guest was the least of his worries.

It didn't surprise Kai that no one assisted Mr. Spencer with his inquiry. Guests often wandered into the forbidden arms of inappropriate lovers. Only to surface hours later. And since there had been a string of minor thefts, his staff was under constant pressure to find the thieves. But like the sophisticated equipment, thieves evolved too.

Noted on the incident log was a minor mention of a drunk man. His colleague noted a minor tiff with a few locals who were on the hotel grounds uninvited. The name of the guest, however, was not Jack Spencer. Logged also was an accident in the parking lot, a missing cell phone, and the cameras that went out of circulation during the storm were repaired. Altogether a hectic day. He hung the clipboard on the wall, just as his colleague entered.

"Hey. I see you had a busy shift."

"You'd think it was a full moon. All the crazies are out."

"I'm looking for Jack Spencer. Room 810?"

"Yes, there was a problem on the eighth floor. A leak or something? They might have moved him. But the front desk should have the details. I'm off."

There, so simple. Staff had moved the guest. It was as simple an explanation as he thought it would be. He reached for the phone to call the front desk, then decided against it. To ensure Mr. Spencer, he'd walk him to the lobby and get the new room number, and all would be well. He straightened his tie and buttoned his coat.

"Mr. Spencer. Good news. Your son had to move rooms." He couldn't help but smile and congratulate himself on a job well done.

"Moved?"

"Let's ask at reception. They'll have all the details."

"Why didn't someone tell us sooner? My wife and I worried."

"I'm sorry about that. I'll bring it up at the next meeting, but we honor a stringent privacy policy. It's against policy to hand out room numbers even if it is family."

John fell into step with Kai. The man was efficient, but still; it didn't quite add up. Even if Jack had moved rooms, why hadn't he called? At the front desk, a pretty clerk looked up Jack's room number on the terminal facing her. She read the comments on the file and made notes.

"It seems we had to move him because of a burst pipe. It says he is now in room 633."

She smiled at John, then at Kai, as if she had solved the world's biggest conundrum.

"Where is 633? The numbers on our floor are all rounded."

"It's on the volcano view side. The rooms are smaller. I'm confident the bill will reflect the change."

"I'm not sure I care about the bill. I just want to find my son."

"Let's head up there now."

John followed Kai like a come-along shadow into the elevator. They weren't alone, but it spared both Kai and John from making that inevitable boring small talk. On the sixth floor, Kai held the door aside for John to step into the corridor.

"This way."

Along this side of the hotel were the smaller, less lavish collection of rooms. They were still very handsome but half the price, which was still beyond the means of someone like Kai. John counted the door numbers going down. An arrow showed which direction, right or left, and Kai knew every corner of the hotel. Kai stopped. Room 633 was in the middle of the corridor; flanked by three rooms on either side of the long hallway. John had never been so glad to see a room number. His fist pounded.

"Jack! It's me. Dad."

Kai fully expected that a somewhat hungover man would pull the door aside. He could even picture a likeness to John mumble something that would make his father happy. They waited. They also strained to listen for sounds of movement.

"Jack! Open the door."

John pulled the phone from his pocket and dialed his son's number. He didn't bother bringing it to his ear, instead; he listened for the ringing on the other side. It was unmistakable. The muffled ring on the other side of the door exasperated John. Why did Jack not answer the door or phone? Could he have gotten that drunk? And be that comatose?

"We can't go in. Can we?"

Kai looked down the long corridor from side to side. Under other circumstances, he would have run it past his superior. But Mr. Spencer had that look that indicated that a no would not suffice. He pulled out a master key and waited for the flick of green light. The door opened. The room was in a state, but John recognized Jack's belongings. He identified the suitcase, the suits, and nautical style garments swinging the closet. Part of the bedding had fallen onto the floor, which Kai picked up and attempted to straighten. Why had room service not done their job? This looked bad for the hotel. He picked up the phone and called housekeeping.

"I'm in room 633. Can you tell me the last time someone used the key? And why hasn't housekeeping cleaned this room?"

Keeping his irritation in check, Kai kept quiet. He allowed Mr. Spencer the privacy to search for his son's whereabouts. But the ensuite and the two closets were empty. Jack had vanished from the room.

"He's been here, but where is he now?" John couldn't tell what was missing. Although he assumed that Jack wouldn't have come without his laptop, it wasn't in the room. The phone, well, it was in clear view. Under no circumstances could he think of Jack leaving without his phone. Unless, John considered, he had gone diving. Or another wet sport. John couldn't tell from the garments hanging in the wardrobe, and folded in the drawers, what was missing. His tuxedo swung from a hanger and stirred by the breeze of the air conditioner set on full blast. Laundry had it pressed. In the ensuite, John saw a shaving kit and Jack's collection of toiletries. He recognized the brand. His son swore the concoction of potions helped prevent ingrown hairs. But where was Jack?

"I want to call my wife. She might want to have a look."

Kai made himself small. He understood John's worry, even if there was nothing wrong. If it were one of his sons, he'd make some indiscreet inquiries too.

"Yes. Seems Jack's room had a problem. They moved him. You can breathe again. His things are all here. Sure. 633. I'll wait."

While John spoke to his wife, the front desk called. Kai took the call and turned away, he scribbled notes on the hotel stationery. "Great. Thanks. I won't."

"Mr. Spencer. According to our log, your son was in the room less than an hour ago."

John flipped his wrist to check the time. It appeased him, but he was joining Team Myra, and he scowled with disbelief.

"My wife is on her way. I'm sorry if I'm keeping you from something."

"No, it's fine. I'm glad we solved the mystery."

Kai let himself out and said he'd wait in the corridor. He left the door ajar. Five minutes later, he heard the elevator ding. Mrs. Spencer was en route to conduct her inspection. While he waited, he made a mental note to call the police. Although his canoe had no monetary value, he needed to report it as stolen. That way, at least, it was on their radar if it turned up. But first, he had to wait on the Spencers, and then get ready for the big sunset wedding.

Chapter 9

Time Warp

It was just like on television. The waves rolled and propelled him up and down, and Jack was weightless. There was nothing to see only swaths of water that he couldn't see beyond. Jack was gasping for each breath, and he was sick of spitting water. For the last hour, he crawled across the waves, relying on his good arm to do most of the swimming and tugging the canoe with him. It was impossible to measure if he made any progress at all. A counter-weight seemed to pull him in an entirely different direction, and he couldn't tell if he was swimming in the right direction either. In any direction. He had only a vague sense of which way to swim and nothing to base his hunch on. His elbow no longer hurt, it was numb, and even his fingers no longer had any sensation in them. Five more minutes, he promised himself, to appease his mind and give himself something to look forward to. He couldn't believe that the water out here was from the same body of water as the ocean running alongside the hotel. It was freezing.

While he swam, he kept a close eye on the waves, looking for any signs of fins coming toward him. And Kilo. He noticed the name painted on the canoe. Kilo. When his body first hit the water, his instinct had been to climb back on board. The cold sucked the breath out of him, and he nearly went under. But if he intended to survive, he had to stay fit. He had to find his own means of rescue.

"One, two, three…" Jack counted his strokes as he would his repetitions at the gym. Small bites. "Thirteen, fourteen, fifteen." He focused on the effort of each stroke. The freedom of movement rejuvenated him. Even when he thought he felt something brush against his skin, he pushed on. Despite being depleted and hungry, he swam. If no one found him soon, he'd be in worse shape with each passing hour. He'd seen enough survivalist shows: now was the time.

He hauled himself into the canoe. His limbs ached, and his muscles twitched from the exertion and being cold. He had tied his clothing to the wooden seat on the bow. Someone had nailed a makeshift plank to create a seat to lean against. Jack could appreciate the effort. Having something to lean on was a comfort he had taken for granted until now.

Although he counted his strokes while swimming, he didn't want to count the hours he'd been adrift. He was loath to use the word missing. To keep his sanity, he envisioned a fleet of Coast Guard ships coming to rescue him. There was no doubt his mother had flown into action. By his count, he was missing for an eternity already. Not that he could guesstimate the time with any accuracy. Without his watch, he was at a loss. Time was like finding a thread in a sticky ball of cotton candy. He could only use the sun as it was making its descent. He already knew that in Hawaii, the daylight hours didn't fluctuate as much as they did in California. And even less than on the East Coast. Back home. What he wouldn't give to be back home. Not his condominium in California, but his home.

"I'm home, Mom." He said, enjoying the sound of his voice.

"There you are!" She'd embrace him. "I've missed you." Jack could envision her smile. Leaning into her embrace, he'd inhale the scent of her perfume. She'd fuss. "You haven't eaten. Silly boy." She'd take his hand and walk him into the kitchen. He couldn't wait for it to happen. To see his mother.

Drying himself with the spare vest and his briefs, Jack was on the verge of tears. He hadn't known men could cry as much as he had and with no control to stem them.

"Mom. Please find me."

Deflated and cold, he sat with his head in his hands. This was, without a doubt, the single and biggest fuck-up he'd ever been part of. Invading Tessa's private life had been a big mistake, but this took the cake. He imagined the scene at the hotel and the confused look on his parents' faces. They would argue themselves through the ritual of giving him the benefit of the doubt. Then they would investigate his whereabouts. He suspected that his mother would want to launch an investigation immediately. But his father would let common sense rule. "He's not a kid anymore. Give him some space."

They'd learn that he vacated his suite because of a pipe leak. Brody would slip some comment about the attractive woman into his father's ear. He wouldn't omit that from the moment they arrived on the island, that Jack had gone full tilt. Brody would list the other young ladies Jack flirted with, and the clues would lead back to the beauty. His last conquest. No one knew of the two goons. No would suspect to look for foul play. Logic would prevail that he was asleep from exhaustion somewhere in the hotel. They'd speculate on the bed of which conquest. His mother would argue and say, "that's not like Jack." Common sense would override sending a search party. Common sense would appease everyone, except his mother. "Please, Mom. I'm right here."

By his count, he'd been drifting for twelve hours. Since he couldn't tell how fast the canoe was traveling, there was no way to measure such things. There were no landmarks, and it wasn't as if he could calculate such distances. He was out of his element.

When he wiggled himself into his shirt, he flinched. His elbow wouldn't bend without sending a brilliant shot of pain up his shoulder and down to his fingers. He prepared himself for the pain when he slipped his jacket on. He suspected night, and the further from land he drifted, would be long and cold. Exhausting himself by swimming was a good idea. It had taken his mind off hunger somewhat though he'd give anything to take a bite of something. Like a plain piece of bread, a banana. McDonald's. He hadn't eaten at MacDonald's since his university days. His mouth watered, thinking of the Golden Arches. He knew for sure it would be the first place he'd ask his rescue team to take him. "Supersize me!" He'd order one of everything.

To save on heat, he curled himself into the larger of the two spaces on the canoe. He rubbed his hands together for warmth despite the excruciating pain. Each movement reminded him of his injuries. It had been a grueling day, but he survived. What drove him nuts was the pesky feeling that he was overlooking something. Something that might seem trivial but was a ticking time bomb. Like that sense of foreboding, he found so irritating in movies and literature.

Chapter 10

Search and Rescue

Myra leaned on the railing and scanned the view below. She was on the cusp of more tears despite trying all day to make the best of it. Smiling, while struggling for composure, she down-played Jack's neglect when anyone asked. When she finally had a minute on her own, a tear took flight on the wings of frustration. She'd been to Jack's room three times and knocked. Everyone in the wedding party told her a hundred times not to worry. "That's Jack, they said. "He's been playing it on both ends." As if she needed an explanation. "He's fine," they added and insinuated much more by not saying what they were thinking.

"You're probably overreacting." Tessa had said at lunch, eating like a sparrow. "Jack's having a good time. You know what he's like."

That was the problem. As his mother, she knew what Jack was like and didn't appreciate Tessa suggesting she knew Jack better. Jack might be a lot of things, but if he was one thing, it was close to his mother. Myra swallowed what was in her mouth, and she felt John's hand clamp down on her thigh. The lunch table wasn't the place to put the bride in her place. There'd be time for that later.

With a quick swipe, Myra put an end to the tears. John had given up prowling on the terrace and was on his way up. To fight for composure, she poured two glasses of scotch, one neat, one on the rocks. She preferred the subtler shades of wine on most occasions, but today she needed a stiff drink. In the mirror, she fluffed her hair and ran a finger along the lash line, drying the tears with a swipe. She also freshened her lipstick. She didn't want John to see her fretting.

"Have a nice walk?" Myra handed John the glass.

"Yes. I didn't wake you?"

"No. I woke up a few minutes ago. You're right. I needed that."

Truth was, she hadn't slept at all. She had wallowed in the tired bed of confusion and then stood at the window and sorted through the people. One by one, she weeded them out as they lay unaffected by the pool, or in the shaded cabanas on the beach. Watching them, she could make out many young men who had a similar build. Some were running, tossing a ball, or a frisbee, or diving into the kidney-shaped pools. But none were Jack. She did, however, spot a familiar figure among the crowd. John. He was weeding through the bodies too. He even mistook a young man of similar build and tapped him on the shoulder. From her vantage point, she could see John's shoulders deflate at the mistake.

"Anything?"

John shook his head. His disappointment was as great as hers; only he was much better suited to making sense out of Jack's no show.

"No. I'm sure he's around. I've never seen such a crowd."

"Did you talk to anyone else?"

"Yes. Everyone assures me that Jack has overdone it on the first three days. They're hinting that he's catching up on his sleep. Still. It's a bit unusual."

"Should we call the police?"

Myra wanted to. She picked up the phone repeatedly, rehearsing how she'd phrase her concern. But aloud, it sounded ridiculous. The evidence suggested it was as his friends predicted.

"And say what?" John drained his glass. He had rehearsed his own spiel.

"Did anyone say if the room change upset him?"

"I asked. It didn't seem to bother Jack because he didn't mention it to anyone. In the end, we have nothing to go on if we call the police."

"Does a mother's intuition not count?" Myra tried to ease John's concern along with her own. But she was right. In her heart of hearts, something was wrong. While John was out, she called the Coast Guard. They were cordial and tried to placate her. They took her details and said to keep them abreast. As gracious as possible, they attempted to sway her concern. And since she had no evidence to link Jack to being in the ocean, they were afraid, there was nothing they could do. Their answer made her feel as if her hands were bound, and her feet shackled, but her heart was wide open.

John stared at the bottom of his empty glass. The amber courage he had swallowed was slow to kick in. The stress of the merger clouded his focus on how to find his son. But he had to keep that from Myra. She worried enough as it was.

"Of course, it counts. I would want you on my rescue team. But I keep telling myself, there's nothing to worry about."

News of the room switch surprised him, and that Jack didn't mention it. Brody hinted that a few other women hooked up with Jack, promising to track them down. And then there was the bombshell from last night. It's her who they should concentrate on. Not that she'd done anything, but she was the last person seen with Jack.

"It's odd. I can't for the life of me figure out that our son would be so thoughtless. It's not like Jack. But like you said, all we have to go on is a feeling."

"You're right, but now I have some bad news. Michael called. I must handle some negotiations. It's not that Michael is in over his head. You know the old boys' club; they want to see an old head served on a platter."

"Go! Do what you have to."

Myra heard John close the door to their bedroom. It was the same at home. The business couldn't tell time, yet it consumed all of John. Since she had eaten little at lunch and breakfast, the lack of calories was catching up. Her stomach growled; she was woozy. On the oval table was a bowl of fresh fruit, she selected a cluster of grapes to nibble on. When the phone vibrated on the table, it burst her reverie. She jumped. For that split second, before she looked at the caller Id, she allowed herself to believe it was Jack. She'd been replaying a memory of last Christmas, when Jack came home for a week, and it was like old times. In the morning, everyone gathered around the tree. Jack sat on the carpet, dressed in his pajamas, and opened his stockings. She took a picture, one that turned out to capture the boy still alive inside the man. "Damn it, Jack. Where are you?" Turning the phone over broke the spell. It wasn't Jack.

"Hi, Hon. No. Not yet."

"That's what everyone keeps telling us."

"I won't. We have three hours, and then we'll hear where Jack's been hiding."

"Yes, the countdown is on. How is the baby-bump?"

"Just like you did to me. I never had worse heartburn. I pity you."

"I'll tell him. And yes, I'll text you as soon as I see him."

Myra set the phone on the table again. Stacy had tried to make light of Jack's vanishing act too. He had done it to her once at university. Only that time, he had a legitimate reason. He ended up in the hospital for emergency surgery on his appendix.

Alone with her thoughts, she drifted toward the window. She missed Jack and worried. Her mind ransacked the catalog she always kept within a finger's reach. There was footage of Jack as if it were a movie reel complete with sound. She saw Jack in everything, she heard his voice whisper, "find me, Mom."

The ocean and its lull had a calming effect. It was an endless blue, falling away in all directions. It was also unsettling. Instinctively she knew it had something to do with Jack.

Chapter 11

Big Brother

Kai ate his dinner alone in the security office. After the tumultuous start of his shift, he finally had a moment to himself. Because of the unexpected demands Mr. Spencer made on his time, he hadn't had a moment to check on his canoe. Luckily, he had a wide network of family and friends who cast their net searching when he couldn't. They understood the importance of keeping the news from reaching his father.

He wolfed down the last bite of his sandwich and washed it down with a medley of fruit juice. His family was nearing the tail-end of their paychecks, and he made do with the remnants in the pantry. He wasn't sure he tasted any of the Spam, but the bread was fresh. Taking a bite of his banana, he hoped he had settled the overzealous worries of the Spencers. He smirked and shook his head. Apparently, they didn't understand that young people had their own priorities, especially on the island. Here, they lived with the lure of other desires. Kai wasn't a betting man, but he bet he knew where their son was. He visualized two young bodies entangled in a heap of sheets, one of the bodies belonged to the stunning woman Jack's friends described.

While he had the office to himself, the urge to check the footage of the previous night took over. Any clues captured on film would lead him to the mysterious tourist who allegedly took his canoe. Or better yet, catch the two goons red-handed. He inserted the first disk. In black and white film, the camera panned the southeast gazebo entrance. He set the replay button and slowed the surveillance footage.

"Well, well. What have we here?" He zoomed in on a grainy snapshot of two people arguing in the corridor to the back entrance. The camera captured a classic dilemma. Without a soundtrack, it was hard to determine the dialog. Kai studied the footage and there was no shortage of words explaining the message in the body language. The woman had crossed beyond the steep territory of peeved.

"What are you watching?" His night-shift partner asked. Engrossed, Kai hadn't overheard him enter. Because of the wedding, they added extra staff as precaution. It was how Kai's schedule became less than an ideal situation to find his canoe. Saving grace— it paid overtime.

"Lover's quarrel," Kai said, aware of the pressure of a person muscling in on his space.

"Triangle is more like it," George said.

"What do you mean?" Kai rolled away from the desk.

"That's the bride for the sunset wedding. But that ain't the groom."

Kai zoomed in and froze the image and leaned closer toward the screen.

"You're right. That's her. She's not so pretty when she's pissed."

Kai couldn't believe the transformation. He focused on the man who had his back to the camera. Then he clicked on the other monitor and rewound the footage. The beauty on the stairs and the man who made her smile. It was the suit that confirmed his suspicions. Same man. Could it be that this was the missing man? The shot was too grainy, but the similarities were there. Tall physique, good looks. He wished he studied the snapshot Mr. Spencer shoved under his nose. Although he glanced at the picture, other thoughts crowded out the face, and he thought then that it was nothing but a silly misunderstanding.

"The dirt. For all that money, they can't keep it in their pants."

Kai leaned even closer toward the screen. There was definitely an explosion of emotion in that scene. Was this a lover's triangle gone wrong? Yikes. He felt the sensation of angst settle in his gut; those rich people could have it.

"She's mad. Wonder what he did to deserve her wrath?" Kai turned to face George.

"Anyway. I wanted to run something by you."

Kai looked at his partner. George shared Kai's ethics. He had mentioned his concern about the two new garden crew members as soon as he met them. But George also had it in for two housekeeping maids. He suspected them of being responsible for the recent string of thefts.

"Shoot," Kai said.

"You know those two goons. Bruce and Wayne. Well, I've caught them a few times on film, trespassing. They were loitering outside the dance club last night, despite my warning. I shouldn't judge based on suspicion, but I watched the footage of them again and again. The lanky one stole some cash from the bar. But there it is. The big but. The video is too dark, and it doesn't show him stealing the money."

"No. I think that's good work. I can't stand those creeps. Not sure why we're scraping the bottom of the barrel to hire them. So why do you think they stole money?"

"I checked with the head cashier, the till tape from last night's bar is short. Not too much, but they figure around two-hundred."

"If it's them, that's clever. Take a little not to draw suspicion."

"I've been asking around. Did you notice their tattoos? Bad boys. Watch yourself."

"You too."

George set a tray of tangled lanyards next to him on his desk. It was their job to update the security files on both the newly hired and newly fired staff. It was tedious work that none of the security staff enjoyed doing, but the hotel also had a high turnover rate. Seasonal work was like that. He untangled a cord, then set it down again after looking at the photo.

"We sure go through a lot of staff. You been here how long?"

"Me. Fifteen years. That's how I got the watch, and probably the promotion."

"Both well deserved. How's your dad?"

"Not great. He hangs on. It's broken his heart to rely on us. Thinks he's a burden. The sad thing is, he's still so young. Only sixty."

"Sad. But many are worse off. At least he has you. Old guy down the street from me has no one."

"The cost of living just about does us in. You know, having two mortgages. But I can't talk Dad into moving. We could build an extension."

"That's the thing. We can't save any money either. Our house is our retirement plan."

"Darn. We better get going. Wedding will start soon."

"I'll do the first round," George said.

Kai switched the monitor to the live feed on the west terrace. Draped lengths of tulle rustled in the breeze on the arbor. It looked like the clouds would comply and settle down for a spectacular sunset. A red carpet led toward the infinity pool, flanked by champagne-colored satin chairs. The stunning backdrop would frame the sunset slipping into the ocean. He heard the bride had hired a man who specialized in sunset photography. Kai couldn't imagine something as lavish as hiring two photographers. When George came into view at checkpoint number one, he gave Kai the thumbs-up. Things were going according to plan. The camera also panned toward the guests who were enjoying the spectacular view of the ocean. Buckets of chilled champagne, hors d' oeuvres that Kai couldn't pronounce floated on silver trays from guest to guest. He knew the soft music piped in through the hotel sound system. For such a lavish venue, they probably chose something classy like Pachelbel or Mendelsohn. He remembered his own wedding tunes: Lady in Red, Caribbean Queen, songs he could still sing without a lyric sheet. He hummed a little.

Over the two-way radio, static snapped. George was on his way to the kitchen while Kai watched the wedding party on camera. Everyone glanced toward the stairway. Any minute, the bride would come into view. The bride had the walk down the aisle, the ceremony, and I dos rehearsed down to the minute. At least the afternoon wedding had gone off without a hitch. He settled into the back of the chair and watched.

Slowly, the terrace filled. Several guests took to their designated chairs and watched. Others roamed, but everyone casually glanced toward the staircase. Kai saw people snap pictures of the assembled guests, the venue, and selfies. He didn't hear their laughter, but he could imagine it. And then he saw the Spencers. There was no mistaking the hulk of a man ushering the attractive woman toward the front. Mrs. Spencer sorted through the crowd without wanting to appear anxious. She kissed cheeks, shook hands, shrugged her shoulders, and laughed.

Kai checked the clock; eleven minutes to go. The bride should be ready to descend the stairway as soon as the wedding march aired on the sound system. Most of the guests ambled toward their seats, all looking backward, expectant of the bride.

But there was a commotion. Lined up near the altar were the groomsmen. Some were dabbing their brow under the sun's final rays and shifted on antsy feet. Something was wrong. Cold feet? Kai leaned closer. A groomsman sprinted down the aisle seeing something the camera didn't capture.

"George!" Kai radioed and waited for the garble to subside. "Come in, George!"

"Kai. We have a problem. The best man seems to be missing."

"What?"

"Spoke to the groom, they can't find him anywhere."

"Did they check his room?"

"From what I'm hearing, they haven't seen him since the night of the storm. They assumed he'd show up for the wedding."

"Is his name Jack Spencer?" Kai heard his chair fall over.

"Yeah? You know him?"

"Houston! We have a problem." Kai felt his color drain. All on his watch. He picked up the phone and pressed the button marked General.

Chapter 12

Despair

The last rays of mauve sunshine fanned across the vast horizon. Jack squinted into the glare and understood he was a mere pawn in an endless cycle. A disposable pawn, but he wasn't ready to admit defeat yet. He had chewed all his fingernails until they bled. He was so hungry. Despair, which set in after he tossed the plastic bottle as far as he could, gripped him. Like the ocean, hopelessness rose in waves and alternated within the highs and lows. But only he was stricken with bouts of panic. Jack regretted tossing the plastic bottle. It was a measuring device for how ill-equipped he was at keeping his wits about him. Things didn't bode well.

Whenever he could, he stood and screamed into the wind, "Mom! Find me. Anyone! Please!" No one ever answered back.

He was grateful for the three inches of water he had found on the other side of the bench. It was warm, and he brought it to his nose to smell before tasting. The plastic bottle crackled when he sucked every drop of liquid from the bottle. Then he did the unthinkable thing and tossed it in the ocean. He couldn't risk going in after it. If anyone were keeping score, the ocean was miles ahead of him.

All-day, his mind jumped from one lily pad of thought to another, but none were stable. He couldn't focus, and his lingering hangover was only partly to blame. It was the situation. Jack understood because of his absence, there'd be no wedding, and drama would take center stage. His mother would buckle from the pain. He could picture his parents like a Panavision moment in a movie, rolling on the giant screen of the sky. Tessa would have the tantrum of all tantrums. Her uncontrollable rage would land on some innocent bystander. He hoped that it would mean they were sending the rescue helicopter.

"Please find me." He said when he sat back down.

Within minutes, the sun slipped from his view. It pegged the time somewhere around ten minutes before seven. Tessa had the ceremony mapped out, down to the minute. He watched while the blend of mauve and orange shattered the steel-blue sea. He wasn't sad to say goodbye to the shades of blue that kept him company. Another tool was about to come into play. Night. Somehow it helped him to overshadow his great disappointment: that no one came to pluck him from his predicament. By his count, he'd been missing for sixteen endless hours. What that measured in distance wasn't something he could extrapolate from the waves. He knew the horizon bobbed close at hand, but in the darkness of night, he hoped to see lights. Not stars, but the lights of Hawaii. So that he could direct the canoe and start paddling toward the shore. He didn't doubt reaching land if fate even handed him the frailest chance on the Ship of Hope.

Jack closed his eyes for a moment. The ocean was calm; nearly as a sheet of glass, and he guessed he should be grateful for that small mercy. A gentle breeze brushed over his body as if to say: there, there. Soon he'd miss the sun and its heat. In the last hours, Jack had learned considerably more about himself than he had in his entire life. One: he was a selfish twit.

To keep busy, Jack thought back to the argument with Tessa. She'd been furious and had reached the boiling point, and he had ignited the fire.

"You selfish, egotistical asshole. How dare you sniff around my private life!"

Tessa had pounded on his chest. She was partly right. He didn't have the right, but he had to know who Brody was marrying. And things about Tessa didn't add up. Where she came from was still a mystery, but his PI had found some clues. She was born in Buffalo. Not New York.

"And you're a god-damned liar!" He spat back.

"So, what! So are you! You used me, and now you think you can make me go away."

"That's not true, and you know it. I realized what you were. But you didn't waste any time to switch your undying love to Brody. You're a sham!"

"Yet you still wanted to fuck me every chance you got. Even after Brody confided his feelings for me. Some friend you are!"

"Don't play Ms. Innocence with me. You offered."

"That obviously was a mistake. But I swear, I will crucify you if you say a word."

"Don't fucking threaten me, Tessa! I can play this game too. I demand you break off the engagement."

"I'm not going to, and it's you who shouldn't threaten. You claim Brody is like a brother to you, yet you took the first chance you got to screw him over."

"I wasn't like that, and you know it."

"Oh, I know it! It was me you screwed. How many times? Do you need me to remind you? Once is a forgivable mistake. But for months…? I don't think so."

"To save Brody from you, I'd be willing to give him up."

"But you won't. You love your reputation and that you slunk so low and cheated your best friend will make you look bad."

A security guard, who came whistling around the corner interrupted them. And Jack was glad. Two days before the wedding was too late to fix anything, and he remembered walls had ears. It's how he found out about Tessa. Walls, he learned, loved to gossip.

The more time Jack spent alone, the more convinced he became that Tessa was responsible for his predicament. He had seen something in her eyes during the last argument that was pure evil. When his PI suggested he watch his back, he had laughed it off. The information he had on Tessa was a weapon that turned the game in his favor. But Tessa saw it differently. Within a month, he packed his bags and moved to the West Coast because Tessa demanded it. His life had become a soap opera, and Tessa was right. There was a skeleton in his closet, and Tessa had done her homework too. She aced it.

Listening to the slow shuffle of waves splashing against the canoe, a rush of emotions got the best of him. He was thirsty, hungry, and frightened. He clung to the life raft of hope. If Tessa had hired those goons to send him adrift, wouldn't she eventually send someone to pluck him from this hell? Was she that evil that she would let him die?

He waited for darkness to fall like snow on cedars all around him. Suddenly, he missed winter and the cycle of the seasons. In California, they were less verbal. In New York State, they took to the stage in four acts. Jack leaned into the wooden plate on the seat and waited on the night to spread its wings. He couldn't wait to see the lights twinkling on the shore.

Chapter 13

No More I love Yous

Kai stood in the middle of the terrace. Daylight had vanished as quickly as the wedding guests. He pressed a wad of tissues to the cut on his face. The bride had thrown her bouquet with much fanfare, and his face caught all of it, thorns included. He had started an apology the bride didn't want to hear. Since he had time to think about it, he could never have finished it anyway.

A bride's maid, dressed in volumes of lilac silk, swooped in and took the round posy before he could pick it up. A group of waiters gathered champagne flutes while another group dismantled the pergola. It all happened so quickly, yet it unfolded in slow motion. Staff stripped and stacked the chairs and collapsed the tables. From his viewpoint, it was difficult to say if the wedding had taken place or not. Spilled wedding confetti, in the shapes of doves and hearts, fluttered when the breeze danced across the terrace. The tulle bows billowed on the pergola. It was over even before it began.

"How is she?"

"The doctor gave her a sedative."

"Awful. And the bride?"

"She's throwing things. What a nightmare! And all on our watch."

"What a dreadful thing to happen."

Kai answered the beckoning finger of the general manager. He squared his shoulders and strode toward the stairway, climbing up, saving his boss the trouble. Most of the staff understood the protocol. No gossiping with guests.

"You're needed in the control room. The police are here. But before you go. Don't give them anything. I've retained a lawyer. He'll be here in the morning."

"In all your years with the hotel, have we ever lost one?"

"Not to my knowledge. Let it go, Kai. It's not your fault."

"Easy for you to say. You didn't hear that sound. I wish I could make it stop."

"Mothers. Everyone said they heard her heart break."

Kai nodded. He'd have nightmares. She crumpled like a house of cards in the wind. One moment she was on the screen, all regal and elegant, dressed in her wine-colored dress. The next moment, they were peeling her off the floor. Her hands beating at the man trying to upright her again. *Missing.* The moan that brought the ocean's sound to a standstill, *my Jack, my Jack* gripped everyone within hearing like a vice.

He'd nudge the police officers toward the two new hires on the garden crew, which wasn't fair. But he needed to lay the blame to rest and get it off his shoulders. He should have investigated when he saw the incident report. He should have taken the father's concerns and handled them. He should have.

Kai took the service elevator to the sixth floor, the police officer in silent tow. They turned down the long corridor passing one or two guests, who shied away and looked to the carpet. He inserted the keycard, and the light flickered red, then buzzed to green. Cooled air greeted them. Kai had already called the maid who last cleaned the room, and she was on her way in. Though her rude tone on the phone suggested that she wasn't pleased. He followed protocol and kept all the necessary details a secret. Kai understood. No time to construe any passable lies.

"Don't touch anything!"

Behind him, Kai heard the snap of latex gloves.

"Yes. Everything in the room appears normal." Kai answered the officer's question. Except that the tuxedo hung and swayed in the draft, the body was missing. A camera snapped. Opening the wardrobe door disturbed the other hung suits. The white linen slacks, silk shirts, the nautical pattern shorts, and T's swayed. The officer opened each drawer. They revealed nothing other than the perfectly folded garments, a leather billfold, a gold bracelet tucked beneath a pair of vicuna wool socks. Nothing out of the ordinary. Room-service finally made up the bed. No one had sat on its corner and ruffled the duvet since.

"Inventory." The cop said. "Doesn't look like much of a crime scene."

He scribbled notes on his pad. Did a full three-sixty, then he turned to Kai.

"Looks like our guy vanished into thin air. Left his phone. I'll be needing the father to go through what's missing. Like what he was wearing for a missing person's profile."

"The security camera should tell us that."

Back in the control room, the scenario played itself out on the screen. Silence fell while everyone stared at the monitor. The security footage explained away the fragile pieces of the puzzle and left gaping holes. Jack had indulged and enjoyed all the amenities. He was on film flirting with several women. Since his arrival four days ago, Jack Spencer had been busy. The cop scribbled without looking at his pad.

"I'll need names."

Jack, however, had saved the best for last. The woman on the stairway.

"Five-ten, one-fifty. Athletic, close-cropped curly, dark-brown hair. Brown eyes."

"Sorry, Officer. John Spencer is ready for you." George intruded.

They had pieced together Jack's last known movements. No surprises. They established from his composure that he was more than inebriated. From the film footage, they had a description of the suit. Navy blue, white piping, a white drawstring. Mr. Spencer added it was Armani, silk, and brand new, a birthday present from his sister. Pale blue shirt and ostrich leather loafers. Same as other groom's men. Small Gucci emblem, the groom texted a photograph. All the details, although not much to go on, sketched a rough draft to go on. They entered the Spencer suite invited and solemn.

Kai swallowed a disrespectful yawn and averted John Spencer's eyes. John pointed toward the door and lowered his voice.

"I'll ask you to be quiet. My wife is asleep in the next room."

A doctor had injected a dose of a mild sedative into her struggling arm. For the moment, she slept in a bed of bliss she'd never experience again. Kai fingered the twenty-dollar bill in his pocket. He wondered when it would be appropriate to return it. He felt like a fraud for having accepted it. But more urgent concerns troubled John. He was ready to listen to what they had discovered. A second officer, a small and quiet man, confirmed the small details. He listed the last known movements of Jack and all led to a dead end. He cleared his throat before speaking; it was a shitty job having to explain.

"One of Jack's dates left yesterday. Name. Emma Capri. We'll get in touch with her first thing in the morning."

John Spencer nodded. Exhaustion crept upon him. His shoulders and neck dropped. His pallor was a shade of ash. He had difficulty listening, and his mind raced to the million places where he hoped his son would be. Alive.

"Second woman. Rose Winter. We interviewed her, and she said Jack came to her room. They had their fun, and Jack left. She said she thought she saw him on the dancefloor with another woman. The night of the storm. The mystery woman who is not a guest at the hotel."

"Find her. She was the last person seen with my son."

John Spencer gained his authority and stiffened his spine. Kai stood quietly at his side, expecting a reprimand, but Mr. Spencer spun on his heel and said, "call me. Regardless of how trivial."

Alone in the control room again, Kai printed the missing person posters of Jack Spencer. The printer ran out of red ink after twenty copies. One copy for each elevator, each public bathroom stall and change room. Although management tried to shield their guests from knowing, they encouraged Kai to be discreet.

"Just make them, you know, non-threatening, or pathetically sad. He might still turn up."

While most of the guests slept, Kai taped a copy of the poster inside each elevator, each stairwell. He knocked on the public washrooms, and anyone using the toilet would do so with Jack's face smiling at them. The night clerk displayed the missing Jack Spencer in a frame. Hotel management canceled all the scheduled tours for the following day.

They kept the extra staff on. Each manager headed a search team, and their instructions were clear. Search in each outbuilding, closet, basement, utility closet, vacant room, waste bin, rooftop. Everyone gathered in the control room. Muster point—posted on the door.

In the morning, the police would quiz the guests. The manager asked to proceed tactfully.

"Decorum demands it," he said, and Kai volunteered to stay on. Somehow, he felt the brunt of the blame. Nothing mattered but finding Jack Spencer. At least for now, Kilo would have to wait.

When the initial rush simmered down sometime around midnight, Kai took a nap on a portable cot asking to switch off with his colleague in the wee hours. Kai dreamed about Jack. When he blinked his eyes open, he hoped the first words greeting him would bear good news.

Chapter 14

Formidable

From time to time, to break the monotony, Jack dipped his toes into the water. Feeling the drag of the water and anticipating that something would touch his foot urged him on. It was a fear he wanted to conquer. He figured it was close to midnight. Although he wasn't sure, he believed the moon traveled at a different pace than the sun. Why hadn't he paid attention in school to such basic information? Glancing up, he had never seen such a multitude of stars, the Milky Way was awash in spilled milk. The universe reiterated how insignificant he was, and he only hoped that of all the five shooting stars he counted, one would grant his wish. Beside him, the ocean was calm, and in the gathering darkness, thick like black tar. But any minute now, Jack expected to see the lights on a shoreline. Or better yet: a rescue boat. Every few minutes, he rose and looked about. They had to be somewhere, but in the darkness, it was difficult to see where the ocean ended, and the sky started. At night they were the same shade of pitch-black.

Biding his time, he tried to make sense of what happened, and each thought led back to the beginning. Tessa. Thinking it through, Jack convinced himself she was behind this. The idea had festered all day, and he rode the possibility around and around like a carousel. He replayed their last argument a hundred times. Dissecting her words to discover what she was capable of. He also rewound his memory tape of the day he met her. It was September, the start of a new term. He was too young to know any better. Something other than his brain made decisions then.

Brody had driven an elbow into his gut, they'd been talking football when they noticed Tessa try out for the cheerleading squad. Watching the women was a sport and ritual of sorting the fresh blood out among the seasoned. On the third day, as Jack was leaving the library, Tessa bumped into him.

"Excuse me." She laughed. Her luxurious curls bouncing in a ponytail. An armload of textbooks weighing her down.

"Not at all. I didn't hurt you?" Jack said. He had grasped her arm to spin her out of harm's way and closer toward the wall. She was grinning. He was too. A hoard of people rushed past them. Jack remembered thinking, wait until I tell Brody.

"No. But would you show me to…" She unfolded a hand-written map. "Quincy House."

"You're off by a mile. Don't you have the campus app on your phone?"

"I do. But it's at Quincy House." She laughed again. "I lost it on my first day. Someone at Quincy picked it up."

"Let me show you. It's two streets over." Jack took an armload of books off her.

"John Spencer, Junior, but my friends call me Jack."

"Tessa Washington."

"This way."

By the time they crossed Massachusetts and Auburn Street, Jack had her number. He couldn't wait to tell Brody. She was so tiny walking next to him. Fragile even. Standing height of five foot four, a hundred pounds, if that, he felt the urge to protect her. But it didn't take long to learn she was as fierce as a dragon and competitive. She harbored secrets that he extracted inch by inch, like her birthmark. Others peeled away quicker: she was a tease.

Jack fingered the scab on his knee. It never had a chance to harden. Saltwater kept it soft, but he couldn't resist picking. He ate what came loose.

Tessa. In the early days, he even believed he was in love. If it hadn't been for the pact he made with Brody, he would have jumped right in. But Brody was wiser with women. He had a patience Jack didn't possess.

"Never let a woman come between us. If both of us like the same one, we walk away."

They shook on it like gentlemen.

Later they changed the pact. "If fate chooses one, let the fortunate one be happy."

That was how Brody ended up with Tessa. It was how Jack ended up cheating his best friend.

Out in the middle of the ocean, it was becoming more evident. Tessa had played them from the start. He had under-estimated her completely.

Sometime between waiting to see a glimmer of light on Hawaii and morning, Jack fell asleep. A chalk mark on his calendar, and his second night of drifting. He slept soundly, and when he woke before dawn, it was to knock on the canoe. It took a minute for his mind to piece the puzzle together.

Sitting up and adjusting his stiff limbs, Jack investigated the knocking. The horizon was busily churning out another spectacular sunrise. A pale wall of orange crept up the gray sky, but it was still too dark to see.

"What's this we have?" He said, leaning over the canoe.

A round, furry creature bumped the wood as if trying to climb aboard. But Jack couldn't allow that. He had to be careful. If it were edible, he couldn't let it escape. If it were dangerous, it could kill him.

Curious enough, he poked it. It didn't bite and was rough to the touch. He had to be patient and wait for more light. Using his briefs, he guided the creature along with the canoe encouraging it to come along. He had a suspicion, but he had learned the adage, "don't count your chickens..."

Drifting along, he salivated. This could be a turning point and save his life. When the sun's yellow yoke broke the horizon, Jack used his briefs and scooped out the object. He flung it to the far end of the canoe. Landing with a thud, it was wet and coarse and rolled back and forth. It was a beautiful coconut.

"Ha ha!" Jack clapped triumphant. Its weight had surprised Jack. It weighed at least four pounds, and he hoped it wasn't waterlogged and ruined. On the island, they were everywhere. He remembered stumbling on the beach, stubbing his toe. And he never forgot the wise words, "never sit under a coconut tree. They can kill you."

"How about a drink of coconut water?" He said while reaching for the nut.

"And meat. Come my precious."

Jack lifted the nut and brought it down on the lip of the canoe. One swift bash against the rim should do the trick was his thought before he made contact with the sturdy wood. What Jack hadn't considered were his long fingers and the instant, excruciating pain exploding in his fingertips.

"Holy fuck!" The hard knock broke the skin on his knuckles, and his hand sought refuge in his mouth. Jack sucked on the blood and glared at the coconut.

Chapter 15

Valium Sleep

A glimmer of the pale dawn fingered its way in through the curtain. John snored in a smooth baritone beside her. He'd been too exhausted to undress, laying on top of the duvet he was ready to spring to action, his wedding shoes still on his feet.

Blinking, focusing on the overlooked details of yesterday, Myra braced herself. The full onslaught of emotions was awake long before she was. They'd been waiting until the injection John talked her into washed through her system. The first feeling rising was resentment. The drug didn't even allow her the pleasure to dream of Jack. Instead, she dreamed up a vivid episode of the Simpsons. One of Jack's favorite television programs. Anger. Why hadn't anyone listened to her concerns? She rolled away from John and swung her legs over the side of the bed, braving the floor. Fear, cloaked in a suffocating mantle woven of desperation, rose with her, slowing her down. She gasped for breath. Last night, the floor had become her solace. Panic had buckled her knees, and she made a scene and crawled on all fours, searching for her Jack. Numbness spread. Fuck everyone else. She should have listened to her gut instinct. She might have saved so much precious time, possibly Jack's life.

In the ensuite, her ugly self greeted her in the mirror. She had cried off all the mascara, but traces of lipstick still contoured her mouth. There'd been no wedding feast to wear it off on. Nor was there enough champagne to stamp the rim of a toasting glass. Myra turned the tap and washed her face, she reached for the toothbrush. Where are you, Jack? Was the question she searched the mirror for. She wished it had the visions of a crystal ball.

Hunger pangs rippled in her gut, she was deflated and empty as if some giant syringe had zapped all the vital juices from her body. Tiptoeing, she closed the door without a thud behind her. In the sitting room, she called the front desk.

"Can you put me through to security?"

"Absolutely. Can we send some breakfast? Coffee?"

"Please."

She waited while the clerk put her call through. A soft Muzak rendition of Vandross played on the line.

"Grand Ocean's Bay Hotel."

"This is Mrs. Spencer. Any news on my son?"

"We're trying. It's a large hotel. Please don't give up hope."

"I'm his mother. I'll never give up hope."

She hung up. Hope. Though she'd embrace any straw at all, she had something far more powerful to wield as a weapon. A mother's instinct. Jack was alive. No one could persuade her otherwise. While she waited on room service to knock, she stepped out on the balcony. Rushing waves toyed on the sand below. In the distance, she saw surfers waiting for their ride. A slender and agile boy vacuumed the kidney-shaped pool stirring the aqua water with a long hose. The sun was climbing up; while another boy swept the tiled terrace where the wedding should have been. Not a trace of any nuptials remained. At least not from her view eight floors up. She turned her gaze toward the ocean again. Although the waves seemed harmless, Myra had a suspicion, and she hoped they weren't her enemy, but she sensed the ocean's humbling power.

She pictured her son, always smiling and full of exuberance. Jack had always been an athlete. The running sort. The ball throwing sort. Swimming and water had come as natural to him as rock climbing, golf, and tennis. If anyone could take on the ocean: Jack could. All he had to do was win whatever fight came his way.

John's warm hand on her shoulders startled her. She hadn't heard him until he was next to her, and his warmth leached into her. If only he held the magic words. If only he could reset the clock so that they could start over. And despite all, it hadn't fully sunk in yet that Jack was missing. She expected him to walk through the door at any moment.

"We'll find him."

"I've no room for doubt."

Myra squeezed John's fingers. Such a knowing gesture. She and John would survive this. Together, they'd find Jack. Regardless. Myra could not foresee conceding to the cruelty of fate. She'd fight with her claws out.

"Any progress?"

"Nothing. We'll play the waiting game."

Over breakfast, Myra laid out her demands. No more sedatives. She asked John to call Brody in for a briefing. In a private sense of foreboding, she assumed Brody had somehow escaped a giant-sized mistake. That Jack had appeased the gods of fate with his vanishing act. But she wouldn't share such thoughts with anyone. What good would it do?

Have you heard from Brody? Tessa?" John asked. He had pulled her into a bear crushing embrace. If only he'd say, it would be okay. That Jack would be okay.

"Not a word. Poor Brody."

"Poor, Tessa." John finished for her. He knew Myra had difficulty admitting that this catastrophe affected more than just them. But instead of preaching, he allowed her to struggle with her emotions. This was not the time to argue.

"The security person you spoke with is on his way up."

Myra had taken the message from the waiter who wheeled in their breakfast. John joined her after his quick shower. It hadn't revived him as he had hoped. With as much kindness as she could muster, she pampered John. She buttered his toast and spread it with marmalade; she stirred cream into his coffee and smiled. What she really wanted was to fall apart. Sitting across from her on the balcony, John jotted notes on the hotel stationery.

"We need to call Michael and Stacy. There's no putting that off any longer."

"Let's wait for Kai to fill us in. Then we'll have a better understanding."

"Kai?"

"Security. His name's on the tag. The more people we'll have on our team, the better."

Myra nodded. Waiting for new information had become her prime focus overnight. Any news. Good or bad. But when the knock sounded on the door, her heart reminded her that she was a liar. She would only accept the good news. Bad news be damned.

"Mrs. Spencer, Mr. Spencer. We've searched in every service room of the hotel. The roof which Jack couldn't have had access to. This morning, we'll start on the hotel suites and any on-site buildings we didn't get to during the night."

"No trace? Nothing at all?"

"Mr. Spencer. No news is good news. And please, if there is anything you need, ask."

"Thank you. Detective Malone called too. Now, we wait."

Chapter 16

Hubbub

Bruce had slept through the hubbub while snuggly tucked away in a storage closet. It wasn't the most comfortable place to sleep, but he had had some extra help via a few puffs, a handful of white tablets that he never left home without. Plus, they helped to erase the sound that that bitch of a woman made on the terrace. Causing a scene and collapsing like a house of cards. It was almost comical to watch the wedding come unglued when the pieces fell into place. The only thing that held up its side of the bargain was the showstopper of a sunset. He had watched the stunning color display while everyone else flew into a flutter caused by the panic. Bruce didn't think anyone in Hollywood could have done a better job orchestrating the fall-out. Fiction could never mimic facts.

When everyone realized what had happened, they flocked to the woman on the ground. Pity all around for the mother. And apparently none for the hot bitch of a bride who was left stranded on top of the stairway. Rich people were a breed all onto themselves. Bruce couldn't stand them, and he believed in karma. They deserved what they got. And Kai. When the bride threw her flowers at Kai, that was a comedy routine right out of a Lucy show. He had trouble containing his laughter. The startled look on Kai's face was worth a Kodak moment.

Scrambling to stand, he eased the stiffness from his lanky body and lit a cigarette. The first cigarette of the day always tasted the best. His boss ordered everyone working on the wedding to be on high alert. Because he was a new hire, they gave him the shitty job of searching through the parking garage and the dank waste management room. Kai had even suggested to his boss that someone should comb through the giant trash tanks reeking to high heaven.

Bruce raised his arms above his head for a long stretch. A drawn-out yawn contorted his mouth. He could taste yesterday on his tongue. Next to him, a musty string mop stank. His shift, clipping shrubbery in the garden, would start in an hour. First, he had to check in with security and report his findings. The hotel promised those who volunteered to search all night a complimentary breakfast. With a quick sweeping motion, he dusted off his khaki slacks and matching shirt. He kicked his shoes into the stringy mop for a quick shine.

Yesterday, while chit-chatting and waiting for instructions, he had speculated with everyone else just for the fun of it. The odds were high that the missing guest was probably lost in the bed of one hot babe. When everyone laughed at the suggestion, he laughed too. He kept the truth hidden behind a knowing grin, and swallowed the temptation to offer his opinion, "or out floating on the ocean."

He'd always had a fondness for secrets and, better yet, keeping them. Once his assigned partner in the search signed out, he scoured places that a reasonable person, even someone as drunk as Jack Spencer, might seek refuge under. He made it look good whenever he was searching near a camera. Then he'd had enough and slept in the storage locker. No one mentioned a canoe.

Chapter 17

No Sign

One by one, the reports trickled in and confirmed Jack Spencer had vanished without leaving a trace. When the last person reported empty-handed, twinges of guilt assaulted Kai.

"I need some air." He said to George, and to the police officer who stayed on duty.

In the garden, he fumbled in his pocket and fished out a roll of antacids. Without thinking, he popped two tablets into his mouth and chewed. *Fruit flavor my ass,* Kai thought while they foamed up his mouth. They usually eased the burning in his gut, but not now.

All night, they took turns sifting through the surveillance footage. They burned copies for the police. Kai saw nothing he didn't already know. Eventually, someone higher-up would ask for the tapes, and the GM insisted they keep copies of everything.

He paced. For a split second, he wished he smoked. It would give him something to do and maybe relieve some stress. Kai didn't hear his boss's approach.

"Anything?"

Kai shook his head. He wished like hell that they had discovered something useful in the video footage. Or even on the ground search. This did not bode well for the hotel.

"The last place we have him on video is in the garden. That's why I'm out here. I wanted to see for myself." Kai gestured toward the lush vegetation as if any minute Jack Spencer would jump out. He waited for a comment from his boss who was always a man of few words.

"Nothing from the search either?"

"Not a trace. Jack Spencer vanished."

"Are you saying he came outside, and we have him on camera? But we don't have him going back in?"

"That's the thing. Because of the storm, that night, we lost three cameras. So we have no way of knowing if or if he didn't come back in."

"We're finding this out now?"

"No. We fixed the problem the morning after. As soon as we could."

"Hmm. Not ideal. But we don't have a responsibility to our guests for their own behavior. If Mr. Spencer was that drunk, why didn't any of his family for friends intervene? We're not a drug and alcohol rehab. If our facilities aren't at fault, we're good."

"I feel bad," Kai said.

"I'm sure you do, but Kai, there is only so much we can do. We provide luxury. The rest, our guests must take responsibility for. Can you imagine one of our staff advising a guest on how to behave and what choices to make? We'd be out of business. Just remember what I always advise. Think first, then speak."

"Will do."

Alone again, Kai moved the stalks and leaves aside, looking for clues. When his phone rang, he answered with trepidation.

"Kai here."

"Yup. No. We haven't found him. Been searching all night. Not a clue."

"No. I don't think so. His parents are pretty sure he'd not go near the water at night. Despite how drunk he was."

"Yes. Drunk people have done dumb things, but they're adamant he wouldn't. He's not that sort of person."

"I appreciate it. And thanks for looking. Yes, please bag me three mahi. Yes, I have a call in to get a wahoo. Thanks."

Kai hung up. His cousin was the third person to suggest the correlation. Was there a link between his missing canoe and Jack Spencer? But it made little sense. Why would he take a canoe without a paddle? And the Spencers said it themselves. "Jack would never go down the cordoned-off section of the beach." It's what they also told the police. They had a hunch that he booked a diving or snorkeling excursion. "He said he had a surprise for us." Officer Malone confiscated Jack's phone and ensured the Spencers, a qualified police hacker would search for a possible link. That Jack would neglect taking his phone and leave without a word to anyone was inconceivable.

In the garden, he heard people laughing. It was sad that despite Jack Spencer's disappearance, life without him moved on. The ground crew already clipped the lush lawn into a plaid pattern. Those not relegated to the search crew went about their routine chores as the demands of the hotel would bow to no one. Kai inhaled the scent of frangipani deeply into his lungs. He dared not imagine a landscape without such star-studded shrubs, maybe on Mars. He pretended as if he were on the sole mission of finding Jack Spencer, and it proved hard work the lies gathering. But he needed Kilo, and the demands of outstanding bills didn't waiver just because Jack vanished. One of them, a double mortgage bill, was due this morning.

Kai clung to the bit of desperate hope that he'd stumble across Jack Spencer. He could picture finding a man waking from his inebriated state. It happened often enough. While brushing his hand along the torch ginger flowers, he imagined Mrs. Spencer. He imagined her shriek with joy at the discovery. What mother deserved to lose her son? He thought of his own wife and her overwhelming love for their sons. It was unlike anything he had ever witnessed. Undercover of the giant blade of a Bismarck palm, he called his wife and left a quick message.

"I'll be home in a few hours. No. Still nothing. But it will complicate my schedule."

To appease his sense of curiosity, he headed toward the beach where he kept Kilo. Stopping at the top of the cliff, he scanned the ocean's expanse slowly. He prayed. He didn't want to be the person to spy a body floating on the waves. A corpse face-down in the sand. No. He'd not be the harbinger of such news. Climbing down, he filled with anticipation. The tide had been in and out four times since Kilo went missing. Enough chance for the surf to return what it had stolen. At the bottom, Kai found nothing, only sand washed a million times. Back up on the lawn, he wiped his shoes with the kerchief he kept in his pocket. His phone rang. It was George.

"We need you here. Police are questioning the guests. They want to start with those leaving this morning."

As soon as he entered through the employee entrance, glad to be out of the humidity, the manager flagged him down. They followed the corridor away from prying ears.

"Change of plans. Our lawyer will sit in with the police. He'll keep you informed, but you can take some pressure off. I only ask that you put yourself in charge of whatever needs to be taken care of."

Kai nodded. There was no one else on the security team who could assist with an investigation. He had tact and diplomacy.

"People like you."

His boss was about to add something. And Kai knew. People trusted something about his brown eyes, and the kind tone in his voice. But this morning, it was a compliment thrown with the speed of a curveball.

"I was on my way to see the Spencers again. I want to assure them we'll assist in any way possible. I've asked the front desk to be extra courteous."

"Great. You'll be compensated."

Chapter 18

Deadly Adversary

Jack remembered the scene in Cast Away, where Tom Hanks pounded on the green coconuts. But he couldn't remember who walked away with the trophy. He reached for the coconut with his good hand and shook it against his ear, involuntarily salivating. Small as the coconut was, it wielded an immense key to his survival. If—and it was a big if, he could crack it. He'd spent enough vacations in tropical climates to know a thing about coconuts. Though he had never harvested or pried one open. On St. Kitts, they had a gardener who could crack a nut in ten seconds with his machete without spilling a precious drop of water. But Jack had no tools. And the way he'd been managing, if he had a knife, he probably would have severed a limb by now. The gardener always chided: Coconuts can crack your skull.

Jack studied his find. This was not the sort of coconut you bought in the supermarket. This coconut was in its primitive state, or better known in its Fort Knox shell. He had seen survivalists use coconut husks to start fires. But on the canoe, he didn't give a fuck about starting fires, and everything was perpetually wet. He ran his nose over the rough husk. A slight fishy odor emanated, but he was so hungry he'd eat anything. His only tools were his hands and fingers, his mouth and teeth if he had to. He already learned he couldn't rely on his brain, but the pain in his fingers was slowly subsiding.

Assessing the coconut, he formed a plan. He'd wiggle the board on the bench loose. If there was a nail or screw, he could use it to poke holes in the husk and slowly tear it. As it was, the board wiggled each time he leaned into it. Using the heel of his palm, he slammed it against the wood. It hardly budged. On second thought, Jack wedged himself into the opening between the two seats. His legs were stronger. He kicked until it gave. Ten minutes later, he came away with a small victory when he cupped the prize — a long nail, rivulets of sweat and no injury.

"Come my precious. Let's get this done."

He poked hole after tedious hole along a natural seam in the husk. But at this speed, it would be sundown before he could have a drink, a meal of fresh coconut meat. He bedded the coconut down in the life vest and kneeled. Repeating his perforating pattern over and over, he concentrated. After three passes, he rose, stretching his limbs and looking if something better than a coconut was coming toward him.

"Fuck! My fingers hurt." Jack said to himself, shaking out the cramp in his hands. A slow burn affected his muscles despite alternating between his right and left hand while poking away on the seam. A rivulet of sweat swung from his nose and dropped. Everything tasted of salt: the air, his skin, his sweat, and even his tears.

"When I get back, I'm gunning for you, Tessa." Jack jammed the rusty nail into the coconut as if it were her face.

"First, I'll confess to Brody." For a second, he wished he had his fingernails back to scratch the surface of the husk. "I'm gonna keep it simple and say, sorry, buddy, but I fucked your girlfriend even after you got engaged. She offered. Not that that's an excuse." Confessing out loud to the coconut made it ring true and with more conviction. Slowly, what he had done sunk in with a hard reality. Maybe he deserved this punishment?

There was no use denying he was scum for what he had done. That no one ever suggested anything about what seemed so obvious, and wrong, surprised him. Theirs must have been the longest-running affair on record. He was sure his mother saw something. Stacy had to know. And Brody? How could he not know?

"How could you not see it?" Jack thought of Brody coming to the house during the Christmas holidays. He had a key. Brody was always welcome at the Spencer home. Tessa had arrived unexpectedly an hour earlier, timing it so that his parents were out visiting friends.

Two days earlier, Brody had proposed to Tessa over Christmas dinner. She accepted the flawless diamond and said yes. Everyone at the dinner table clapped and said, "it's about time." Jack assumed a yes meant their affair was over, which was a good thing. Being entangled as he was, he dreaded that the truth would surface at any moment. But Tessa had other ideas about how marriage would work and insisted on a long engagement. Her excuse, she wanted time to plan the perfect wedding. It's how they ended up in Hawaii. Tessa wanted it all, including him as her slave. What was worse, he allowed it, and she fueled his addiction. He didn't have it in him to refuse what she was offering. Things escalated from there and spiraled out of control.

It was at that moment when Jack heard the door open and saw Brody in the foyer; he froze, and his guilt caught up to him. The scent of fresh pine hung in the air; soft jazz music played in the background. Red poinsettias lined the stairway up to where Jack was standing on the landing. Seeing Brody below, it was too late to tuck his shirt in, and his heart pounded in his ears. This is it, he thought. He was sure a blind man would have been able to read the guilt imprinted on his face. But Brody said the most incredible thing when Tessa came out of the kitchen, a glass of water in her hand. Somehow, she adjusted her dress, her hairdo.

"I figured you'd still be here. Sorry, I'm late, Babe." He kissed Tessa on the mouth and lifted her off the ground. Tessa squealed. "Put me down, you oaf."

That Tessa had risked everything blew Jack away. She had shown up unannounced, and within minutes she had his clothes off. Later, when he found out she knew Brody was on his way over, the truth stared him in the face. He had to untangle himself from Tessa.

"Come on, you!" Jack spoke to the coconut. "It's lunchtime, and I'm starving."

Slowly, a tear was forming in the husk. Head down; Jack worked furiously until he got his finger into the crevice. The sun hung on the west side of high-noon, and Jack could taste his victory if not the coconut. Clouds were boiling on the eastern horizon, and he was glad the ocean was calm. He wanted it to rain, yet he dreaded terrible weather, knowing he wasn't equipped to survive. But he'd give anything to stick his tongue out and lick the raindrops from the sky. Anything? He asked himself.

Jack only laid the coconut down when he thought he heard something. A faint sound. A vibration that moved closer, then slowly vanished again. Sometimes he thought he imagined the sound, that it was the sound of hope fading.

Chapter 19

Expanding the Circle

A long list of people had access to the Spencer suite. The general manager allowed himself in after knocking and waiting for the "It's open." Everyone stopped talking when he entered.

"I wanted to offer you the use of the penthouse suite. And to say we're doing all we can."

"That's very kind. But we're fine here." John had expected better news. Myra saw it in his eyes. John didn't like to rely on others either. He was a doer.

Myra was grateful for the intrusion. She'd been sitting for three hours with Detective Malone. The man had the tenacity to dig into Jack's personal life, leaving nothing to chance. But he had so many phone calls that it made the interview rather challenging to sit through.

"To summarize. Jack was wearing a navy-blue suit. A gold chain with his initials etched into the link. We have a photo of him. And we know who he was with last."

All during the interview, Myra battled the urge to get a lint brush and roll it over the detective's suit jacket. The fabric shone from wear, and winter had dusted the shoulders and lapel with dandruff. Myra had no faith that this man was qualified to find Jack.

"Enough for now. You have a description. Let's find him."

Everything was moving too slow. No one had the same sense of urgency to find Jack as she did. She felt a scream sitting at the base of her throat, and she wanted nothing more than to take over the search. But they'd never allow it. She had to hand the life of her son over to strangers and trust. She rose, excused herself, and shut the bedroom door behind her. Above her, the ceiling fan whirled gently, caressing her bare arms. Directly ahead of her, a native woman with lush hair stared out from a painting. The woman was braiding her hair in the portrait, unaware of the sadness that followed Myra into the room. It was unfair that life went on for everyone but Jack. Even the lifeless painting, teeming with movement and depth, breathed life. The artist had done an excellent job.

Every hour, room service delivered some offering to heal the wound. Plates of fruit, crackers, and cheese, steaming urns of coffee, and bottles of mineral water cluttered the table. For the first time in many years, Myra had foregone her hour-long workout at the gym. Her perfect life had toppled in a matter of hours.

Michael had already booked a flight, and he'd be arriving in the late hours of the morning. He had asked the same questions as Stacy and said, "not Jack." Their infallible brother was out there. "They're not looking in the right places." Stacy had said. In her condition, the doctor would never consent to allow her to travel by air. Instead, Stacy volunteered to make the arrangements to send someone to search for clues in Jack's condominium. If he had left any.

Myra smoothed her skirt and then rose. With her phone in hand, she scrolled for pictures. The overwhelming urge to

THE LUCKY MAN: AN ACT OF MALICE

see Jack's smiling face won out over every other need. Not that she'd ever forgotten what he looked like. It was torture looking into his eyes; it was torture not seeing those eyes. "Where are you, Jack?"

John knocked softly. He understood she needed a minute to balance her emotions into an upright composure. She felt like a game of Jenga. One wrong move and she'd tumble.

"It's open."

John leaned into the open door but didn't invade the small sanctuary she had sought.

"Officer Malone just wants to wrap up. But if you need a minute, I can manage."

"No. It's fine. We're in this together."

During the invasive probing, she and John answered truthfully, yet Malone wanted more. Blood from a stone. Taking a seat across from him, she readied herself for more.

"No, Jack isn't suicidal." Myra snapped at Malone's cruel tone.

"I'm sorry. I have to ask these questions."

Myra noticed for the first time that his eyes were permanently sad. Even during happy times, his eyes were upside down.

"What about finances? Did he have a lot of debts? Gambling?"

"We're working on getting you his bank and investment information. Although I highly doubt that they have any bearing on his disappearance."

"What about a domestic relationship? Back in California?" Malone drummed his pen, painting his own version of Jack Spencer. He'd already been corrected, rather harshly, by Mr. Spencer when he inadvertently used the word *was*—a slip of the tongue.

"We know your son liked to drink. But what about drugs? Street or prescription meds?"

"No drugs! You're going the wrong way with this." Myra couldn't help herself.

"Religion?" Malone veered the interrogation back to calmer waters.

Myra didn't understand the simple yet complex question. But her answer settled the matter.

"We're Christians, but no affiliations."

"Have you identified the woman on the stairs yet?" John asked.

Impatient, he asked again. His entire hope lay with the women who spent time with their son.

"Not yet. But we have an answer from Rose Winter. She spent the night with Jack. He gave her his number in case she ever headed his way."

"Nothing else?"

"What about the Coast Guard? Why is it taking so long to get his search going?"

"We don't know if your son is in the water. Nothing is linking him to being on the water. You said yourself he'd never go near the ocean at night. That he had a healthy respect for it."

Officer Malone shook his head. Exhaustion half-closed his eyes. He didn't have the manpower, but he agreed with the Spencers, the woman on the stairs was a suspect. Her looks were bait. But so what? Another dead end and a term he'd better not let slip off his tongue. No one on staff confessed they knew who she was.

"So, the window we're looking for is after the last camera captured Jack in the garden?" That's the gap we need to fill. Malone snapped his notepad shut, and it vanished inside the deep pocket of his rumpled jacket.

Myra swallowed the panic when she rose to shake Malone's hand. "Thank you. Please excuse our bad manners. We know you are doing what you can. But you must understand."

She left off the obvious that at least thirty hours had passed since anyone spoke to Jack—that they knew of. That not everyone was on high alert rattled her nerves.

John shook hands with Malone and ushered him out the door. Myra turned her back on them and walked toward the balcony; the view had become a mental hideaway. Seeing the stunning expanse of the ocean and sky, she knew Jack was looking at the same thing at the same moment. Logically, she couldn't account for it, but with each beat of her heart, she felt Jack's beat within her own rhythm. Jack was alive.

Kai entered just as Malone was leaving. He and John discussed something in a low voice, and Myra didn't care. They could hash all the dread of hopeless speculations. She'd swim alone on the deep end if she had to.

"Myra. Kai offered to raise a search party. Family, islanders, volunteers from the staff. He's already amassed twenty people. He'll manage them. As Malone said, the police just don't have the manpower."

"A bit of good news supported by action. I'll have the hotel arrange a luncheon afterward. I'm grateful. Kai seems a decent bloke."

"He is. I think I'll join the team, but I suggest you stay here."

"What? You're afraid of what they'll find."

"I am. I'm realistic."

"No, you're not. Jack's alive. Don't ask me how I know, but he is."

"I'm glad you have faith. I've also called Jason Rockport. He's clearing his schedule and hopes to catch the last flight."

"Spare no expense. Jack's out there, and I sense he needs us."

John leaned in and kissed her when she saw the sadness. She pitied him. John didn't have that invisible string attaching him to the children. Not that he loved them less, but that bond, no one could steal that from a mother. The umbilical cord the doctor cut and never severed.

"I find the helpless waiting the worst. You?"

"Not seeing his face. Yet when I look at his photograph, it cuts me. I miss him so much."

John brushed the wayward tear rolling down her face with his thumb, he pulled her into the safety of his shoulder. They stood in a long embrace, words left unspoken, sentiments exchanged by osmosis.

"I'll call you the minute I have any news. And I mean any. We can do this."

"We can do this. For Jack."

Alone, Myra stared out toward the ocean. The answer lay in the waves that relentlessly sent their offerings and deposited them on the shore. Regardless of whether you wanted their gifts. The waves did not discriminate. They gave, and they took. As a family, good fortune and good health blessed them. All that their lives needed to be comfortable and successful was at their fingertips. Was this the price? Was Jack the deal they had somehow made with the devil in exchange? "Take me instead, you nasty piece of shit!" Myra argued with her thoughts. Give me my Jack back, and I'm all yours. But don't do this. She closed her eyes, and snapshots of Jack flooded her mind and unleashed a torrent of tears. The dam breached and let go. A collage of Jack playing on her memory smiled and waved. Jack was everywhere and nowhere.

Myra clutched the balcony railing for strength. She missed how Jack said, mom. A word used a million times per second around the world. But like the instinctual scent of an animal, the word belonged to her alone. Mom. I won't let you down, Jack. I'm gonna find you no matter where you're hiding. And wherever you are, Jack, don't give up. Wait for me, and I'll come.

A soft knock intruded on her connection.

"Mrs. Spencer. Flowers for you."

The young porter carried an extravagant arrangement of tropical flowers into the room and set them on the round table. He left the room soundlessly except for the click of the door.

The small card read, *Whatever it takes! We'll find him. Love Brody.*

Poor boy. His wedding was ruined. The bride, according to John, refused to see anyone and had thrown the flawless carat ring at Brody's face. Brody and Jack were like brothers. Suddenly, the urge to wander among the shrubs and palms kicked Myra into gear. She grabbed her sunglasses. She needed air, nature, and solace.

In the long corridor, she sidestepped the luggage awaiting the porter in the hallway.

Before she reached the elevator, a cleaning cart wiggled toward her. A housekeeping maid, dressed in the standard mustard yellow uniform, looked up, saw her, and quickly ducked into the stairwell abruptly abandoning the card. All Myra saw was the neatly coiled bun and a slim figure wearing a uniform two sizes too big before she could call out. Myra was confident it was the young maid from the day before. The pretty one.

Chapter 20

Vigil

Kai suppressed a yawn. He had learned all the tricks of staying awake years ago when his father suffered that severe injury in a work accident. For hours at a time, he sat next to his father's hospital bed. Praying, worrying, and occasionally falling asleep for minutes at a time. There were moments when his father took a turn for the worse and moments when the praying paid off. When his father recovered enough, the hospital bill left them on the border of being almost destitute. If it hadn't been for the hotel and their generosity, they would have been. They loaned Kai the money to pay his debts at a minimal interest rate and in return earned Kai's loyalty. Even if the fees were still horrendous, his family could float if not outright swim. Kai took on fishing for money and peddled his catch to anyone willing to pay cash. Though he never wanted to look a gift horse in the mouth, he vowed to take only what they needed. Kilo was a crucial element in the plan, and now Kilo and the means of making money had vanished, and for what seemed like an eternity, no echoes of an abandoned canoe reached his ears. When a moment of privacy finally opened, he called the police station.

"Kai Hale. Name painted on the wooden canoe is Kilo."

"Can you provide us with a photograph?"

"I'll send it."

"And you said what night?"

"Thursday. The night of the storm."

"You work at the hotel where they're looking for Jack Spencer."

"That is correct too."

"Come in and sign the statement when you can."

The miracle he prayed for hadn't come to fruition with the phone call to the police. Kai half expected whoever answered to say, "Oh, yes. Someone called in a found canoe."

When he looked up, he spotted Mrs. Spencer. She was kneeling and looking behind a stand of heliconia for something. No. Not something. Her son. He swung wide and allowed her the privacy she needed. Jack, he knew, was not in any of the gardens. He had done a thorough search and instructed the garden staff to remain vigilant. A life was at stake. Kai dared not think of the emotional beat down the Spencers endured with each waking minute. He kept his head down and prayed Jack was safe. Someplace. He couldn't say why he felt that, but then this was not about logic. It all came down to instinct.

His cousin offered to haul in at least three fish a day. No charge. A favor exchanged for a favor exchanged among family didn't come with a price tag. So far, whenever he mentioned the missing canoe to his cousins, he heard their breath catch. They fished from a long-reaching heritage too. Canoes were a sacred family treasure. Promises to keep an eye out for Kilo didn't warrant verbalizing. Like Mrs. Spencer, he knew in his heart Kilo was out there. Floating somewhere within reach, if only he believed hard enough. Not that Kilo and Jack were on an equal footing of importance. But Kilo was Kai's lifeline. He daren't stab a guess of what Jack meant to his mother. Kai knew.

The muster point for the search party was strategically located in the Orchid garden. He assessed the assembled crowd wondering how to best split them into teams since he volunteered to oversee the search himself. Mr. Spencer had such hopes rise in his eyes when Kai suggested it. So far thirty people waited on his instructions, and they were eager to find Jack Spencer. The police promised to conduct their own search. The Coast Guard was searching for the proverbial needle in a wet haystack. Kai was on a list of first to know. That list came with the honor of pride. But who wouldn't offer the utmost?

Kai cleared his throat before speaking. Some staff members doubled as family and friends. He knew their faces, and he tried to instill the importance of the search by gazing directly into their eyes.

"Last known position of Jack Spencer is in the Rose Garden. We have a video of him. He's suspected of being injured and assumed disoriented."

Maybe he shouldn't have stressed the word injured. Mr. Spencer flinched when the brevity of the word landed on him.

"If you find any object in the garden, bag it. Note on the sheet where you discovered the item. Let's find Jack!"

Kai handed out clipboards and pens. Small pegs that were used for solar lamps on special occasions were to mark anything of interest. Even the most minor thing like a button, a footprint.

"Let's meet back here in an hour, and please be thorough."

John Spencer approached him on the soft lawn while talking into his cellphone. There had never been a good time to return the tip Mr. Spencer had given him. They had trespassed beyond that time zone, and he didn't expect John to hold out his hand. But Kai's conscience enjoyed reminding him that Jack had been missing longer than anyone assumed. Jack was lost to the charms of that stunning woman. Behind the stunning facade of the woman hid another secret Kai hadn't shared. There was something familiar about the woman in the video. Although he didn't know many local beauties with blond streaks in their long brown hair, there was something familiar. She was young, too young, and he hated using the term girl because she had an innocence about her that shouldn't charm a man. Yet captured in the footage of her on the stairs, she knew exactly what she wanted. Her eyes didn't betray her. Jack Spencer was her target.

"Kai. Thank you again for arranging the search party. I'm in your debt."

"No need. We'll find Jack."

"I have a very specialized PI coming in tomorrow. I'm hoping we won't need his services, but can I rely on you to be his main contact? Show him around, answer his questions."

"Absolutely. Whatever it takes, Mr. Spencer."

"You have our gratitude."

"Let's find your son." Kai pointed. "I spotted your wife, she's in Orange Blossom Garden. That way."

Chapter 21

War

Jack's fingers throbbed just where his cuticles met the start of his nails. Despite the initial pain subsiding, an electrifying ache reminded him each time he moved his fingers of how stupid he was. And it had cost him more than a layer of skin. It surprised Jack how rusty his blood tasted and that the force split his skin more precisely than a cut. A red stain grew persistently beneath the strip of cloth he had torn from his sleeve and tied like a tourniquet around the wound.

He sat with his legs wide apart, the naked coconut lumbered on the canoe floor and mocked him. Despite the pain, he had finally finished stripping the husk off. Now he was considering his next plan of attack. Jack was sure of one thing: he could not afford to allow the generous offering to escape. The coconut, whether it knew, represented survival. And the water, he hoped to drink, was not only a thirst quencher but also an antibacterial immune booster. At least he remembered reading that in a fitness magazine.

However, he decided he had to be smart about his next move. He couldn't subject his body to another beating. An infection would minimize his chances. Lord knew what deadly collection of bacteria inhabited the canoe; or the water that continually touched his skin. There was no escaping.

"Listen here. You're my lifesaver, and I plan on using you." He spoke to the coconut, wagging his finger. "Regardless of how long that might take. Or how deviously vicious you are. You hear me!"

Jack reached for his prize. He knew coconuts had a natural fault line. The gardener at St. Kitts had shown him how to split one into two perfect halves and seldom wasted a drop. Jack could picture the man's white grin spill out with laughter, and he always cracked the coconuts with deadly accuracy. Now it was Jack's turn to practice what he learned.

Jack weighed the coconut in his hand. Its eyes stared up. He remembered to feel for the natural line and to smash it against something hard in one swift motion. Like swinging a club or racket, Jack feigned the movement and paced his arm, lining it up with the lip of the canoe. This time he calculated his fingers into the equation.

"One, two, three."

The whack landed just as Jack planned, and the coconut broke cleanly in half. He hardly spilled any of the water. Although he wasn't the praying sort of man, he looked up toward the sky and acknowledged the gift. He saved a mouthful for his cut, the nasty boils that were sprouting like mushrooms on his body.

"Thank you, thank you."

A fat rim of white meat lined the coconut but chewing on it was hard. Jack hacked away on the pristine flesh with the rusty nail. He couldn't get the meat into his mouth fast enough.

"Oh, so good." He nibbled his way around the rim.

"I can do this!" He yelled while chewing.

He also remembered how the gardener tapped the coconut against a rock. Going in circles until the meat came away from the rind. A basket of brown burlap skin cradling the meat. Jack had plans for the cup-like shells. He couldn't afford another folly like the water bottle, and he had learned his lesson. Chewing as fast as he could, he ate half of the meat while debating if he should save half for later. He knew there were two schools of thought. One: eat what you can when you can. Two: save something for a rainy day.

Rainy days were coming. Jack knew that despite not wanting to be a pessimist. But waiting could also mean losing what precious resources he had. His stomach decided for him. Jack rubbed the residual oil onto his chapped lips and skin. Overcome by joy, he clapped the empty shells like horse hooves and rose to stand and celebrate. How many victories would he need to survive? He wondered, and was anyone keeping score? Squinting, and his hand at attention, he scanned the horizon. The undulating waves danced in all directions and sent running white caps in a haphazard pattern across the blue expanse.

"There! What's that?" He pointed, straining to see it again. But the ocean was nothing but a pathetic liar. He fell for its tricks repeatedly. His eyes were willing to see the mirages that didn't exist. This time, when he blinked, he saw the movement again. A bubbling white breech. Undoubtedly something significant: a whale. Knowing they were that close terrified him. His heart thundered, but he had to keep his irrational emotions in check. Or else. He took a seat and paced his breathing. It would take more than a coconut to save him.

Jack's hope lay in the blue sky and blue ocean. He didn't care which one as long as it happened. So far, Jack had counted ten airplanes that streaked across during daylight, and thirteen blinking lights streaked across the night sky. They weren't looking for him. They didn't even know he existed. His airplane would have to fly in a little lower and be loud enough for him to hear. But there was no doubt it was on its way.

"Mom!" Jack yelled. "Mom!" Waves carried the word into the open arms of the breeze and vanished. There was nothing on this earth that would stop his mother from launching a search. He simply had to have faith; she was doing everything she could from where she was. There was no doubt, only it was taking longer than he thought it should.

Feeling revived by his small success and food in his stomach, Jack clapped the coconut shells again. The rain was coming, and he'd have to bail. Clouds had steadily amassed on the horizon as if they were jostling for position in a race. The shells might save his life yet again, and he vowed to take care of them.

"Stop that!" He said, chiding himself. He jammed the shells into his jacket pocket. Jack hadn't been able to resist clapping and enjoying the hollow clopping. But they weren't a toy, and no matter how bored he was, he couldn't sacrifice them for a moment's satisfaction. To keep his mind occupied, Jack concocted lists which he rambled off every hour to keep his sanity in check. He rotated them for the sake of the moment, but there was one sensation he couldn't harness. It took the top-spot even after a meal of coconut meat.

Hunger. Jack wished he had access to the brown doggie bags he hauled home from the countless restaurants. The ones his cleaning lady disposed of for him.

Thirst. Cruel joke. He had drunk himself to oblivion and ended up in a gigantic bowl of water that he couldn't drink from. Was that irony?

Fear. People paid to see whales, sharks, dolphins, and whatever wildlife. He preferred to watch them for the safe angle of his leather recliner on his high definition television. Whales, sharks, even those bull-faced fish that chased the canoe and boldly knocked, scared him.

Boredom. Without a single gadget, Jack felt trapped in a mindless time-warp. Is that what prison was like? Was he stuck in jail without walls? For some sort of crime that he was being punished for? Was that what the universe was throwing at him as some sort of revenge plan? Regardless of the answer, there were too many hours in a day.

Panic. It rose in his gut and spread like warm floodwaters upward. Depositing silt as it went on its way.

Hopelessness. Sun and sky and nothing between. He sensed his own insignificance. A week ago, he would have argued the point. Now he was ready to drop, humbled to his knees.

The urge to chew. Jack had feasted on his fingernails. Toenails were on the menu.

Frustration. Jack would have never guessed this, but frustration stemmed from his teeth. Until now, he hadn't known that teeth were responsible for the aggravation. But the sensation set in his jaw and his teeth took hold.

Despair—the stage curtains. It fell and rose. Jack wanted to punch the person responsible for pulling the rope.

Loneliness. He'd never look at another person the same way. He'd reach out to the elderly and homeless if he ever got the chance to remedy his mistakes. Loneliness, he learned, wasn't an emotion at all. It was a physical and crippling affliction.

Chapter 22

Itching

Bruce leaned against the wall. With his leg braced, he pretended to enjoy his coffee break in the afternoon sun, but his eyes were elsewhere. Through the mirrored lenses of his sunshades, he glared toward Kai Hale. That fucker had been strutting around the hotel and gardens as if he'd become the head honcho overnight.

"What a cunt?" Wayne hissed. Plumes of yellowed cigarette smoke catapulted out his nostrils and mouth.

"Keep your voice down!" Too many fucking ears around." Bruce kicked off the wall and ground his cigarette butt into the soil.

Kai Hale was a cunt. But he had been good on his promise. Bruce no longer needed to sweat. Instead, he rode the new-fangled mower because of Kai's influence. He'd have to be careful how to tread around him. He had to keep the game in play.

"Whatever. So how'd you sweet-talk your way into getting off the push mower?" Wayne crushed his Styrofoam cup and flung his butt into the bushes.

"Charm and skill." Bruce pulled his cap lower. Irritated, he sneered. Wayne was a blabbermouth and didn't need to know about the bargain he struck. He had a runaway mouth.

You seen her?" Wayne lowered his tone.

"How many fucking times do you need to be told!"

"Sorry. It's not like I used her name?" Wayne took offense. It seemed that lately, he couldn't get anything right for Bruce, who was perpetually miffed.

"No. She's not taking my calls. Her big fucking brother is acting as a bodyguard. I can't get near. But she's gonna get what's coming to her."

Bruce flicked a salute to Wayne. He had a lawn to cut, and he wanted to keep this lucrative job for a little while. Boring as it was on the mower, it was better than sweating. He kept his head down. There was no point in having one of the volunteers harass him again. And Kai would freak out if he had seen them smoking on hotel grounds. Kai was anal about following the rules. Or at least that the staff followed the rules. It seemed no matter where Bruce worked, management always lived by a different set of rules. Kai was no exception. From his vantage point, Bruce observed. Comical really, that the volunteers scoured every shrub and flower bed for clues of that missing fucker, Jack Spencer. Good riddance. If he wasn't smart enough to paddle home, then that was just God's way of weeding out the trash. Natural selection.

"One down, one to go," Bruce said aloud while glaring toward Kai, who was busy explaining how to log a clue on the clipboard to one of the brain dead-bimbos who thought she found some vital evidence in the search. Bruce guessed it was a case of too much CSI.

Making his way back to his mower, Bruce wondered if Kai's status would diminish if they found out about the canoe.

That it was no longer moored to the post. And how it was so dangerously accessible to guests who wandered off the path on the beach. How would they react if some anonymous bird sang that Kai's precious shit-canoe vanished overnight? That it was roughly in the same place as they guesstimated Jack Spencer's last whereabouts? And that Kai withheld information that might have saved a man's life.

The engine of the sparkling new mower kicked over and purred. Bruce shifted gears and dropped the blade. He grinned. Wouldn't they like to know?

PART 2

ANOTHER LIFE

Chapter 1

The Missing

The ground beneath Rose oozed with water when her feet touched down. She had nearly fallen asleep on the outlook that Ron crafted from a salvaged palm. On this crow's nest, she had two options: wedging herself in place and sitting; or standing for the duration of the four-hour shift. No one enjoyed the job of watchman, yet it was a crucial aspect of their existence. At least it dried the pink soles of her feet, that alone was a luxury.

"Ron. What's that?" She asked after climbing down from her perch. He was oblivious to her approach, the endless, rushing noise drowned any sound and movement. With her finger poised, she pointed toward the horizon, that space between blue sky and blue ocean and the other side of the world. Ron set his fishing rod down, clamping it with his foot, and followed the line of her finger. He saluted to shield the glare from his eyes and rotated his head ever so slightly, then stopped. Without taking his gaze off the object that he thought Rose wanted him to see, he reached for the binoculars strapped around his neck. It seemed an eternity for him to find what even she wasn't sure existed.

"Shit! That's a container."

Their set of communal binoculars had precisely one spot that wasn't distorted like a kaleidoscope, and everyone else, besides Ron, felt dizzy when they tried to focus on that object, they all expected to discover every day. He tested the existence of the foreign object against his naked eyes, squinted, and then reached for the binoculars again. Rose waited for instructions. Her breath stalled in her chest, and her eyes strained to keep the object in view. As if merely blinking could make it vanish.

"Get the others!"

Running was impossible. The ground moved beneath her weight, and each step had to be measured to reach the next platform without sinking. Despite being lithe, it was a challenge and all she could think of was the sharp corner protruding on the offing. It represented salvation and also the unthinkable. That they missed out on something far greater. A ship.

The others were busy preparing for the next series of storms. It had been her job to be on the lookout, and this wasn't the first experience she had with something that she saw crest on the horizon. She'd seen ghost ships shrouded in a white mist, tankers that crawled like ants on the spine of the horizon. And airplanes that streaked across the forever blue and never saw her frantic wave. Those were signs of hope and also the dangling carrot keeping them alive. There was a permanence to their lives, yet it hinged on the intangible endlessness that they all, from time to time, couldn't stand.

Seeing her run haphazardly toward them alerted the others. They stopped mid-motion in their chores, everything happened at moon landing speed, trapped in the web of the surreal.

"Get on the raft."

She yelled, missed her next landing, and fell into the water. She should have used the standup paddleboard, but she thought this was quicker, and if they happened to see her, they'd detect that sense of urgency. With her forearm on something semi-solid, she pulled herself up, spitting water, gasping. This wasn't the time to go weak in the knees. When she reached the raft, the others were ready and guided her on board with their outstretched arms. Mark hunkered down in the stern and shouted orders.

"Rose, you're with Li Wei."

Rose had a designated seat. Everyone did, and they balanced their weight. She grasped the roughhewn oar and dug in, without getting a chance to catch her breath.

"What did you see?" Mark shouted, looking directly in her eyes while keeping the raft steady as they found their rhythm.

"A container." Her lungs burned from exhaustion. But ultimately, if they could salvage anything, she'd be a hero.

"Ted! Ease up. You're pulling too hard; the others can't keep up."

The cumbersome raft was veering away from the direction they were heading toward. They needed to pick up Ron, who stood motionless, his gaze focused on the object. Slung over his shoulder was the lunch he'd been busy reeling in, and not even this urgent mission would allow Ron to waste any precious resource. The raft came to a stop when it bumped into the wall of plastic, and Ron clamored on board. This is what they trained for every day when they weren't busy trying to survive elements beyond their control.

"Pull," Mark yelled. He had his position as coxswain well-rehearsed, his eyes lingered a second longer on Rose than the others. If there was a message in his gaze, now wasn't the time to read it. Rose dug deep and kept pace with Li Wei, and

Ron rose to stand at the helm. He'd be the eyes forward, and the signal to guide Mark.

With every pull, Rose inhaled the sweat of everyone on board. But she was used to their odor. If anything, she could almost distinguish one from the other, based on their scent. Each muscle in her arms and legs burned from the strain, but it was now or never. When she first glimpsed the corner of the container, it was as always, a test to separate fact from fiction. While on watch, she'd been struggling to keep her eyes open. The morning glare was challenging to look through, and a haze of heat shimmered above the water. Any minute she expected to see a mirage or fall uncomfortably asleep. She guessed the container was at least 1200 yards out, and she wasn't any good at measuring distances without any landmark to go by.

"How far out do you think?" Mark was straining to see something in the direction Ron was looking toward. But from ground level, it was impossible to see beyond the waves rolling at a lulling speed next to them. The raft was cumbersome to maneuver, a flaw Ron was still working on solving. But the fact was, it either stayed upright in whatever storm came their way, or he had to forsake speed. Nothing came easy.

"Hard to say, at least a thousand yards or so. It's hanging just on the lip of the horizon."

Mark was panting, and even Ron had trouble catching his breath. Rose bit down on her teeth and dug into a source of strength she didn't know existed. Adrenaline. It made her lightheaded, but she couldn't risk what was at stake. She focused on Mark's muscular legs and watched the serpent tattoo around his calf muscle come to life. His skin was heavily inked and explained away at least part of his mystery. And she didn't want to look in his eyes again. He had plans that he included her in, but she wasn't sure she agreed with the unspoken demand. But at times like this, the team banded together for the cause. Nothing else mattered. And as suddenly as the thrill began, it ended. Ron slumped down and covered his face.

"What is it? Ron? What the fuck?"

"I lost it. It's gone." Ron wouldn't look up.

"Take over." Mark held his hand out for the binoculars.

Everyone dropped their oars, as they coasted, allowing their breath to catch up while Mark did a precision scan of the endless blue before them. They knew disappointment like a close acquaintance and recognized it when hope barely clung on.

"Row! I see it." Mark gestured northeast and away from the gigantic disc sitting comfortably on the skyline at ten o'clock.

"Steady. Go straight!" Mark didn't take his eyes from what only he could see.

"You see it?"

"An easy 800 yards."

Distance on water is deceptive. But everyone trusted in Mark's and Ron's opinion, and they had nothing left to lose. Rose dreamed of eating something. Anything. Although here, the choices on their daily menu were simple. It was either fish or fish. Seaweed when they were lucky. When she looked up, she saw Mark's superhero pose reflected in the shadow that fell backward onto the raft. There was no doubt she needed to have faith. In them. Trust wasn't something she owned any longer. She had given all of it Ron two years ago.

"Steady now, 600 yards."

On land, 600 yards is a comfortable distance, on the ocean, on a raft that wouldn't comply with their combined effort, excruciating. The wind had stopped completely, they all glistened with sweat, their core temperature was set on boiling. But they all clung to the glimmer of survival and what lay at the end of the rainbow. Rose wanted nothing more than a container full of pizza, or hamburgers, thick milkshakes. Cases of peanut butter. Even stale loaves of bread. She swallowed what she imagined she could taste.

"I can see the back end. We're in luck. It's door side up."

Chapter 2

Bounty

As the raft drifted closer, everyone held their breath, what they saw and wished for wasn't a secret. Rose believed in miracles even when they seldom surfaced. Looming on the waves, the rectangular shape, partly sunk, bobbed on the water. Any second it could take its last breath and sink before their eyes, sending out a small set of tsunami waves. Despite this being a salvage operation, they hadn't any reliable tools but their own will and the residual strength in their bodies to harvest what little came their way.

"It's not locked. Not a good sign. Probably empty." Mark reached to touch the metal corner and prevented the raft from drifting. The container door was skimming above the lip of water.

"What's the plan, Ron?"

"Well, it's not listing. So, whatever's in there has shifted slightly toward the back in our favor. I'll take any positives I can."

"I was thinking the same. Should we just go for it?"

"First we should prop it up. Get the buoys."

Straining to untie a set of handmade buoys, Rose stretched as far as she could without falling into the water. Because of Ron's ingenuity, they had a raft, an island and a means to keep dry. She dug her fingers into the knots that tied the buoys to the raft and were also part of the raft. Her handmade life vest cut uncomfortable into her ribs, but everyone wore them on Ron's insistence. Following orders saved lives.

"Get three more." The urgency in Ron's voice was reminiscent of a military command. He understood what was at stake better than most.

While Rose was struggling with the knots, Mark and Li Wei wiggled themselves into the ill-fitting wetsuits that were also from a salvage operation. Mark's neoprene suit puckered at the knees and crotch, the man it was tailored for was a giant. And Li Wei's suit was pink in all the wrong places.

Before Rose arrived on the island, she'd been swimming in a public pool with seniors. Learning the benefits of aerobics. It still made her laugh to think about it. But pool water and ocean water were two separate species, both could kill a person, but ocean water had a mind of its own. Ron tied Mark and Li Wei off with the hand braided cord. There was no way he'd let them go in without keeping his hands on them.

Whenever anyone entered the water, their lives were at risk. Although it wasn't shark season, what lay beneath the surface remained a mystery. Mark dived in first, the water rippled, and Li Wei followed. Li Wei was an amazing free diver. His small stature and agility made him adept at many chores. Mark could rely on his physique in most instances, but his lungs were no match for Li Wei.

Rose held her breath while waiting for them to surface. Ron stared at the place in the water where they had vanished. All around them, the shifting water reflected the color of molten glass, sometimes green and then without notice, a shade of ultramarine, but always dangerous.

"What do you think's in it?" Ted said behind her, voicing her own curiosity.

Beside her, Ron stripped off his shirt, exposing a roadmap of scars. He still joked that feasting on the scabs he pulled off his skin kept him alive. Whether there were any nutritional benefits to the salt sores didn't matter. He said his teeth enjoyed the benefit of chewing on something. Because Ron's skin tone enhanced the blank spaces even more, he looked like a man made of polka-dots. The spots no longer tanned, or even burned. He'd eaten his own pigment along with the scabs. He survived on a diet of fingernails and scabs that he claimed was the cure for obesity. Toenails, he said, are the best dessert.

"I hope it's something edible. Anything. Even shoe leather."

"Me too. Pizza would be nice."

"Shepherd's pie with a cold beer."

"A bleeding steak, a baked potato. Yes, I'd cut my arm off for a cold one."

"Pasta. Oh my god, I can taste the garlic from here."

It was true. Rose could taste that perpetual linger of something similar to a metallic garlic in her mouth too. Whenever a palm tree floated into their corner of the world, she flossed with the fronds. Despite not enduring the grinding whir of a dentist's cleaning gear for several years, her teeth felt clean. A diet of fish, saltwater rinses, and her exploratory tongue did a decent job.

"Some rice for Li Wei."

Ron fed the long cord into the water. Bubbles surfaced, Mark and Li Wei were beneath the container, but it proved impossible to drag the buoys under, no matter how hard they tried to drag them. They popped out as fast as they could shove them under because the cords kept breaking apart. And disturbing the container was perilous.

"We need traction of some sort." Mark hoisted himself onto the raft. Li Wei followed. Both spitting and panting. After an half an hour of trying, the container hadn't budged and every handmade buoy fell apart from pulling.

"What are the chances of Mark and I lifting just the lip of the container and then sliding the paddleboards under?" Ted offered his suggestion. "We have enough to stretch the width of the container. Shoving the buoys under isn't working."

"Worth a try. Rose. Get the boards. Mark, Li Wei rest a minute."

Rose didn't mind being the lacky. Being busy and instrumental was ultimately better than being a tool in a box of tools. During the last year, they salvaged five new boards. The one she enjoyed using most was carved from exotic woods. Mark even suggested that a board like that would cost upward of fifteen-grand. Yet they discovered it drifting on the ocean, its owner missing, the possibility that the waves took him, always a reality. But it suited Rose. The footpad was worn from sun and saltwater and standing on it in the middle of the Pacific was humbling. It wasn't lost on her.

"Do you want just the plastic ones?" Rose floated the first two boards over.

"For now."

"Actually, Rose, can you get the wooden ones for Mark and I to stand on."

"That might just be the footing we need to brace ourselves."

"Good thinking."

Good thinking was crucial, but at times instinct took the leading role. Ron quadrupled the braided cords, they had enough length, and tied them together, making a net of sorts.

"Let's give it our best shot. Li Wei, you okay being in the water and shoving the boards under if we can lift it?"

Grinning, Li Wei nodded. He was a man who needed to be needed. Even if it could kill him. Ted and Mark found their balance on the boards.

"On my count. One, two, three."

Ted and Mark strained, Li Wei vanished and slid the first board beneath the container, Rose fed him the second one.

"Easy, easy." Ron directed.

After they wedged the third board under the container, it became more buoyant and lifted an inch above the water line.

"Should we try for one more?" Mark asked panting.

"Fuck it. Let's try as is. If we need another, we can add it."

Mark scrambled to standing and drove the first bolt aside. Three more to go. Rose fed a line of cord through the corner to anchor the container and prevent it from drifting, but she was to let it sink if it came to that. Mark tested the buoyancy with his weight, bracing his weight against the metal frame.

"It should hold Li or Rose."

"Me do."

Li Wei wearing his slick suit squeaked with every movement. Mark cupped his hands for Li Wei to use as a step and hoisted him onto the container. It bobbed but didn't sink. Everything rested on the two men, there was no guarantee that the MAERSK container held anything of any value. A shipment of electronics, or appliances was completely useless. They all craved food, something that would bring comfort.

Rose held the floating can steady. Ron braced himself and kept Ted and Mark steady, Trish and Amanda waited for instructions.

Balancing precariously, Li Wei scrambled like a cat on all fours to the top end of the container. His weight made no impact and the lip remained above the watermark. The rusted bolts grumbled at being forced to move, barnacles had already taken up residence, and Trish was already concocting a menu of barnacle stew. Something that Rose hoped would be foiled by the contents of the shipping crate.

Li Wei walked the tight balance while Mark, and Ted forced the door open. Ron was on standby with a piece of lumber to jam into any opening. They had no idea how to gauge the weight of the metal door.

Mark strained, his teeth a wall of white cinderblocks, ready to burst from his exertion. Rose couldn't see Ted's face; a woolen head of hair obscured his features. Whatever happened next could ultimately change their lives. Inside the container could be many things. She had had a nightmare once when in the dream they discovered a ship. But once they boarded, it wasn't what they hoped for. Dead bodies littered the cabin, on the deck, in the rigging. Despite being dead, they stumbled toward her until she woke screaming. Rose never forgot their dead eyes.

Rose kept her eye on Li Wei. His agility and strength, pound for pound, Rose thought he was the toughest of all the men. His muscles were smaller, but he also knew what strength it took to survive. Mark, Ted, and Ron didn't know hardship until circumstance taught them the lesson.

The metal door groaned. And inch by inch it allowed daylight into the darkness. Trish latched onto Ted's leg to keep him from slipping on the board. And just like that they reached the turning point, the door crashed open, and Li Wei nearly fell off from the blow.

"Fuck. Hold on Li!" Mark yelled and Ron tightened his grip on the rope.

Sometimes not knowing was better than knowing. While the mystery of what the container held was alive, they could all cling to hope for the impossible. Within a minute they'd all know the truth. Rose hoped it wasn't for nothing.

After an excruciating afternoon, Rose could no longer move her arms from exhaustion. She could have sworn that even her eyelashes hurt. Lying on her back, she watched the top hat of the sun sink yet again, and in the east a pale paper moon was already lining up to follow in the footsteps that the sun made. An explosion of shades, violet, purple, yellow, and orange painted every corner of the evening canvas in the west. Within minutes it was over.

Next to her, Mark stared at the sky. His fingers within inches of hers. She hadn't seen him this happy in a long time. The container sank. It burped, expelled a bouquet of bubbles and then sent small rippling waves that set the raft on its course.

"That was something," Mark whispered and turned to face her. "You did good." He smiled and hooked his fingers over hers.

"It's something all right. Too bad we couldn't reach the Whiskas before it sank."

"Some might float up. The cat food would make good bait."

"You still have a chocolate mustache."

"Oh yeah?" Mark rolled over and trapped her beneath the weight of his body. He kissed her, smearing the traces of melted chocolate across her lips. "Now you do too."

Rose giggled and ran her tongue across her mouth. Although she was feeling nauseous from eating too many Mars, M&M's, and Twix, it was the best feeling. Li Wei hadn't stopped vomiting. He had never tasted chocolate before in his life. But one of their wishes came true. Rice for Li Wei. It was the one staple he said he couldn't stand living without, and he was thin enough as it was.

"Rose?" Ron moved toward them. "Guess how many cases?"

"A million. At least my arms feel like we salvaged that many."

"Ten cases of Uncle Bens, twelve cases of Mars bars, twenty Twix, sixteen M&M's and four bags of Pedigree. And of course, seventeen cases of Flavia. Four cases of Dolmio sauce. Trish is already preparing a menu for the next three months. We did good."

"That's amazing. But right now I don't think I can eat another candy bar if you paid me."

"Gluttony. I told you so," Ron winked. He'd only eaten one. "You should have eaten your portion of fish first."

"Live and learn."

"Get some rest. I'll steer us back toward the island."

Ron could read currents like most people read a road map. Their island was built around a racetrack of docile, yet powerful, currents. If a person wanted to go where the current was heading, it was like a prepaid carriage ride in the park. If a person were heading in the opposite direction, it took not only muscle power but also ingenuity to break free from the undercurrent's pull. Only storms had the power to slingshot them out and away. But storms were costly. Hence Ron had manufactured the cumbersome raft, a feat he hoped would survive the next series of hurricanes jockeying to come their way.

While Rose watched the last of the diamond waves fan out across the wide arms of the ocean, Mark pulled the nearest tarpaulin over her and wiggled his body closer. Although the evening air was still warm, he wanted something else altogether from her that only she could give him beneath the crackling sheet.

Rose woke in the morning when a foot gently prodded her shoulder. Ron pressed his finger to his lips; the sun was just climbing over the horizon. She had slept soundly but when she moved her arms, they felt like the weight of the world was anchored within every torn piece of flesh. As gently as possible, she extracted herself from Mark's legs and arms. The crackling noise from the trap was sure to wake him. But if she worked hard yesterday, Mark and Li Wei did triple duty. Ron extended his arm and eased her up.

"I thought you'd want to be first," Ron whispered through his smile.

During the night, Ron brought them back to their island. He and Trish secured the raft, and from where Rose was standing, she could see that Trish was already flourishing in her element. A small black puff of smoke chugged from the chimney of the yacht she arrived on. Ron handed her a cup of steaming Flavia coffee.

"Great work finding that container. Proves once again we have to remain diligent."

"Hmm. So good. Did Trish sweeten the Flavia with chocolate?"

Ron nodded. Despite the bounty, he insisted they stick to a stringent schedule and catch a ride on the first storm heading their way.

"Couldn't have happened at a better time. These supplies might just make the next adventure bearable." He almost said survivable but caught his lips from tripping him.

"What about the rice? Can Trish do something with it?"

"She's working on it. Even if she can just get the rice to boil for a few minutes, you know our wood source is precious and cardboard only burns in bursts, then she thinks she can set it into the sun and keep as hot as possible."

"That might work. What if we made like a hotbed and covered it to trap the heat?"

"That's the plan."

"I can gather whatever materials you need, though I doubt we'll be two days lucky."

Chapter 3

Blow Hard

One by one, the others woke, stretched, and yawned. Rose returned with an armload of gear from the makeshift store. She had a plan. If they were going to eat rice, it would take team effort. But everyone deserves a break when nature handed them out and sleeping past dawn was like Christmas on an island where even time didn't keep pace with the days of the calendar. On the south side, and straining, grip by tenuous grip, Trish hoisted the red bucket that Ron submerged yesterday toward the heaving surface. From its weight, she had high expectations. It was loaded.

"We got a big one!" She yelled above the hustle. Ron swung down from the yacht. He'd been busy re-stuffing the gigantic hole in its keel. It was the only way to keep it upright and floating. Although he caught a string of healthy dorados yesterday, he wouldn't pass up an opportunity to eat calamari either. On his knees, his bad cut-offs soaked to the waist, he took over and brought the bucket on board. An octopus, who had taken up residence, fingering with its long tendrils through the grate, wanted to live too. But not on Ron's watch.

He spilled the contents on the hard planks strapped to-gether as a killing ground. Octopus moved with stealth; a lesson he learned early, and because Rose was closest, she drove the pointed end of her spear between the docile eyes staring up. It was another of mother nature's miracles to watch the color fade from the jelly-like body, change from browns to translucent, as its life spilled out as a sacrifice so that they could live.

"Thanks for this wonderful token," Ron looked toward the sky.

"Now, we can have a true feast," Trish said, taking the car-cass and hacking off the limbs. Trish didn't kill things, but she was an expert at salvaging the best parts and skillfully avoided the inkpot and intestines, which they used as bait for other fish.

"Do you need help with the fire?" Ron leaned over her shoulder.

"I don't, but it would speed things up."

Ron climbed back aboard the old yacht on the handcrafted rope ladder he fastened to the railing. The Windseeker wasn't much good for anything other than keeping the driftwood dry, and its galley kitchen had miraculously survived almost intact, as had Trish.

"Breakfast in half an hour, and Ted, Amanda, finish where you left off yesterday. We're now behind schedule."

Ted was about to argue but thought better of it.

"Rose, Mark. Finish storing what we can't take with us. Li Wei, see to the fish."

Rose was prepared. Mark had whispered all sorts of plans to her last night under the tarpaulin. He wanted to set out. Just the two of them and take their chances.

"Listen, Rose. There's no point in putting it off. How much longer will we be slaves to Ron's demands? We've got a better chance on our own. Especially with all the food you found yesterday."

"Not now. I told you last night. If we find a more ocean-friendly boat, I'll consider it. But not right now."

Rose grabbed the closest paddleboard and leaped on, landing on her knees. The push set her off before she could hear what Mark had to say. Balancing herself upright with the oar, she paddled toward the makeshift shed. Mark was right behind her. His long-reaching shadow outdistanced hers even when he stayed behind her.

On the dock, she dragged the board up and set the oar down. Without looking for Mark, she headed toward the shed. Everything was dilapidated, yet it was also familiar. She slid the aluminum door aside, the tarps snapped in the draft as she stepped into the stifling dead heat.

Ron had taken her into his confidence again this morning before the others woke and voiced his concern. He could read the swell and skyline for signs of weather like a prophet. Overnight, the waves increased and rolled like bowling balls spilling over the lip of the raft. Hurricane seasons weren't always a death sentence, at least not under Ron's command.

She heard the tarp crackle when Mark entered the shed. It wasn't a surprise he was that close behind her.

"Listen. We have to figure this out."

"Not right now, we don't!" Rose bristled at the pressure of choosing between loyalty toward Ron and accepting what Mark was offering.

"When then?"

Rose didn't know the answer. Something was keeping her trapped on the island, and it wasn't just Ron. Leaving with Mark, well, she thought about it constantly, was a dangerous option in many more ways than staying put. The glint in his gray eyes however suggested he was impatient with her answer and being under Ron's thumb.

"I have stuff to get ready. As do you." She picked up the first carton and set it on the hammock. Above ground, goods had a chance of surviving unscathed if they remained dry. She tested the hammock for strength. Mark handed off another case, and his warm arm hairs brushed against hers. Rose lived in a world divided. Either direction had consequences.

They heard the bell chime. Breakfast was on the table, if only they had one. Trish served steaming bowls of rice with calamari for breakfast. But tensions had arisen like the building wall of cumulus clouds in the southeast.

"Hey, we gotta get a move on." Ron set his plate down first. All during breakfast, he kept his eyes on Mark and the skyline. Deciding which of the two he had to deal with first; which of the two was the most dangerous proponent to his plans made him solemn.

"Mark. Can I have a word?" It wasn't an invitation or question.

At times, she thought Ron could read minds. She felt guilty, yet she hadn't done anything. It was Mark who needed a reminder of what was important. And although she had enjoyed the portion of Uncle Ben's rice, she had difficulty swallowing. Mark stomped off behind Ron. It wasn't difficult to decipher their conversation from the body stance Mark had taken on and what the argument was about. Rose had heard it all a hundred times. About the dangers. About the consequences. Next to Rose, Ted whispered to Amanda and Trish. He shot a look her way, knowing she could hear him.

"Can't have mutiny." His shadow in the sun's glare looked like a giant phallic symbol. "If we don't, you know what happens?"

"Shark bait," Li Wei answered.

"We wouldn't want that."

Shark season petrified everyone, and life on the island kept them in a constant danger they couldn't escape. Once a year, in early spring, when the silver tips sailed toward their makeshift home, they were even afraid to breathe. As it happened by the unwritten laws of nature, their turf lay smack in the middle of a migratory trail of great white sharks. Although when Rose first arrived and Ron gave her a stern warning of the imminent visits, and frequent bumping, nothing in life had prepared her for the terrifying ordeal. The fear wasn't something a person could slough off with experience, it affected them all equally. There was no arguing the point, the menacing sharks knew they were there.

At first, the sight of a hundred or so jagged sails slicing like a steel blade through the water took Rose's breath away. How bad can they be? She thought. Then, one after another knocked on the plastic ground beneath her. A razor-sharp muzzle only inches away, separated by a bundled layer of plastic, grinned menacingly beneath the thin layer of water. One time, when she tripped, her hand plunged into the water, touching the scarred, sandpaper skin of the shark's back. She was in hysterics for hours afterward.

Regardless of what anyone said, they would never persuade her that sharks weren't intelligent. These sharks used a fear-mongering tactic of knocking that was an intimidating and calculated stalking method. But when the sharks switched the game plan and attacked with silence was when the real terror took hold. Sharks reinforced their threat by periodically flashing a threatening fin, circling in the water, and sniffing the air like bloodhounds. And year after year, they remembered.

After Ron and Mark ended their bitter discussion, Rose busied herself with sorting through socks and flip-flops. Dry feet were a crucial element to survival, and it was a constant battle to keep clothing from growing blue beards of mold.

"You need help?" Mark kneeled next to her. Whatever Ron said had sunk in, and Mark consented to live under Ron's rule for another undetermined length of time. But it wasn't difficult to see it took all of his resolve to comply. Rose handed him a bundle of shirts to sort through.

"You okay?"

"Whatever. I swear if we come across anything like a rubber dinghy, I'm out of here."

Rose wanted to say, *careful what you wish for*, but Mark wouldn't appreciate the idiom.

"Let's get these on the raft. Then we can seal everything. It's the last of the chores before we leave. I assume you got your water duties done?"

"Yup. Still's gushing like Niagara."

On the raft, Rose stuffed all the mismatched socks, shoes, and clothing into the airtight tubes and set them into the sun to seal them properly. Then she had to see to the bedding, which was a ludicrous chore because as soon as they set out, everything not in containers was wet before they even lost sight of the island. But it was about following orders and rules. That's how they survived. Trish was busy packing the dry fish, the rice she set in the sun to cook, and fresh fish Ron reeled in for lunch. Surviving was a full-time job.

"Thanks. I just need to secure the store. That's all I have left."

"I'll meet you there. I just need to tap the keg of water."

Rose didn't need help securing the store. They had an hour until lunch, but the makeshift store was also a hideaway. Despite Ron wanting to keep an eye on everyone, he also understood the need for privacy. He and Trish had the yacht, Amanda and Ted met on the small island next to the dock when Ted fished. Li Wei honed the skill to find solace by meditating.

Mark slid the aluminum door shut, the heat was stifling, but at least they were out from under the demands of the ferocious sun. Inside the shed, Ron had crafted a platform

149

for Rose to use from an industrial refrigerator door. She had woven blankets of plastic to make it a comfortable place to lie on. Although it wasn't wide, their bodies fit without falling off.

With her long fingers, Rose unbuttoned her blouse. It wasn't a mystery what was beneath the sheer fabric bleached by the sun and salt. She seldom wore a brassiere or panties. Without so much as bending, she stepped from the nylon shorts that once belonged to a boy. It wasn't difficult to see that Mark was ready.

"I'm not pretending. If we ever get off this shithole, I would still want to be with you." Mark saw no point in mincing words. His thumb brushed over her shoulders, and his breath followed. Rose never saw herself as beautiful or even desirable until she came to the island. But here she was everything a man could want in a woman.

When their lovemaking was over, Mark pulled her into a spoon position, his skin stuck to hers in the humidity. He nestled her into the curve of his lean body and held her close, the bedding crackled whenever they moved. He was always softer and kinder afterward.

"Please give it some thought?" He spoke into the curve of her neck.

"I will, but it's been too crazy. And you know, I'm torn."

"Is your loyalty with me, or them?" Rose felt Mark's body tense.

"This isn't just about loyalty. It's about surviving, and like Ron, I think there's power in moving as a team."

"So, you're willing to die here because of Ron's beliefs?"

"Yes. Ron saved me. In more ways than one. He's the glue that keeps us together. I feel a sense of loyalty. I know you have other ideas, but you don't know me as Ron does."

"Well, you've always brushed me off. You have this fortress around you."

"As do you. After nine months, I still know nothing about you. I don't even know your last name. You could have been a criminal." She teased him, trying to lighten the tone.

"Same here. I know you fell off a boat. That's it! Why the secrecy if you have nothing to hide?" Mark played with a long strand of her corkscrew hair, stretching it out. Rose twisted away from Mark so that she could see his eyes.

"You know the chocolate that made Li Wei sick? Well, I used to gorge myself on anything sweet and bad for me. Unlike Li Wei, my diet didn't consist of rice, fish, healthy meats, and leafy greens. I was fat."

"You? I doubt that."

"Ask Ron. I was grossly overweight. My idea of exercise was going down into our basement and stuffing myself with bite-sized chocolates that I kept in the bags of frozen vegetables like broccoli, lima beans."

"You wouldn't know it to look at you now."

Mark did just that. He looked at Rose's lean legs and stopped when he reached her contoured biceps. They were as strong as his, pound for pound.

"You know, we all had lives before this marvelous one. Mine is pathetic."

"Don't be so hard on yourself. In a way, we're all products of our environment."

"What would you have done differently if you could go back in time?" Rose rested her fist on Mark's heart.

"Can't think of anything. School. A degree of sorts? That's the only regret. You?"

Mark pulled her closer, despite her shifting away. Acknowledging her past made her feel vulnerable.

"That's the million-dollar question. I should say that I wouldn't have gone on that cruise, but that would be a lie. I was desperate. For anything. My life wasn't perfect like yours."

"Perfect? Are you kidding! I've screwed up so many times, I sort of deserve this lesson. I was playing Russian Roulette with my life. I'm not sure I've learned all there was to learn."

"I knew you had a dangerous edge lurking. The tats give that secret away."

"Tell me what happened before you went overboard. And before that? Ron hinted it was a cruise ship, but people don't survive that sort of dive without being rescued by the Coast Guard. Sounds like the makings of a miracle."

"I'll tell you, but I really need to get the store battened down." Rose reached for her clothing and dressed. Mark did too.

"Lunch," Trish yelled down from the yacht, she rang the bell three times.

"Grilled sardines! Yum." Rose realized that despite the big meal at breakfast, she was hungry. There hadn't been time to snack on the candy bars.

"And coffee again? Wow, we're spoiled." Mark took a heaping of rice and sardines, biting the oily head off without any revulsion. Li Wei had regained his pallor and ate a serving of fish and rice, but he adamantly refused the packages of candy.

"I'll say, let's have a siesta, and in an hour, I think we should be on our way. The wind is shifting." He held a wet finger into the air.

They woke to the gentle prodding of Ron's foot. The clouds had already swollen in size and were no longer docile. Feeling the raft beneath, it rode the herd of waves like a bronc. Ron motioned for them to look east. In an hour of peace, the sky plainly spelled out a warning message, storm ahead. They set off at dusk. Adrift on the raft, everyone scurried and busied themselves. Ron checked the netting securing the bundle of floatable plastic that the raft was woven from again. Their lives depended on it. Li Wei checked that all the containers were tightly strapped down, even though Mark and Ted had done the same minutes earlier. They resembled the cast in an apocalyptic movie.

After Rose survived her first squall, or typhoon, cyclone, gale, or whatever the fuck a meteorologist called the brutal weather blasting them, she learned a valuable and momentous truth. The ocean current liked to circle back. If a person didn't drown during the first onslaught, the ocean always offered up another chance later. Just in case a person changed their mind about surviving. On the upside, after floating for days in no man's land, the current swiftly deposited what it took back in one form or another. Regardless, the ride was always a risky business.

"Okay, we're set. Strap yourselves in." Ron gave the command.

One by one, they struggled themselves into their pouches. Last-minute smiles were exchanged, reassuring one another was futile. They had rehearsed this drill every week at Ron's insistence but were at the blind mercy of luck. Distance and direction were preordained by the wind and ocean.

Within minutes, Rose was soaked. It wouldn't be long before uncontrollable shivers would join her in the plastic pouch. The pouches were this year's brilliant addition and already seemed like a bad idea. Water seeped in through the smallest holes and spread quickly. There was a good chance they'd all die. Ron never minced words when it came to preparing them for the voyage. He had survived by his wit for seven years, but he also understood that other elements like luck played a crucial role. Others, who had drifted in and out of his life, were now ghosts in a watery grave. But he promised if they took his advice, their chance of surviving increased. The rest was up to them.

Rose stilled her breathing and tried to meditate. Lying flat on her back, she could feel the undulating rise and fall of each wave. But the worst feeling happened when the raft came unglued and shot upward like a rocket with the water. No matter how she braced herself for the eventual impact, the pain was always extraordinary. She groaned when she couldn't endure another minute. She screamed as if she had bought tickets to ride a roller coaster.

What would her parents say if they could see her now? How many prayers had they offered up for her? Did she still have a leading role in the words they tele-typed to their God? Of course, she never wanted her parents to know what she endured. There wasn't a psalm in the Bible that fit her vulnerable and exposed state.

Eventually, she passed out. She never knew if it was for a minute or an hour.

"Wake up! Rose! Rose!"

Mark roughly shook her shoulder. He had unfolded her pouch. Blinking, she could see the pale-yellow glare of the gibbous moon. The storm wasn't over. Rain pelted them, and unfurling waves hopped aboard the raft. Ron yelled.

"The storm's merely reconfiguring itself. But it's as good a time as any to eat." He didn't say, tend to personal urges, which they did while everyone's backs were turned.

"Here. Eat something."

Mark handed her a dish of rice and sardines, a bottle of cold coffee. Ron gave care packs to Ted and Amanda. Li Wei shook his head and declined, motioning to his upset stomach.

"Any idea what time?"

"Hard to say. Probably six hours. Maybe more."

"Too bad, the pouches aren't working."

Ron nodded and hunkered down next to them. He was as cold as the rest of them. Nighttime was infinitely worse, and the temperatures would plummet even farther. Rose bit down on her teeth to stop them from chattering. A sickening feeling rose in her gut. Could she stand this for days on end? Again. Instead, she forced herself to smile, when she swallowed the last of the fish, she answered Ron.

"You know where we went wrong? We didn't test them."

"Your right. We relied on theory instead of execution."

"No matter. We're soaked with or without."

"Can you see a break in the weather?"

Everyone perked their ears at Rose's question. Ron's eyes darted in all directions. But he was stalling; searching for that break in the clouds that raced across the sky.

"Not yet. But who knows? I'm not the weatherman, and I've been wrong before."

Ron excused himself and busied himself by testing the netting. It was true, Ron had been wrong before but never about the weather.

"Stay down!" Mark yelled into the wind. Since it was dangerous to stand, they crawled. Next to them, waves the size of mountains crested. Any such wave might strike at any moment and wash them off the raft. Although they were all tethered to long plastic cords, once a person went overboard, their chances of surviving decreased. It also risked the lives of those still aboard.

"Get in! I'll tuck you in."

Rose felt Mark's hand on her back. He smiled at her through the rain. It would be the last she'd see of him for hours.

When she opened her eyes again, darkness had taken over, and the storm returned full of vengeance. Her body convulsed from the cold. She tried to roll herself into a ball, but inside the pouch, there wasn't enough room. Instead, she brought her hands to her mouth and caught her warm breath. She felt a rage fester deep inside and fought the urge to scream at the universe and those who sold slices of happiness for a buck.

"Fuck! Fuck! Fuck!"

She could feel the raft rise on a wave; she prepared her body for impact. When Rose came to again, the urge to urinate strained in her groin. Without shame, she allowed her bladder to open, and its delicious warmth spread from her crotch down to her legs. It wasn't something they needed to explain—to anyone.

For what seemed like an eternity, they were mummified. The storm tried to kill them. But Ron had designed their raft with an iceberg in mind: impossible to overturn. Yet the force of the wind and ocean chewed away on the plastic, and the raft could easily break apart. During those rare moments in the storm cycle, when the storm ebbed, either Ron or Mark climbed from their pouch and tugged on the netting keeping the raft in one piece. Re-knotting, shifting, pulling, and sometimes kicking plastic parts back into place. Once or twice while in her cocoon, she felt fingers squeeze her shoulder. She was so cold she'd do anything for a minute of warmth.

For some predestined reason, the ocean took revenge on the raft. Slowly pieces came off, but faithful to its design, it righted itself. But there was still a trick to staying alive. One could never practice luck.

In her mind's eye, she pictured her mother, always a step behind her father and eyes shied to the floor. Rose had imagined her rescue a hundred times and had every detail, down to her mother's dress and hairdo rehearsed. Magically, her mother was always in the kitchen when the news of her rescue arrived. Hovering near the stove or sink, the shock on her mother's face, setting the teapot down, grasping the counter to steady herself as the news sunk in, was almost comical. The enormous ordeal Rose endured would buckle her mother's already weak knees.

Luckily, her mother had other ideas of where Rose ventured to. Sometimes death was a blessing, and her parents would find solace that their daughter's assumed death had been relatively painless. They'd shuffle the memories of her childhood and say, "do you remember when our Rose won the blue ribbon for baking? Or when Rose got it into her mind to make the track and field team." Those vague memories would be the net they'd cling to for their survival. But her parents certainly didn't have the fortitude to imagine their daughter strapped to a raft in the middle of the violent Pacific. Most certainly not still alive. It went beyond comprehension. Those on the winning side of surviving were made of sterner stuff than their Rose.

After moments of relative calmness, another monstrous wave rolled. The impact, when it crashed, nearly shattered Rose's back. Who knew that water had the same hardness factor as a brick wall? And suddenly, just as quickly as the storm exploded, the waves relaxed, rolling entrancingly calm next to them. This time, Ron unfolded her from the pouch. He looked worn out and aged. He squeezed her hand to assure her that he was fine when her concern broadcast on her own face. He pulled her to standing. The dark gray clouds had thinned out, and through the white mass, they could see the faint outline of the sun coming over the horizon. Someone coughed, Li Wei stretched his limber body. And Ted teased Ron that he had built them an ark, to which Ron replied with a hint of humor twinkling in his eyes.

"Then, some of you had better get off!"

In their painful past, a man named Joe did get off. The circumstances were too painful to speak of, and Ron never forgave himself. Since they were a cast of missing people, who appreciated what the word found truly meant, missing didn't have an expiry date. The worst thing they could do was to allow Joe's smile to vanish from their memory. Then he'd be genuinely missing.

PART 3

GUILTY

Chapter 1

No Sign

The click of the ceiling fan woke Kai. Slightly confused about his surroundings, he blinked with the smoothness of sandpaper, despite the five hours of uninterrupted sleep he had just woken from. He swung his legs over the side of his bed while his wife rolled over, searching for him in her dreams. She knew he kept a vital secret from her. She had a built-in radar for things like that. He hadn't seen his father either since the afternoon when Kilo vanished. Or more urgently, the day Jack Spencer went for a predawn stroll and never returned.

Once during the initial interview, when the police officer questioned the Spencers, Kai considered telling them about his missing canoe. But based on the answers the Spencers supplied, Jack wasn't the sort of man who'd steal or do something as reckless as going for a ride in the middle of the night. Even if he was as drunk as the evidence suggested. Logic prevailed. Jack had nothing to do with Kilo's disappearance.

He struggled his feet into his flip-flops and raised himself off the bed, careful not to disrupt his wife's dreams. Because he usually rose early, and because he always suspected the urgent middle of the night phone call, Kai had his uniform ready in the kitchen. His wife had packed his lunch after supper. This morning, he'd indulge and have breakfast at the hotel. His biggest job today would be to walk the hired PI through all their discoveries and answer questions about the hotel. Although no one had given Kai the details of his arrivals, his flight number, or what room was reserved on his behalf. All Kai knew was that the first flight into Honolulu didn't arrive until 7:00 am. Give or take a few minutes. He wanted to be on hand when the PI made his appearance.

Kai slowly rolled the truck from the driveway. Keeping the lights off until the gravel drive met the hard road. There was nothing he could do to silence the crunch of gravel beneath his tires, the throaty purr of his four-cylinder engine. However, everyone on his street slept through the small noises his truck made. He envied them their sleep. While cruising quietly, he spotted a random yellow light shining through a window. Two hours till sunrise.

Ten minutes later, he parked his truck and looked at the massive structure that paid most of his bills. Bills that the mailman brought continuously. Two mortgages, food bills—though they ate frugally, his father's medicine and physiotherapy, electrical, water, taxes, phone, cable, and loan repayments to the hotel engulfed their money quicker than they could earn it.

The hotel was both: a fiend and friend wrapped in salmon pink paint and opulence he would never be able to afford. Twenty floors of grandeur for him to patrol and monitor via cameras. He buzzed himself in with his security tag and walked the short distance to the security office. In the solitude of the corridor, Kai speculated. Questions that seemed to vibrate louder inside the walls of the hotel.

Was it at all possible that Jack hid someplace inside? If so, what reason could he have to play such a cruel game? If anything untoward happened to Jack on the grounds what happened to his body? Kai wouldn't allow the only logical answer to take hold. Speculating was an invitation to open the gates of hell.

At his desk, he relieved the night guard who appreciated the early send-off.

"No news is good news." The man moaned.

"What about the bride?" Kai set his upcycled lunch bag down.

"Bitch left last night. Alone."

Everyone suffered from exhaustion and from the turmoil of upsetting a perfectly good routine. Kai perked a pot of coffee and read the reports addressed to him. No one had yet found any trace of Jack Spencer. A tourist discovered a small mother-of-pearl button washed up on the beach. No one could say for sure it belonged to Jack's shirt or that it wasn't just part of the continual flotsam the early morning crew cleared away. They'd check with the manufacturer. But so what? Kai thought. They knew Jack had been on the beach.

While Kai worked at his desk, an occasional knock on the door intruded on his routine duties. But the staff were curious and hungry for an answer to quell the rumors of a hefty reward. Kai, however, knew better than to play that game. The Spencers had set a new light of hope on their PI; as if the man conjured miracles. Reward or not, the ticking of the hands of time were twisted by fragile fingers and slowly fading. Minutes and hours could only stretch so far. Kai hoped that Jack was somehow, by an intervening fate, alive.

Kai logged the night camera footage and dated the new tapes. His job wasn't complicated, but it helped to have an eye for details. Sleeping on the job didn't necessarily mean being asleep and vice versa. He slipped the tape of Jack Spencer climbing the stairway into the machine and fast-forwarded to the footage marked 11:10. The exact moment when Jack laid eyes on the beauty heading toward him. No one at the hotel would admit the practice, but club staff often allowed friends to sneak in and party among the hotel guests. The hotel didn't really frown on the practice either, because the guests appreciated the influx of local beauties. Regardless of sex. Of course, those trespassing had to act the part. The woman on the stairway had her role down pat. Her dress looked expensive, might have been a hand-me-down. It wasn't unheard of for a guest to give a favorite maid a token for her service. Then there was the lost and found that staff had access to, albeit that the articles should have been sent to the local donation center. But poor people didn't need gowns and fancy shoes.

"There she is."

Kai froze the frame. His heart raced when he recognized something trivial about her. He didn't like to stereotype or play favorites and strained to see her more clearly in the frozen frame on the monitor. Something about the dark hair streaked with sunshine ringlets, the big almond eyes, and aloha smile seemed familiar. And yes, he'd argue anyone black and blue that Hawaiian women, hands down, were the most beautiful in the world.

Based on his own bias, he felt their ethnic roots favored them from the start. Their outdoor lifestyle contributed. The glorious climate they lived under was enough to make anyone more attractive than the pasty tourists who hailed from the mainland. Island men also had a reputation of being blessed with the physique of warriors. Kai laughed aloud to himself. He could name only a handful who fit that description. Of course, tourists coddled the notion that all native women were adept at hula. And by rights, they were misled for the sake of the tourist industry. But the woman on the stairway was two things for sure: local and she danced the hula professionally. The graceful extension of her hand while Jack reached for it was a pure Hawaiian dancer stance. He printed copies of the still frame and planned to investigate further. Something about her didn't sit right with Kai. Aside from that, no one had been able to explain the mysterious entries into Jack's room. With his own key. They were perplexing questions to a puzzle he wanted immediate answers to.

Kai checked his watch. In ten minutes, he'd approach the managers scheduled for the morning meeting. Someone had to know the woman in the picture. Why were they coddling the secret when the life of a man depended on it?

As usual, Kai arrived first. The boardroom was eerily quiet at this time of the morning, and for a moment, he enjoyed the serenity of not having staff, or a guest, intrude on his thoughts. Today, he hoped to get his canoe back. He could feel it in his bones.

Most of the department managers found these meetings a waste of their time. They argued they had more important duties to manage than to rehash duties they knew every intrinsic detail of. But Kai disagreed. The weekly meetings were a vital link in strengthening the operations of the hotel, even if on some mornings they seemed trivial in comparison to the last catastrophe concerning missing laundry, broken dishes, or irate guests, and temperamental chefs.

At promptly six o'clock, the hotel manager called the meeting to order. He gestured for Kai to sit next to him at the long koa wood table.

"Morning everyone." He looked about the room, including everyone with his eyes. "First duty, people, we must find Jack Spencer. Kai is still your main contact. Anything you think might be a clue, run it past Kai. Don't be ashamed if it's as minor as finding a pair of *slippahs* abandoned in a hallway or on the beach."

Kai nodded to confer that his opinion was the same and shouldered the importance of his duties. They looked up, suddenly, as if they no longer knew who Kai Hale was.

"And I want to add that you can call me anytime. You have my cell number. I want to ask again about this woman. Please look at this picture again and again."

Kai handed the copies around and waited. A consensus that they'd remember someone as beautiful as the woman depicted in print softly rumbled. To Kai's disappointment, everyone shook their heads in denial.

"Does anyone recall seeing that dress before? There can't be more than one."

They pointed to the picture in agreement. The dress, even on flat paper, shimmered like the tail of a fictional mermaid. No one could forget a dress like that. He urged them to ask their staff as well. He waved the extras he printed.

"I also invite you to come and watch the footage. Maybe something about the way she moves might trigger something."

The manager concluded by reiterating, "let's find Jack Spencer today. Also," He cleared his throat when he rose, "despite Jack's vanishing act, we have a first-class hotel to run."

Kai made his way toward the lobby. The first wave of guests would be arriving in under ten minutes. He wanted a good vantage point for pinpointing the expected and highly revered PI. The shuttle driver had strict instructions to text him once the airport van was within five minutes of the hotel. Kai rechecked his phone out of habit, but it was silent. While he waited, he scanned the lobby. He had worked at the hotel for fifteen years. Management, at the behest of the silent owners, even bestowed an award on him and promoted him for his dedication. Scanning the room, he tried vainly to look at the guests, the staff, and the lush and verdant decor through the eyes of a person coming through the revolving doors and seeing the refined interior for the first time. It was stunning, and at this hour of the day, not a leaf, chair, or smeared fingerprint mired the elegant lobby. He could smell the faint odor of the saltwater pool that a crew member had just finished cleaning. Towels shaped like turtles, elephants, hearts, and elaborate flowers sat in waiting for guests on the lounge chairs circling the pool.

Kai realized he took the grandeur of the hotel for granted and the effortless precision with which the staff executed their daily routine. They were the blood pumping in the veins of the hotel. Even though they had lost a guest, they surged on as a unit. The limbs of the hotel didn't feel the turmoil he felt. Watching from his perch on the upstairs landing, he had a grand view. Guests mingling in the lobby didn't seem inconvenienced by the possible loss of a person. They scurried and scuttled like mice in a maze. Oblivious. All they cared about was finding the cheese: their breakfast, the day's planned activity, an opportunity to take a selfie next to the gorgeous orchids. Or the spread laid out for them at the breakfast buffet.

The incoming text made Kai's head snap up. The shuttle was three minutes out. He already checked the day's booking log, ten guests were on their way out. A constant shuffling of precious merchandise. He saw the white van parked under the portico. Porters rushed to fetch the suitcases, and six guests piled out, eager to find their way to their hotel room after a long flight. Their excitement always sizzled in the air. A young woman dressed in a vibrant colored sarong, hibiscus flower behind her ear, greeted the arriving guests and draped a frangipani lei over their necks. She had rehearsed her smile a thousand times before a mirror and guests alike. Kai couldn't imagine just what lands all the guests issued from or where they went to afterward. He'd never been off the Island, except on excursions on Kilo. Once, he caught a ride on a yacht that took him to a sister island. But he could never imagine living elsewhere, despite the hardships. This was home.

When the newly arrived guests vanished from the lobby, Kai checked the register. No one had asked to see him. He'd have to wait it out since he could not remember the PI's name and pride would not allow him to ask the Spencers. But regardless, Kai wanted a heads up. Mrs. Spencer had taken the first report from the Coast Guard rather badly. This time she didn't have a melt-down, but disappointment sunk in her eyes like the setting sun.

This morning she'd get her second installment, and he wanted to be present. He took the service elevator and prepared himself. There was no joy in being in the same room as the Spencers. Not that they were rude or condescending. It was just that their sadness sapped Kai's energy, and walking on fragile eggshells wasn't a ritual he had much practice in. He filled his composure with a deep inhale, knocked on the door, and waited for the password, which came at him directly. The kitchen had sent up breakfast, and the maintenance crew had brought up a treadmill and a set of hand weights for Mrs. Spencers' personal use.

"Good morning. Is there any news?"

What a stupid question. If there were, the results would be painted onto the faces and composure of the Spencers. But what does one say? Kai closed the door behind him.

"Nothing as of yet. The Coast Guard is supposed to be calling any minute."

"We held a meeting this morning, and I've handed out posters of the mystery woman."

"I hope it jogs someone's memory. Good thinking."

Mrs. Spencer plodded on at a running pace on the tread-mill. For a woman of her years, she was fit. Her shoulder caps were well defined, and the power of her leg muscles reminded him of women he'd seen on the Olympic team. It was good that she kept busy. The treadmill had been Kai's suggestion. Mr. Spencer poured a cup of coffee for Kai and handed it over. Such a personal gesture made Kai uncomfortable. He owed these people an answer to the whereabouts of their son, and yet he had nothing to loan.

"Was there anything else I can arrange to make your stay more comfortable?"

"No. We're good. We appreciate the treadmill."

Myra stopped running when John's phone rang and padded the beads of sweat on her brow. Silence exploded into the room while John listened to the other end. Myra put her finger up and mouthed, "speakerphone."

"One moment, please."

John laid his phone on the table, and Myra reached for his hand while she joined him.

"Mr. Spencer, I'm sorry not to be calling with better news. But we've found nothing so far. The storm that happened the morning Jack disappeared must have swept him further out than we first calculated. Plus, we don't even know for sure he is in the water."

"For the heck of it, what resources besides a boat and he-licopter is at your disposal?"

"We have state of the art search and rescue equipment. A seventy-seven percent success rate when we've deployed the latest software. But with your son, we've nothing to go on."

"He is out there. It's the only logical place. What does your drift trajectory come up with?" John paced while he asked the questions. Myra stood stock still.

"We've searched out as far as we can. There is weather coming in, and the water is choppy. There are squalls brewing. If he's out there …"

"Don't you dare say it!" Myra cut in, ready to fight anyone who might say to the contrary of her heart's dialog. Her fingers curled into a fist.

"We're doing everything we can. But I agree. Don't give up hope. He might not ever have made it into the water."

Myra stared at the phone a second longer, and in the stifling silence, Kai shifted on his feet. The land search party found nothing. Strike one. The Coast Guard found nothing. Strike two. Kai hoped their magical PI played ball better than anyone else.

When neither John or Myra said anything for a few minutes, Kai bowed out and left them on their own. For all the money they had, he did not envy them. And suddenly, his family's struggles seemed insignificant in comparison. His father had survived, and they were slowly getting a grasp on their bills. His sons were healthy and doing well. He was so proud of their achievements. No, he could not envy the Spencers their luxury. Everything had a price.

Maids with cleaning carts pushed past Kai and mumbled their morning greeting. He had the elevator to himself for two floors. When he got a call on the sixth floor, he got out, a maid and her cart took his place. She found the tile more interesting than Kai. Before Kai could react to a thought that popped into his mind, the elevator dinged on the seventh floor. Then it skipped on to the eighth, ninth. Something about the housekeeping maid wasn't right. Her uniform didn't fit properly. It was much too large for someone so slender.

Chapter 2

Milk, Water, Whatever

"I'm fucking sick of it!" Jack yelled. But on the open ocean, not even an echo kept him company. His limbs ached, his tongue was swollen, and his brain had gone to mush. He was utterly exhausted, and it was impossible to tell how many hours and days had passed. When he fell asleep, he often woke, not knowing if he slept for an hour or a minute.

Jack had seen the fins of sharks' circle, a fleet of what looked like dolphins in the distance, and the sails of those green and gold bull-faced fish that knocked on the canoe relentlessly. He knew they were harmless and swam with them from time to time, their inquisitive bodies brushing against his. Some of their faces were starting to distinguish themselves from one another, and he knew he was only steps away from insanity.

"Mr. Spencer. Can you tell us anything else about the two suspects that sent you adrift?" Jack dropped the tone of his voice, pretending to be a detective assigned to his case.

"Yes, officer. I remember the tall one had pockmarks on his cheeks and red lesions down his neck."

"How could you see they were red? You said it was dark."

"True. I don't know how I remember. I just do. There was something else about his neck that bothered me. I can feel the answer sit on the edge of my memory, and I'm sure that if I try just a little harder, it will come to me."

"Did they have names? Something you might have overheard."

"I know it sounds silly, but Batman comes to mind. I know, I know. It doesn't make sense." Jack caught himself, gesturing with his hands.

"What time would you say you saw them the first time? When you went outside?"

"The window, I'm thinking of, is sometime between midnight and when the storm hit."

"What about a watch? You don't wear one?" The officer looked up from his notepad. Or at least Jack imagined he'd have one of those flip pads he'd seen cops use on television.

"I have a Rolex. But I don't recall checking the time. My focus was on her. The woman I was dancing with."

"And her name? She didn't give you a name? Don't you think that's strange?"

"She told me. But like I said, the music was loud. Kelsie, Chelsea, Elsie. Something along those lines. She didn't say the last name."

"You think it wise to associate with people whose names you can't remember?"

"Officer. I was drunk. I admit that. And I've told you. I think someone spiked my champagne. The vague sensation that my body was beyond my control followed me to the beach. It wasn't a symptom of being drunk. It was something else."

"Let's get that straight. The two men you remember, with the menacing look about them, remind you of Batman. And the woman didn't have a name? Is that correct?"

"I know it sounds ridiculous. But yes. That is all I can tell you. Has no one else come forward with information?"

Jack caught his forehead in his palm, the weight smacking above the sound of waves.

Rehearsing his statement, with an imaginary cop, was about as helpful as an empty cup in the middle of an ocean.

"Look for a connection between them and Tessa Washington." Jack squinted his eyes shut, trying to see the invisible connection that surely existed. "You know, phone records. That sort of thing."

"Now you're telling me how to do my job? Mr. Spencer." The officer cocked his head and pursed his lips. Jack understood, under no circumstances would he appreciate anyone telling him how to do his job. And cops, he doubted, were any different in that regard. Even imaginary ones had an ego.

"Please," Jack whispered. He was starting to recognize despair when it knocked. He'd been over the same scenario what seemed like a hundred times. All fingers pointed at Tessa. Somehow she was connected to the two goons and he had underestimated her he had underestimated her.

Adrift, he was so many things: vulnerable, hungry, thirsty, bored, lonely, frustrated, and always on the verge of panic. But something else lurked in his psyche. The will to survive. Every day, he forced himself to swim, to wash, to paddle the canoe in the direction of what was north, based on the rising and setting sun. But north was nothing more than a vast expanse of nothing. Water that at times loafed like liquid glass next to him and a sky that really was infinite.

He was starting to eat the coconut shells. The half with the three holes. His teeth craved biting as much as he craved eating. He ate his scabs as they came off, and he tried to catch the darting fish that teased him. He had caught one and ate it. Guts and all. Which was a mistake.

What surprised him, however, was how constant the canoe was. It climbed the waves as if it had trained for such an occasion as this: effortlessly. But then hadn't they traveled for long distances in these types of canoes? The Polynesians and Samoans. Or were they the same? Didn't they sail from Australia and New Zealand? If they survived, why couldn't he?

Frustrated by his hopeless situation, Jack no longer fought the urge to sleep. He allowed his eyelids to shut down whenever. Sleep was a gift. A fantasy escape even if his dreams were a jumbled mess that had no bearing on reality. Fighting through the conflicting surges of the fluctuation temperature alone was enough to wear a man down. Too hot during the day, too cold, to the point of freezing, during the night. And being constantly wet grated on his nerves.

When Jack woke in the dark, his teeth were chattering. He had made himself as small as humanly possible, not that there was room to stretch out, and hugged the life vest close to his body in the small space. He cupped his nose, anything to produce heat and store it.

The third time Jack awoke was just before nautical twilight. He regretted his long legs. He unfolded them slowly from the cramped position. Cheered by the sun, just slipping onto his side of the horizon meant another notch on his precarious string of survival. He loved the rising sun, but during the day—he despised her. He gingerly tested his fingers and wiggled them. Giving life where none seemed to exist. He had survived another night. Only there was no one to share his joy or success with. Next, he wiggled his toes and half expected to see the signs of frostbite: black rotting skin. He was cold, but so far, his limbs were intact. He rubbed his palms together for heat.

"Mom. Please find me." His eyes were crusted over and stung each time he blinked. He chewed on the hard callous that bloomed on his thumb and index finger, and his neck crunched with each movement. A waft of familiar body odor made his nose twitch. He stank. Another ingrown hair had sprouted overnight on his jawline, but the ocean was too rough to act as a mirror. His fingers knew the way and poked. He missed his pouch of Benjamin's specialty products. He couldn't resist and poked the swollen bumps tenderly. One, two, three, four.

When the yellow coin on the horizon ventured to his side of the world, he noticed the southeast skyline. As beautiful as the orange and red cloud formation was, he suspected trouble. It reminded Jack of smoldering lava. But if rain was on the way, he was ready to lick the clouds.

"Okay, Jack. Time to paddle home."

He leaned over the front, the narrower end of the canoe, and reached for the water. With a steady rhythm, he clawed the water. Because he couldn't gauge the distance, he counted the waves instead. Each time he set a goal for himself and this morning, he was hoping to get past twenty rolling tops. Twenty was his goal, but secretly he was hoping to make thirty.

This morning he awoke with new wisdom. He had been mesmerized by the utter darkness during the night and had played the hand game and never won. Under no circumstance could he see his fingers, even when he waved them directly across from his eyes. He felt the breeze his waving hand created and smelled them rather than saw them. He was utterly blind amid the darkness. Another strange thought occurred to him. What if? What if the exact opposite happened and light overpowered all color. Would that make a person invisible? What if he applied the same theory to any color? Would that turn him blue, or green, or pink? Those random thoughts, Jack feared, were a sign of insanity.

While the sun slowly rose and warmed his limbs, he finished counting twenty-five waves. He couldn't bring himself to do thirty, for the burning in his muscles. Jack rose and urinated over the edge of the canoe into the blue water. That he had anything left in his tank to dispose of came as a surprise. Of course, he briefly considered drinking his own pee. He had heard of that too. He just wasn't ready for such drastic measures, and he perpetually scanned the ocean for anything swimming toward him.

Impatient to the point of anger, he longed to hear that strange sound of life in the distance: a boat, a plane, the hum of a helicopter.

Instead, he heard the rumble of thunder. A storm was brewing.

Chapter 3

Action

Myra waited for John to leave the hotel room, and as soon as the door clicked shut, she sprang into action. She no longer cared what the lazy police officers and Coast Guard had to say. Or the hotel with their kind simpering. While in the bath, she had searched out the numbers of private helicopter tour operators and Cessna airlines. She had meetings scheduled with both. The concierge had booked a town car for her, and she had lied to John.

"Just need some time on my own. Away from here."

John believed her. Because it was another weekday, he needed to deal with the nagging business of the merger. He booked a conference room to substitute as his makeshift office, and when Michael arrived, he seldom left his side. They were in a constant flux of new demands. Michael would do anything to keep busy, and to keep away from the emotions neither man dared to face. That they resigned themselves into the hands of others perplexed Myra. Someplace, far away, Jack was running out of time. It seemed only she understood the dire circumstances and the complex demands of time.

She swept her hair onto the top of her head with a clip, grabbed her purse, light jacket, and sunglasses. Walking past the room that had been Jack's, she rested her hand on the door for a minute. She hadn't stopped communicating with him telepathically. Promising help. She repeatedly told him to hang on, repeating her promise like a prayer. Crazy as that might sound to anyone else, she believed in its power.

In the car, Myra calmed herself. She instructed the driver, and when he pulled alongside a long row of blue hangars, she told him to wait. She looked for a man-door marked number three and knocked.

"It's open."

"I called. Myra Spencer." Myra poked her head inside the door. She heard a voice, rustling, but even with the door open, she saw no one.

"Up here."

A man wearing a green flight suit hung suspended from the rafters, swinging from a harness he looked down. He yanked on a string and jumped onto the thick mat.

"We spoke. You said you'd be interested."

"Yes. But tell me, what's the Coast Guard found?"

"Nothing. No trace. But as his mother, I don't buy it. Jack's out there." For a second, she regretted the statement that made her sound vulnerable. It was the sort of tool unscrupulous men used to their advantage. But she also saw a hint of kindness flicker in his eyes.

"Show me on the map where they suspect he was last seen."

Myra peered at the gigantic map pinned to the wall and followed the curve of the island around the half-moon beach of the hotel. She pointed.

"You take credit cards?"

Back in the town car, Myra's hopes rose. At least she was doing something instead of relying on others. Although the pilot didn't say he was hopeful, he didn't laugh at her either. And Jack needed her. She'd fight tooth and nail for her beliefs and to bring Jack home.

John had scheduled a meeting with Jason Rockport, but she declined to attend. John put all his faith in the PI. He had arrived on the first flight in but suggested he should remain incognito until he had a lay of the land. And under the disguise of a guest, he could watch the premises unperturbed. He had brought his girlfriend; she registered the room under her name.

Myra didn't care for Jason Rockport, but she agreed with his bold prediction. Someone in the hotel knew more than they led on. He would hunt them down.

This morning, Stacy had reported that the cleaning woman found nothing suspicious at Jack's condominium either. Jack kept everything with such conciseness, nothing stood out. All his suits swung on their hangers, his cleaning woman said nothing seemed amiss since her last visit. Of course, they hadn't notified his boss yet. They conjointly held out hope they'd never need to know. But the hours that rushed past, one after another, uneased Myra, and John, Stacy, and Michael. None cared to admit they suspected the worst. Admitting it—was like believing it.

To fool John, Myra asked the driver to stop on the strip. She had seen a boutique that specializes in babies and would serve as a logical diversion. And since Stacy was due soon, buying an adorable baby garment might fool John just long enough until the bill for the private helicopter came due.

It was John's fault that she had to go behind his back and invent this charade of needing to get away. She argued with herself while browsing in the aisle and selected two pink jumpers, a yellow dress, and a rabbit with oversized floppy ears. Something about the stuffed toy with its woeful oversized eyes tugged on her heartstrings. Jack used to love Bugs. While she caressed the plush fur of the rabbit, she rehearsed her excuses. John didn't understand everything.

Biting her tongue, she would never accuse John outright. But the sour taste of resentment didn't always wash down with bourbon or copious amounts of wine. Myra allowed her fingers to linger over a soft pineapple motif blanket, but it would clash with Stacy's sugar pink decor. The pilot had promised to set off within the hour. His partner, he promised, was on his way in. They knew the ocean surrounding the Hawaiian Islands like the backs of their hands. To verify the accuracy of the statement, she looked at her own lined palm. Was there a prediction etched into her skin that foretold this catastrophe? The pilot's smooth conviction teamed with his expertise raised the flag of hope up the flagpole. She wished she could have taken to the sky with them. But her prolonged absence would rouse John's suspicion.

Time had become her enemy and moved with the speed of molasses. For Jack, she wondered, did the hours of his precious life trickle away too quickly? Was he drifting, helplessly wondering why his mother hadn't rescued him?

Myra brushed her finger along her nose, preventing tears from falling. They were always on standby. She'd never been an overtly, outwardly, emotional person, but then she had never needed to resort to crying. Her life had been one blessing after another—until now.

She paid for her items and asked the clerk to gift wrap them. While she loitered, she spotted a man walking along the street. He frightened her. His inked-up arms alone told the story loud enough, and the pockmarks on his face made her flinch. He seemed dirty. She watched him amble along, a cigarette dangling from the side of his mouth. His hands resting at the ready on his hips, like a gunslinger in a shoot-out. When she looked down, she noticed something strange. She expected the typical high-top sneakers, tongues flapping, and laces untied, or at least the standby slippahs. Instead, he wore brown shoes. Shoes that didn't belong to the image he portrayed. They were much too good for someone like that creep.

The clerk handed her the shopping tote, and Myra pushed through the door and strolled toward the town car. The man with the shoes had vanished. When she looked at her surroundings, he didn't really belong in this posh atmosphere either. Yes, it confirmed that she was a snob, and in her segregated world of luxury, hadn't suspected that she was admittedly a bit racist. The irony of it caught up.

When the driver asked, "where to?" into the rearview mirror, she simply directed him back toward the hotel. She had done enough damage to her credit card for one morning. John's eyes would pop when the bill came in. Ten thousand to start. Not that they couldn't afford it. And Jack—was worth every dime.

Michael and John were in an in-depth discussion when she joined them in the conference room. Water bottles, cups, and saucers, napkins littered the massive boardroom table. Their laptops and cell phones within reach.

"Have fun shopping, my darling?"

John pulled her close. Michael kissed her cheek and squeezed her fingers.

"It took my mind off things for a short while," Myra lied. Jack had never wandered far. She wanted to ask for news but instead waited for them to bring it up. From their expressions, nothing changed in the three hours she'd been gone.

"Jason's still incognito and scrutinizing everyone in the hotel. But he's hopeful."

Myra glanced at her watch; another three hours Jack had survived on his own.

Chapter 4

I spy

The small luxury of being in command allowed Kai a few opportunities to manage his business and when he could he sauntered toward the beach and scanned the area for Kilo. His cousins promised to fish for him, which alleviated some small stress. Although it didn't cut the disappointment whenever he looked for Kilo and found the post on the beach standing as a solitary marker on the sand. He called the police station twice a day.

He was just rounding the garden when he felt someone draw near. He sensed rather than saw a figure follow him on the flagstone path. He stopped abruptly. But no one crossed his path or came closer. It was the second time that day that a ghost loomed near, then vanished into the shrubs or the long corridors. Just when he picked up the pace again, he saw the two gardeners whisper something to each other and laugh. The creepier, lankier one, Bruce, looked over his shoulder and glared. This morning they were assigned to trim the faded buds on hybrid roses. The weaker one returned to pruning, afraid of another confrontation.

"Everything all right?"

"Yup. Why wouldn't it be?"

Bruce stepped closer toward Kai. The snippers poised like a combat weapon for action.

"Just asking." Kai inflated himself.

"Thanks for getting me on the riding mower."

Kai thought about calling an emergency dentist and wondered how anyone, despite money difficulties, could allow their mouths to rot like that. And who hired these two goons? Kai held his breath. The accumulation of gunge, stale booze, and tobacco assaulted Kai's nose. He stepped away and tried a new tack. He didn't want to be on the bad list of Mr. Green Teeth.

"Thanks for volunteering with the search. It's appreciated."

"Not a problem. Hope they find him. Soon."

"Still. Keep an eye out. Search is ongoing."

"You find that canoe yet?"

Kai took another step backward. The question rang with a hint of malice and stabbed him with the pointed end of insinuations.

"Still looking. It's not important when a life is at stake."

He wondered how often people made fun of their names. Bruce and Wayne. He could imagine the jokes. Bruce Wayne. Although this duo seemed a perfect fit for the underworld, the public garden was a stretch.

"If you say so."

Kai felt dirty. Even speaking with them seemed to contaminate him. He made a note to talk to their manager. Appearance was everything, especially when it came to high-end clients. He couldn't think of a woman who would feel comfortable within a 10-mile radius with men like them. He followed the path leading away from the Rose Garden when a shadow stepped away from the sizable Bismarck palm and scurried into the

Orange Blossom Garden. A stout figure. The faint scent of hot chocolate pipe tobacco lingered. Kai conceded they may just be symptoms of weariness, but he felt as if someone was stalking him.

But this morning, he had a follow-up appointment with the Spencers. Not one he looked forward to, but he hoped they'd introduce him to their PI. Up the service elevator for the umpteenth time, Kai dragged his knuckles along the wall and whistled. In another hour, he'd be free to go home and catch up with his wife. And his father.

He knocked and waited for permission to enter.

"Mr. Spencer. Mrs. Spencer."

"You've met our son? Michael."

Kai shook Michael's hand. It wouldn't require a DNA match to prove that Michael was a Spencer. He was shaped like a man who should be tossing footballs instead of running an empire.

"Is there nothing we can do to help the search along?"

Michael asked. His oversized eyes were eager to jump into action. Anything to ease the frustration of waiting and thumb-twiddling.

"We're doing everything we can. Our paragliding crew and catamaran crew are keeping a diligent watch. I've asked my fishing friends to keep a careful watch."

"What about security footage? Can I go through it?" Michael added. "Mom wants to see it too. There might just be a clue we're overlooking."

Kai shifted on his feet. The suggestion seemed authentic enough. But at the same time, it suggested that Kai hadn't done all there was.

"I'll run it by my superiors, but I can't think it will be a problem."

Mr. Spencer stepped closer.

"Kai. We know you've gone beyond the call of duty. We appreciate that. But from our perspective, we're helpless. More urgently, Jack's running out of time."

"I understand. May I ask about your PI?"

"He hasn't checked in yet?"

"Not with me."

"That's just like Jason. He keeps things private."

"I'm at his disposal." Kai didn't like the idea of a PI running around asking questions.

"I'll remind him to seek you out."

"Give him my number. I can meet him anytime."

On the elevator down, Kai breathed a sigh of relief. It would do him good to spend a few hours at home. More importantly, confessing the missing canoe to his father. Before leaving, he checked in at the office, and Jack Spencer remained the only glaring issue on the duty roster.

Early in the afternoon, Kai walked through the door of his house, and he heard laughter. A refreshing sound. The television hummed on low, but the unmistakable clatter of domino tiles rumbling on the glass table explained it all.

"Hey. Can I play?"

Kai set his keys on the counter and then squeezed his wife's shoulders.

"As long as you promise not to cheat."

His father swirled the tiles on the table without looking up. On the scoresheet, he was miles ahead and smiling.

"Any news on that missing boy?"

His wife's eyes narrowed. She understood the additional strain Kai had taken on. She always said he should never play poker. He didn't have a face for it. Kai shook his head.

"No. Sad business. But everyone's doing the best they can."

"You given up fishing?"

His father's question shot like an arrow through his heart. He might as well admit the truth while it stared him in the face.

"Dad. That's the other sad business. Kilo is missing."

A domino tile slipped from his father's hand. His mouth snapped shut, trapping the question that didn't bear asking.

"I've looked everywhere. All my friends are looking as well. It happened the night of the storm, but I can't imagine a storm untying my cleat."

"Me neither. Do you think it has any bearing on the missing man?"

"No! Absolutely not. Jack Spencer isn't the sort of man who would steal. Or do something reckless and take a canoe out on the night of the storm. No. Highly unlikely."

"People been known to do dumber things."

"True. I'm so sorry. That canoe means everything; to us. I still hope it will float home any day now."

"You're the same as that missing man's mother then."

Cindy rose and left the table. She seldom corrected Kai, but her assumption hit on the sensitive target. It was the absolute truth.

"Look, son. What's important is you. Not the canoe. We're survivors. So don't take on any extra guilt as you always do."

Kai laid his hand protectively on his father's withered fingers. Despite all Jack Spencers' money, he didn't have access to something as simple as family. Poor Jack: he was just discovering what luxury meant.

"Let's play."

Chapter 5

Liar, Liar

Despite accumulating many overtime hours, the paystub didn't
match what Kai would tally if he had had a canoe and the time
to fish. But he wasn't the sort to look a gift horse in the mouth
either. Once they found Jack Spencer, whether dead or alive,
he'd make up the loss. Yesterday, while playing dominoes with
his father, they had discussed renting out part of the house.
But it became apparent that his father was an intensely private
person, and the thought of anyone seeing his father during
weak moments made him uncomfortable. With a smile on
his face, Kai put the suggestion on the back burner. His father
didn't need to know how dire things really were. He'd find a
way, he always did.

Kai scanned the day's incident report and had already
heard the rumors that the Coast Guard had surrendered. The
search came to an end when the distress call of a tanker in
trouble commandeered them away. Their precious resources
always stretched to the max. But the paragliding team made
mention of a private helicopter flying in a search pattern since

yesterday. They were flying again this morning, hovering above the ocean at 300 feet. Crisscrossing. Looking for Jack Spencer, the proverbial needle in the haystack. Kai assumed the family had hired someone when the Coast Guard failed them. The Coast Guard's termination suggested that if Jack Spencer was by some miracle alive, he had crossed beyond the boundaries of their survival model.

"The Spencers are relocating."

Kai spun. His colleague's statement surprised him. The hotel had offered to fit the bill of their stay, which Kai thought of as a generous gesture. He wanted to dig deeper, but he wasn't the sort who gossiped or speculated.

"Where to?"

"They're moving to the condominiums on the other side of the cliff. Someone donated the use of their unit."

"Oh, that's nice." Kai nodded.

It would feel more like a home and allow the family a sense of privacy; however, he'd miss being a vital link to the search. Although he had never met Jack, he found himself deeply affected.

"Anyone ask for me?"

Kai still hadn't heard from the PI, and he assumed the invisible man would vacate the hotel with the Spencers. Or maybe not. Maybe he didn't even exist. No one had mentioned a man asking questions relating to Jack Spencer.

Kai wanted to say goodbye to the Spencers and assure them he'd not lost hope. He took the elevator up and knocked on their door. He heard movement on the other side. A minute later, the door opened, and a maid with cloth in hand surprised him.

"The Spencers?"

She shook her head and held the door aside for Kai to get a good view of the empty suite.

"They checked out. About an hour ago."

Passing Jack Spencer's room, Kai noticed a new guest emerge. A woman with a baby in her arms. He said aloha and bowed. Life moved on. At least now, he was free again and returning to a semblance of his routine. He could explore the pier for a substitute canoe and fish again.

While he waited at the service elevator, a guest approached him. Something in the way the man moved made Kai understand the guest wanted to speak with him.

"Guest elevators are down that way."

"Have a minute? Kai Hale, right?"

The PI. It made sense. Kai allowed the elevator doors to open and close.

"Someplace private?"

Kai led them toward the stairwell, opened the door, and waited for the PI to step past him. The man reeked of hot chocolate tobacco.

"I have a few questions you can clarify for me."

"Of course. I've explained to the Spencers I'm at their disposal."

"You've been put in charge of the Jack Spencer disappearance from what I understand. By whom exactly?"

"I offered, and hotel management asked me to because I have the most experience."

"Experience in what exactly?"

"Investigation. The hotel layout. I watch guests come and go and have an eye for detail."

The PI squinted as if those talents were a visible attribute. He huffed. Then dug in his coat pocket for his notepad.

"You've worked here for fifteen years? As security and were promoted to supervisor."

"Yes."

"Run what happened the night Jack vanished past me. What did you see from your perch in the control room? Give me details. I've seen the footage."

"Then, you know. We have Jack on camera on the stairs meeting the beautiful woman. We also have verbal confirmation that he was on the dancefloor with that same woman. Footage of him taking the elevator."

"Fine. Fine. But what did you see when the camera shows an inebriated Jack Spencer leave the hotel and a storm brewing outside? You didn't think to leave your post and investigate?"

"I didn't. It's not protocol. If we followed every drunk guest, we'd have to hire hundreds of guards."

The PI made a note; flipped the page. He tensed as he readied himself to throw the bomb toward Kai. His halitosis reached Kai's nose before the verbal assault.

"If you had, you might have saved Jack's life. Live with that!"

"That's hardly fair, Sir."

"Fair? Is it fair that you withheld vital information that might have spared Jack? The enormous amount of grief inflicted on the Spencers?"

"I did no such thing. I've gone out of my way to assist in the search."

"Guilty conscience?"

"No. Absolutely not. I feel bad."

"You do? Imagine how badly the Spencers felt after they trusted you. After they received a phone call in the middle of the night suggesting the worst. You know what those calls are like that come in after midnight?"

"Are you accusing me of something?"

Kai had had enough. He had gone above and beyond. He had put his own life on hold for Jack Spencer, his family, and the hotel. How dare this man treat him like with such disdain.

"I am. That midnight phone call sheds new light on things. The caller simply said, "Ask Kai about his missing canoe.""

The bomb landed squarely on Kai's heart. He flinched; took a tiny step backward.

"Thought so. Your dirty little secret has surfaced. Imagine how disappointed the Spencers are. The Coast Guard would have taken an entirely different approach and been able to map their lateral range curves more accurately. Jack might be safe if it hadn't been for your omission."

"My canoe has nothing to do with Jack. It's out of bounds and didn't have a paddle."

"Well, Mr. Hale. You'd be interested to know that I have your paddle. And guess what else washed ashore this morning?"

The PI scrolled on his phone and shoved it under Kai's nose. Nearly spitting on Kai when he said, "It has your name on it, so don't deny it."

"My cooler. I always leave it tied on the canoe."

"Exactly!"

Although Kai had sported a permanent tan since he was a kid, all color drained from his face. They were accusing him of negligence. And he desperately wanted to ask but was afraid. Did they find Kilo?

"I never thought for one second that my canoe had anything to do with Jack Spencer. Drunk as Jack appeared, from what I heard of his character, he wasn't the sort of person stealing a canoe and going joy-riding ahead of a storm."

"So now you're also a character expert? Listen here, Mr. Hale. I've already spoken to the hotel management about you."

Kai felt the finger stab his chest, but in his mind, he clearly saw his boss's face register the disappointment. That he hadn't been summoned yet surprised him. In a matter of a week, he had really screwed up.

"I don't know what to say. I'm sorry. I had no idea."

"And that's why you're not qualified. You'll be lucky if the Spencers don't sue you."

Kai watched as the PI abruptly inflated himself then stormed and yanked the stairwell door wide open. The door snapped closed with the help of the manual elbow. Kai stilled his breath. Wow! He hadn't expected that. But it explained the Spencers' quick exit. They'd be so disgusted with him. Kai doubted Mrs. Spencer would ever look him in the eye again. Although now that they are gone, he'd never have to worry. Not that his pesky mind wouldn't remind him and rub salt into the wound repeatedly.

With his hand firmly on the cool railing, he took the stairs as his somber mood dictated how to proceed. He wasn't in the mood to meet a guest or employee along the way. His best option lay in knocking on his boss's door and explaining himself. Even if that rude man was correct about the canoe, Kai hadn't done anything other than comport himself professionally. He could wait for the fallout to settle instead of preempting the summons. There could only be one answer as to who called the Spencers during the night. The Batman Duo.

Before confronting his boss, Kai decided to track his nemesis into the garden. If they were going to sacrifice him, he'd mow them down too. More urgently, he needed to understand the reason for betraying him as they had. Their cowardice explained why they made the call anonymously. Face to face, they'd be harder to take seriously. But why? They had to be up to something. And from experience, he read something in each of the encounters with them: malice.

Kai exited through the delivery door and headed for the landscape office. He might lose his job because of those two goons. But he'd not go down without a fight. The door to the office was ajar. A rake and long-handled clippers, left carelessly abandoned next to the trash bin, were the only clue of recent activity. The entire crew had strict instructions to continue the search if they finished their duties. He scanned the shift schedule posted to the door. Bruce and Wayne. Off.

That settled one dilemma. Kai retraced his steps and headed toward the hotel again. This morning he hadn't a moment to enjoy the lush beauty of the garden or inhale the intoxicating scent deeply. He had always been a man of the moment and something went sideways on the morning his canoe vanished. Yet, he hadn't had the chance to upright what leaned toward a slow and painful tumble.

He took the stairs two at a time and then briskly walked down the corridor. The teak door marked Hotel Management lay straight ahead. On his way in, Kai prepared an explanation. It didn't warrant a lot of rehearsing because he simply planned to tell the truth. Fact after fact. No conjecture. He double-checked the shine on his shoes before knocking.

The chipper assistant buzzed him in. She obviously hadn't heard of the dire accusations and smiled at Kai as always. Or she had a gift as an actress. She gestured for Kai to take a seat, then she vanished behind the double door separating him for his boss.

"Go on in." She held the door aside, still smiling with her eyes and mouth.

"Kai. Take a seat."

Kai had sat in the same chair often enough. On the first day, after he was hired, he'd been summoned. His stomach had done a number and churned acid. But this upper echelon superseded Kai's expectations and had always treated Kai on equal footing.

"You know why I'm here."

"I do. But rest assured, I've never doubted you, Kai."

"Thanks. I had no idea that my canoe could have any part in Jack's disappearance. I understand how it looks."

Kai blurted his confession, twisting his fingers into the same shape as his soul. Afraid to look up.

"I agree. I told that PI the same thing. Not that I'm not sorry. For Jack. The Spencers."

"He implied that the Spencers might sue the hotel."

"Kai. The Spencers can sue, but it has nothing to do with you. Or your canoe. Leave it to our lawyers. Just do your job as you've always done."

Back at his desk, Kai breathed easier. Any other boss would have made his life more difficult and probably fired him to erase any blemish on the hotel. He rehashed all the accusations the PI had tricked him into believing. What sort of man gets off on sinking a man's life like that? He also remembered smelling the scent of the odious man's pipe tobacco in the garden. He'd been following him and sniffed around the dirt pile. The dirt pile: the two goons he needed to track down.

Chapter 6

Change of Scene

Myra closed the door to the bedroom and leaned against it. Not that she expected anyone to come barging in. She needed a minute to gather her thoughts and to contain her emotions. She'd been doing a lot of that lately. Holding herself together when she really wanted nothing more than to fall apart. At least in pieces, she'd feel less. Michael had tried to intervene, but John could hardly keep the contempt from his voice.

"What? You go behind my back and rack up a ten-thousand-dollar bill, and I'm supposed to keep my mouth shut?"

As soon as the words fell into the room, he was sorry. Anger and frustration got the best of him too. She brought the tissue to her eyes. At least now, she'd not have to suffer through the waiting. Waiting until John discovered the credit card bill. How could he deny Jack that resource? If she had to, or could, she'd swim as far as her strength allowed and bring Jack home. Even if that meant dying while trying. A soft knock prevented her from floating away with her thoughts and following Jack into the water.

"Come in."

Michael's head entered the opening. He was John's replica physically, he smiled before asking,

"Can I come in?"

"Of course."

"Look. That was just strain talking. Dad's okay with you booking the helicopter now. But you shouldn't have gone behind his back. You have to remember to work as a team."

"It's not right that my son has to play marriage counselor."

She took Michael's hand and squeezed. As big as Michael was, he was a softy.

"Look, Mom. We just have to focus on doing what is best for Jack. And I agree with what you did. Dad won't spare any expenses either. Money isn't the issue."

She led Michael toward the settee at the foot of the bed and sat for a minute in silence.

"I know. It's just that sometimes your father doesn't hear me."

Michael patted her thigh. Was it possible to love one's children any more than she loved hers? She smiled into Michael's kind eyes.

"Dad and I are also going to hire a boat. I thought maybe you'd like to come?"

"Give me a minute. And yes. Absolutely."

At the pier, they passed an old fisherman sitting on the bench. He tipped his cap to them. The dock swayed gently with the combined weight of their hefty steps. Between father and son, they weighed close to five hundred pounds. Guessing from John's stride, he knew exactly what he was searching for. Third dock, tenth boat, The Mariner. As they neared the tenth slot, John's urgency increased. Myra lagged. Next to her, fish swam in green, murky water, oil and gas shimmered in rainbow colors. The Mariner wasn't an attractive yacht or sailboat. Instead, it lumbered like a whale beached on the sand and was impossible to miss.

Michael held out his hand for her, and she climbed aboard the imposing ship. The captain matched his vessel. Stout and slightly banged up, but both exuded the sort of confidence that made them right for the endeavor.

While John and the captain discussed the finer points of the search, Myra looked around. A flag snapped in the breeze; a yellow dog wagged his tail but didn't bother investigating the intrusion. She overheard the word storm, and both John and the captain looked to the southeast. Myra saw clouds nest on a blue horizon and even bluer sky. Ten minutes later, they shook hands, and John hopped down from the wheelhouse. Negotiations over.

Myra knew nothing of ships, sailing, or nautical lingo. Port and starboard, she could never remember which was which. They had been on several cruise ships, but she had never had the inkling to learn more. And John, though he claimed he had sailed in his youth, hadn't a spare minute in his day to indulge in anything other than family. At times they took vacations, but Myra always organized. John showed up when he could, and most often, St. Kitts was the most natural solution for a getaway.

"There. He's heading out soon, but he's worried about the storm. Seamen like him have a built-in radar for such things."

"Thanks, John. I appreciate what you're doing. I'm sorry about the other."

The helicopter search had revealed nothing. On its two-day tour across the Pacific, their range was crippled by fuel restrictions. They all hoped a ship of us such magnitude as the Mariner would have a more extended reach.

"If Jack is out there, we'll find him."

John took her hand, and they walked back toward the Land Rover that came with the condo. The condominium was a blessing. They had more privacy and freedom. The hotel had done all there was. And Jason was still on-site to investigate. No one dared mention that five days had passed since they started the search. No one dared to mention what they feared most. She pitied John for an instant. He didn't have that long-reaching cord she had to cling to. Jack was alive. He was out there. Somewhere.

"I'm sorry to say this, but I have to head back. There's pressing business at the office. The merger is becoming another nightmare."

"That's fine, but I'm not leaving until we find Jack."

"I'll stay with Mom for as long as I can."

"That's settled then. I'll make the arrangements. Let's stick together, and we'll find Jack."

John was about to add something that Myra could not bear hearing. She cut him off.

"One of us needs to call Stacy. She's bound to be sick with worry."

Chapter 7

Small Treasures

Gale force winds delivered the rain sideways, and churning waves breached the hull time and again. Jack bailed water with half of the coconut and held the other up to the storm that offered him a much-needed drink of rainwater. He drank each accumulated inch greedily and asked for more. His mission to rescue the floating object he had seen rock on the distant waves came to an abrupt halt. A building squall had come at Jack out of nowhere and blindsided him. He'd been intently clawing the water to get where he was going when the first bracing hit launched the canoe almost airborne. The bellwether had chimed, and Jack had missed the warning of incoming weather clearly written on the canvass of the sky. He was illiterate when it came to reading weather lingo spelled out in cloud formations.

While crawling toward the object that he saw from time to time crest on the waves, Jack took comfort in the monotonous duty. For however long it took, or however tedious the chore, Jack's mind enjoyed being busy. He had kept his eye on the prize, but when the wind suddenly shifted, and the temperature plunged, it caught Jack off guard. He just managed to struggle his arms into the life vest and slipped the second vest over his hips like a diaper. He held the lifeline to the canoe firmly in his hand while considering his options. If he tied the string to his hand or foot, the force of the turbulent waves had the power to sever his limbs. But without the canoe, he'd be dead too. For a while, he rode the canoe leaning from side to side and keeping it from tipping. But it was an impossible task to balance and bail the incoming water. One wave nearly washed him overboard while he rode uphill on such an angle that the crest was directly above him like a roof. He entered the tunnel and sailed out of it by the miracles of nature.

After some time, he contemplated swimming alongside the canoe. He planned how to submerge himself without risking his hold on the one lifeline he had for even one second. Fear of the frigid water kept him on board too long. Then again, dying from hypothermia might come as a blessing. But that thought only lasted a second. Whatever the ocean was throwing, he was ready to catch, but he wouldn't risk being washed overboard. He'd rather die trying, and his options for dying were limitless.

When another rogue wave filled the canoe, Jack bailed frantically using both hands and the makeshift coconut cups while being forced into letting his grip go. He had to concede it was futile. The ocean filled the canoe quicker than he could empty it.

At least, the strenuous movements warmed his body. The scorching temperature that had seared his skin all day was now remiss. Jack sunk to his knees and bailed with his head ducked low into the spitting wind. If he survived this storm, he promised himself he'd never take anything for granted again. He made the same promise to the universe. Had he somehow asked the universe for this? Did he think the wrong thoughts too often and ended up here to test some secret theory? No.

This had the makings of payback. But just exactly which wrong was this a payback for? He bit down and braced himself for whatever it was that nature was throwing.

He promised to see people in a different light too and learn to value small relationships. He vowed to learn the name of the barista, the security guard at the office, the waiter at his favorite restaurants. He'd donate to various causes. To animal shelters. No, he'd volunteer his time and really make a difference. Whatever happened after his rescue, he'd be a changed man. A kinder man. He bailed scoop after scoop without taking his eyes off the deepening lake forming in the canoe. Jack dug deeper still. He could taste the diluted saltwater on his lips.

When he looked up, the canoe had found its groove and sailed effortlessly over the water. Like a surfer catching his ride. It would be interesting to know how fast he was traveling over the rough sea. Maybe he'd google it one day and calculate the knots based on wind speed, weight, and conditions. Maybe Alexa had an answer on stand-bye. He bailed without looking up.

He'd move closer to home. He'd take the job at his father's firm back. He'd have lunch with his mother every week. He'd be the best doting uncle he could be. Maybe he'd join that enormous church he drove past each morning on the way to work. There had to be a reason it drew such a large congregation, and, suddenly, he also felt the urge to belong to something. He'd settle down.

He'd study history, cooking, and sailing. Maybe take up painting. Yoga. Go to India and study with Sadhguru. Jack even considered becoming a minimalist as he had seen in that documentary. He laughed. "How is this for fucking minimalism?" He clapped the coconut. He'd write a book about his experience. His: Voyage Lost at Sea. He thought about Hemingway's "The Old Man and the Sea," a book he had scorned in high school as boring. How in his youth the message of the book had nothing to do with him. Yet, suddenly, Jack felt as if he were the old man. His arms ached from reeling in the rain and the waves. The rain was winning and filling the canoe. The waves were winning and filling the canoe. He couldn't separate the two any longer. Regardless of how quickly he scooped up the water, he was losing the battle.

Jack stopped bailing. The puddles deepened, and the water quickly accumulated and sloshed past his ankles. Past mid-calf. He decided that bailing was futile, and he didn't have the energy to keep going. He clutched the long string and stuffed the co-conut halves into his pants. He swung his body overboard and plunged into the welcoming waves. His heart clenched, and his teeth were chattering. With the last bit of strength, he flipped the canoe bottom-side up. He clutched the bars of the outrigger and swam next to the canoe. Massive waves rolled him, and the canoe, along. Up and over. He drank a ton of seawater and spit. Rinsing his mouth with rainwater when he could.

Large fins were the least of his worries. Any shark trolling in these waters had a right to feast on his limbs. At least it would be over quickly. He decided then, he'd never vacation near water again. If—he survived this ordeal. He'd change his ways. He made promises that the wind quickly stole from his lips. Jack knew his end was nearing, and the disasters that he had seen befall other people had caught up to him. God didn't discriminate or play favorites after all. A fact that became clearer by the minute. Jack Spencer was a person, no special distinction. He held on tighter, and luckily the life jackets made floating along easier. But if he wanted to die, he'd have to strip them off. Keeping them on would only prolong his agony.

While surfing the top of a rolling wave, filling his mouth with water, he caught a small fish between his teeth. Jack nearly spit the flopping body into the water. But on instinct, he bit down and crushed its body. It tasted awful. It tasted delicious. While floating, he kept his mouth open: if there was one, there were others. As if by some miracle, he had somehow ended up among a school of small fish. He never knew if they were sardines or herring. He feasted on three of them. Raw fish contained so many benefits, including vitamin C.

When the storm finally calmed enough, he rolled the canoe over. Exhausted and cold, he passed out instantly, the coconut halves pressing into his gut. Jack awoke in a puddle of water. A soft rain fell from one remaining dark cloud, but sunshine streaming through the splitting sky warmed his body, an uprooted palm floated next to the canoe. He opened his mouth. Rain.

Chapter 8

Blackmail

Bruce grabbed Wayne by the collar and slammed him against the wall. This is what their friendship had come to. All because of that fucking tourist. And it was becoming harder to keep his temper in check. Things hadn't gone according to plan.

"Don't you fuckin dare!"

Bruce saw his own spittle fly and spray Wayne's face. No-way! He was not going to go down for some fucking tourist. The contract didn't have contingencies either. Shit happens.

"If he's stupid enough to wander on the beach in his condition, then I'd say survival of the fittest."

"We might have sent him to his death."

"You don't know that!"

Wayne's eyes widened at the suggestion that Jack Spencer's vanishing act had nothing to do with setting him afloat.

"It's been over a week. I told you we should have gone after him."

"With what? A dinghy?"

"But if we had told the authorities they might have been able to pinpoint his trajectory or whatever bullshit theory they use."

"Not my problem. But I swear if you say a word, I'll fucking kill you."

Wayne turned his face away. And for good measure, Bruce gave him another shove into the brick wall to reiterate his vow. When he let go of Wayne's collar, he didn't step away, forcing Wayne to slink sideways. So much for friendship, and all because of some stupid bitch and that loser tourist.

He lit a cigarette and glared at Wayne, who didn't dare look up from his shoes. What was obvious now was that Wayne hadn't held up well to the light of scrutiny. And because of it, Wayne morphed from a friend into an enemy.

If only he could convince that pussy not to cave to some feeble moral convictions under pressure. He had already dealt with Kai and his arrogant gloating. Soon that jerk would be out on his ass, serving him right with all that brown-nosing. Subservient schmucks like Kai deserved to be tuned in. And Wayne. He'd deal with Wayne, but there was one other uncomfortable feeling that shadowed him. Who was that fat fucker? The one who smelled of hot chocolate and smoked a pipe? Something about him didn't sit well with Bruce. He had to be careful. Now wasn't the time to fall apart.

Chapter 9

Left Behind

A soft breeze stirred the curtains while Myra served lunch on the balcony. John and Michael discussed further details about job transitioning and hardly noticed her intrusion. It was the scent of garlic bathed in a wine sauce that made them both look up and end their discussion. Michael couldn't allow his position to remain vacant for an extended spell either, and, luckily, they had just the man to fill his shoes. It would also serve double duty and help Brody to keep his head above water. That Tessa had dumped him so unceremoniously deflated the ex-groom as much as losing his best friend. The feeling of helplessness was contagious and inflicted the entire wedding party—except Tessa. Besides, Brody knew the job as well as Michael. He'd been with the firm long enough and deserved a crack at the junior executive position.

Myra filled their wine glasses and cleared her throat. Although they had stopped discussing business, they had switched to another topic just as sensitive. Brody and Tessa.

"Lunch."

While she grilled their mahi-mahi steaks, a token delivery from Kai, she wondered if Jack had eaten since he disappeared. She hoped he had access to something— especially water.

"Look delicious."

John kissed her on the temple and put his laptop on the rattan footstool. Their last meal. His flight would whisk him away this afternoon. Such was the nature of the beast of running an empire. Thousands of people depended on John Spencer's leadership, and Stacy deserved to have one parent next to her when she went into labor. Although Myra still held on to the tail-end of some miracle, that they'd all be there for the event, which would change their family dynamic.

"I'm really disgusted with Jason."

Myra had to get it out. Jason Rockport was an unscrupulous PI. He had frightened Kai into believing that Jack's disappearance and the missing canoe were his fault. Would it have changed the search? Probably.

"He's a PI. He gets his answers his way."

"This time, his ruthless tactics got us nothing. Kai, that poor soul, has bent over backward for us. And he lost his canoe to boot. We should buy him a new one to make up for Jason's lack of decorum."

"We'll deal with that later. If Jack did have access to a canoe, his chances of surviving have doubled. We can't go moping around saying if only we had known."

"Michael? What is your opinion on Rockport?"

"Mom, I'm with Dad. I don't agree with his methods, but he's gotten us answers in the past. I'm sorry he had to complicate Kai's life, but it's for Jack. That's what matters. And Jason thinks he has a lead on the mystery woman."

"That's good news. Maybe she can enlighten us."

"Let's hope. I'm sorry to be leaving you. But both of you stay positive and keep me posted. Remember, we make decisions as a team."

John cleared his plate and drained his glass. He had thirty minutes before the taxi would whisk him to the airport. And he wanted his last few moments in Hawaii to pass on a high note. The mystery woman. She had to have a reason for keeping silent.

While Myra cleared the table, John zipped up his suitcase. He was reluctant to leave Myra, but he was needed elsewhere. And Michael could handle anything on this end. If it weren't such a crucial time in the company merger, he would have traded places with Michael. But such was not a luxury he could afford. Plus, he didn't want it leaked that Jack was missing. It could spoil the deal. Gossip fed the rumor mill and churned out trash. The merger hinged on him being in control of every aspect.

Poor Jack. Where are you, son? Your mother and I are worried sick. And despite all the evidence, John still idled in the surreal world that it was all a big misunderstanding. That Jack wasn't missing at all but had left for reasons he wasn't yet ready to share. He suspected that misunderstanding had to do with Tessa. Kai had shown him the footage of the fiercely contentious argument between Jack and Tessa. And which he hadn't bothered to share with Myra or anyone else. A silent one-hundred-dollar bill asked Kai to keep the explosive footage quiet unless it was needed as evidence.

Staring out the window calmed him. The ocean rolled in and out with the tide and didn't give up her secret. At least not yet. Myra was right, though. Rockport could have softened his tone with Kai. Poor chap. To be hung out like that was cruel. But Rockport must have had a reason, and it wasn't his place to instruct the notorious PI and his tactics.

At the door, he kissed Myra goodbye. There wasn't anything to add. Michael walked him downstairs to assure him that he'd take care of his mother, that they'd find Jack.

Coward. John was strong in so many aspects of life, but when it came to facing emotions, he was weak. Myra pressed her face against the cool windowpane and watched the taxi drive away. John had concocted a million reasons to be on his way back. That the office needed him, and he was the captain at the helm of a sinkable conglomerate. So what? What did any of it matter if Jack wasn't part of the equation? She'd sell or give away every bauble or trinket in her possession to have her son back. Anything. If the devil knocked on the door right now, she'd hand over her soul. But it was only Michael who waltzed through the door again. He smiled.

"He's off. How about a walk along the beach?"

"I'd like that."

Something so simple. A walk. Myra was glad Michael suggested it. She smeared a layer of preventative suntan gel on her skin. In the foyer, she reached for her hat and sunglasses.

"Ready."

The beach was only accessible from their condominium by crossing a busy boulevard. Michael hooked her arm through his, and they dashed among the cars stopping for the light. Down a flight of cement stairs, they touched the sand. A constant breeze lifted the brim of her hat and the frills of her satin blouse. Hot sand seeped into her sandals, but Michael had been right. A walk on the beach was just the ticket.

Walking on the dry, shifting sand took effort, and each step sank into the soft dunes washed ashore up to the seawall twice a day. Once they reached the strand, which the leaving tide had just wetted; the going was more comfortable. The ground beneath their feet was almost solid. Automatically, they headed in the direction of the hotel. From their angle, they could see just the corner, the salmon pink paint peeking through the foliage. Michael slipped his sandals off, and she did too. For a second, she felt like a little girl and walked into the foaming water. Since they arrived on the island, she hadn't had a moment to dip her toes and enjoy the pleasures of being on this gorgeous island. Everything had happened so fast and so slow at the same time. It was as if time had come face to face with time and neither version knew which was which.

Michael stooped and scooped up a pearlescent harp shell and rinsed it in the tide.

"For you."

He laid the shell on her extended palm. His towering body acted as an umbrella while she examined the miniature conch. What a miracle its intricate design represented.

"Thank you. I'll treasure it always."

Together, before walking on, they stared at the grand and humbling Pacific. Both were looking for Jack and knowing the impossibility of finding him on the waves. Myra hooked her arm into Michael's elbow, and they continued to stroll in silence. Sandpipers ran in a choreographed pattern along the shore looking for a meal

Walking next to the ocean, Myra felt a calmness settle over her. She knew inexplicably; she was closer to Jack here than anywhere on the island. As if the water rushing over her feet had somehow touched Jack. A conductor of messages. She wondered again if Jack was thinking of her at this exact moment. She knew he was. "I'm coming for you, Jack. Don't give up."

"Did you say something?"

Michael had overheard her thoughts. She nodded. Without being ashamed, she explained herself and clung more possessively to his arm.

"I was just telling Jack to hang on. That I'm on my way."

"Funny. I was telling him the same thing."

Michael patted her hand. So she wasn't alone in talking to Jack. She only hoped that Jack had his ears open and received their messages. They stopped in unison at the great rock formation separating the beach from the hotel when she asked the question.

"Do you think he took the canoe?" The possibility that he had, had parked itself. It hadn't moved on despite the improbability.

"I've asked myself the same question. But I don't know. He was very drunk."

"He's never been reckless before. Has he?"

"No, Mom. Not in that sense. His choice concerning drinking as much as he has, has been reckless to some degree. And his record with the ladies is reckless too. But I can't picture him getting into an old clunker of a canoe."

"You think Jack is too wild?"

"Honestly? I would have thought he'd grow out of his ways by now. Especially now that Brody was almost married. I thought that he'd follow the example and slow down."

"Did you like Tessa? As a man?"

"To look at? Absolutely. But for some time, I've seen glimpses that she's not a nice person. I'm almost glad."

"Me too. Brody would have ended up miserable with her."

"He's miserable now. I'm glad we talked him into leaving with Dad. Keep his mind off things. If that is possible."

"And he'll help Dad keep his mind off things as well."

"What do you think is on the other side of these rocks? Just the beach of the hotel?"

"Must be."

"I hope Rockport has more tact with our mystery woman."

Myra nodded. The mystery woman. The woman who lured her son away. Myra was curious, yet she didn't want to know the truth either.

"Ready to head back?"

They stopped again and stared at the horizon breaking the blue ocean apart from the blue sky. Soft white clouds dotted the heavens, the waxing moon, a pale reminder that the days were quickly adding up an entire week.

Chapter 10

Stalker

Bruce ducked behind the large shrub planted on the far edge of the back deck. Inside the house, the lights were ablaze. But he hadn't seen any movement. The television light flickered, and he was sure someone was at home. But he had to be careful of the motion detector lights. They were set to a hardwire trigger, and he couldn't risk setting them off.

His instincts told him Kelani was at home. Where else would she go? Hidden as he was behind the shrubs, he had dialed her number. Holding his breath, he heard her phone ring inside the house. She didn't bother to answer, and it didn't come as a surprise. He had already phoned her ten times without avail. Something hadn't gone as planned, and she had backed out without giving him any warning.

Bruce craved a cigarette, but Kelani's brother had a nose for tobacco. If Akim even got a whiff, he'd come storming out the door and blow Bruce's cover. Akim was his boss on the landscape crew and fiercely protective of his sister. If Akim knew, well, there was no telling what he'd do to him and Wayne.

Turning them over to the police would be a blessing. At least, he had that sort of a reputation.

His phone vibrated in his pocket, and in the stillness, it sounded as loud as if a bomb went off. Bruce fumbled and managed to switch it off without anyone hearing. Wayne. Fucking asshole. Crouching low, he made his way along the dark fence. He moved slowly and carefully. When he reached the neighbor's fence, he jumped over. With a few long strides, he cleared the short distance, and his feet slapped the pavement of the sidewalk. He lit a smoke and inhaled. Then a plume of smoke danced among the threat, "I'm gunning for you, bitch!"

Chapter 11

Not Enough Hours

Kai tucked his ball cap lower and headed away from the beach with his head down, watching his feet as he walked. He'd seen them as soon as they descended the stairs but didn't want to intrude on their private moment. After all, he was out searching for the same reason as they were. Looking for that precious something.

Mrs. Spencer stood still in the protective shadow her youngest son cast over her and gazed toward the relentless sea. Kai heard the news that Mr. Spencer had returned to the mainland. It couldn't have been easy to do so. Kai shared an intrinsic bond with Mrs. Spencer. He believed too. He could feel it in his bones that his canoe was out there. Floating aimlessly. Just as Mrs. Spencer believed in her son. He believed that if for some unthinkable reason Jack Spencer set off on Kilo, he stood a chance to survive. The old canoe had weathered many storms, and like a cat had many lives to spare. If anything could take on the ocean, it was the canoe built to glide. And it came outfitted with a few tools which had the power to spare a man's life. No canoe and the absence of a body implied hope.

Kai had parked his truck at the restaurant next to the condominium. He had made his delivery of the fresh fish he didn't catch. But that hardly mattered. Out of an inherent need, he ran across the busy street, sidewinding his way among the cars. He was still teeming with anger that someone had defaced a poster in the elevator. What sort of person painted a mustache on a missing man? A man presumed dead by many. Whoever thought it funny enough probably laughed at Jack Spencer's misfortune. Callously not caring about those who were faced with such an excruciating loss. Sometimes, some people were shit.

Within a week, Kai had witnessed heavy lines of loss carving their initials into the Spencers. Mrs. Spencer had aged a hundred years. Not that she wasn't still attractive, but she looked deflated and haggard despite trying to look her best. Kai imagined she often stared toward the sea, finding some solace that her son, despite the odds, was out there. Wishing for him to miraculously return home.

Back in his truck, Kai headed away from the beach toward his home when he spotted a stout figure on the sidewalk. The PI. Fucking Rockport. Slowly rumors trickled in that he had harassed several of the guests and staff. Often unjustifiably.

Rockport was in deep discussion with a woman. A beautiful woman. Hawaiian. What troubled Kai was the aggressive posture and that the PI had a firm grip on the woman's arm. Forcing her to walk with him. She tried to get away, a look of panic confirmed her fear.

Kai double-parked the truck and jumped out, leaving the engine running, the door ajar.

"Do you need help?"

Kai planted himself between the PI and the woman. An overpowering scent of stale cigar smoke assaulted Kai. Whatever this was, the annoying man overstepped his bounds. Under no circumstances did he have the right to physically detain anyone.

"This man thinks I'm someone I'm not. I've never heard of a Jack Spencer. Or ever been to that hotel." She turned and looked over her shoulder, indicating the hotel, tears of exasperation ran freely down her cheek.

"Mr. Rockport. Let go of her. This is not how we do things on the island."

"Mind your own business, Mr. Hale."

"Let her go."

Kai inflated himself. He had watched the footage of the mystery woman ten times, if not more. Although this woman was just as pretty, she was not the one.

"He's been stalking me for days. I have no idea why."

Rockport loosened his grip, and the woman jerked free. She ran into the nearest shop, vanishing among the colorful T-shirts and sarongs. Rockport squinted and flared his nostrils.

"Don't ever interfere with my investigation again!"

"Don't ever accuse the wrong person again!"

Slow-motion waves of anger lifted Kai's arms, and before he could stop himself, he shoved Rockport, who was not expecting the act of aggression toward him, out of his way. Kai spun on his heels. Behind him, Rockport yelled obscenities. Words like, how dare you, you'll pay for this, you fucking.... But Kai only cared about escaping from the fat finger emphatically accusing him. Seated in the truck, he waved an apology to the person honking. Rockport remained on the sidewalk and glared.

Chapter 12

Benches

Jack ran his tongue over his chapped lips. He chewed on the skin willing to come away until his lips bled. Hunger played on his mind like a broken record. There was no escaping the thought, the feeling, the result. The storm sapped him of all the available resources his body produced and took more than he had on reserve. He didn't think he had the strength to move.

After the storm had settled enough, he struggled to upright the canoe again and with much difficulty crawled aboard. Completely exhausted and cold, he understood he had crossed the border into hypothermia. His mind was playing tricks, and his limbs dragged as if they were full of lead. Sluggish. Breathing heavy, he appreciated being back on the canoe. Periodically, the wind, mingled with a tropical breeze, blew its soft breath over his shivering body. A fever was trying to start a fire. But Jack knew that much about survival: wet and damp things were impossible to ignite.

During the long and unendurable bath in the ocean's revengeful swell, Jack longed to let go and end his misery. All of him, except that tiny voice in his head, asked him to let go of his hold and drift away. The tiny voice, however, didn't belong to him. It belonged to his mother.

While intermittent sleep rocked him on the canoe, he felt her presence and received the message. Hang on—transmitted in Morse code sent directly from her heart. She was his first thought upon waking. He pictured her, staring at the ocean, looking for him on the horizon. He could see her clearly framed against the morning sky. If he kept his eyes closed, maybe he could touch her.

Jack stretched his legs; the sun was slowly exploding in little diamond waves on the ocean, tenderly warming his body. The sun must have been a mother too, she could be tender and strict. His limbs ached from swimming for hours, and each muscle burned down to his toes. He closed his eyes again. He wasn't in the mood to face the endless blue again, or the pangs twitching in his gut. As much as he wanted his suffering to end, he also wanted to live. To survive for another day.

Jack slowly wiggled his toes. His shoes wouldn't have survived the ordeal out on the ocean, but a pair of socks would have been nice. He hoped wherever he left his shoes, they'd serve as a clue in his rescue. Besides being lost and starving, Jack knew he was his own worst enemy. He was a wimp, a spoiled baby, and terrible company to keep. Was he such a horrible person that he deserved such punishment? Yes and no.

He had already admitted, if only to himself, what he had done behind Brody's back was unforgivable. Yes, he owned the truth, and even if Tessa was just as culpable, he deserved a life-sentence of guilt. He earned this misery. If Brody discovered what he had done, the fall-out would wreak devastation. Consequences harsher than he could endure. But it all happened innocently enough, and, on that day, Tessa had, literally, fallen into his arms.

Jack shook his head. This morning wasn't the time to remind himself and trudge around in that nest of guilt. Today, he had some surviving to do. He shifted himself upright, his legs propped up on the bench seat. The prevalent whitecaps from yesterday had played themselves out, and soft waves lollygagged alongside the canoe. His latest find swam without a struggle, tied securely to the ribs of the outrigger next to him. Could he eat the palm leaves? His stomach growled and insisted he could. During his struggle in the ocean, he lost the slippery frond of seaweed, and right now, he'd bite the head of a turtle. He was so hungry; his thoughts were as clouded as a storm.

While raising himself to sitting, he saw a glimmer of something foreign to the canoe.

During his entire week at sea, he had always commanded the more substantial portion of the canoe. He had stepped over the bench in the middle once to pry the board loose from the seat on the far end. But that was it. His long legs required room to stretch out. But in the wee hours this morning, after he righted the canoe and climbed aboard, he didn't have enough stamina to struggle his limbs over the bench in the middle. He passed out in the cramped side of the canoe.

He reached forward and tugged on the corner of what looked like a Ziploc bag. What was it doing under the seat, and where had it come from? When he pulled, Jack realized something crucial. A miracle. The bench seat had a lid. With a quick kick using the heel of his hand, the top gave way and fell onto the other side with a thud. Suddenly, there was no doubt in Jack's mind, he was the luckiest man alive. And the dumbest.

There was a five-inch wide secret compartment. It was like a Christmas miracle and a gift he hadn't dared to count on.

He pulled out the big baggies. "Hallelujah!"

Three bottles of crystal clean water steamed up the plastic bag. Beneath it, there were others. He ransacked his discovery. A collection of soda crackers, cookies, and jerky. Yet another contained a greasy bottle of suntan lotion. Fishing line and rusted lures floated in the puddle of water. A rusted knife and wooden mallet seemed to smirk at Jack and sing. All were nestled on a soaking Hawaiian flag.

Jack guzzled an entire bottle of water in one go. This time he kissed the empty bottle instead of tossing into the ocean. He coveted his precious offerings. He ate half a package of stale crackers and then sniffed the piece of jerky. It expired months ago. There was no question if he should risk it. The smoked smell of meat brought out the carnivore in Jack, and his teeth clamped down on the strip of beef without waiting for consent. Salted tears of joy ran down his cheek and into his mouth.

If God existed, He had just sent Jack a message. You can do this, son! Jack took another bite and then wrapped the remaining goodies into the Ziploc baggie. While his fingers squeezed the seal, the strip turned green. What a miraculous invention, Jack thought. Could it be possible that something as simple as a Ziploc bag had the power to save his life? He could taste meat and stale crackers as his answer.

Jack rose. He scanned the ocean using his hands as make-shift binoculars. The natural curve of the horizon ran on forever on either side of him. Not a ship, or fleck, or land in sight. But swaying on the waves were tiny fragments of hope sparkling in the sunshine. He could do this. Although Jack had never fished before, he made it his first chore. He unwound the length of fishing line and fed it through the eye of the hook. He knotted it ten times for good measure and for good luck, kissed it before flinging it as far as it would. Without weight or a lure, the hook floated on the waves. Would any fish surface and take a bite?

Jack had no idea. But he'd perfect his technique, he knew it wasn't going to be as easy as they made it seem on television. Clamping down on the jerky he had set aside as a reward, he tore a piece off to sacrifice and rewarded himself with another. While chewing, he counted the days on his fingers. He stopped on the index finger of his right hand. Seven. For each hour he survived, he increased his chances of being found. But after a week at sea, he understood that nothing came easy. He'd have to fight for each piece of comfort and for each minute and hour.

Kneeling, he reached over the hull and started sawing away on the palm tree floating next to the canoe unhindered. He could sleep on the fronds, and if he had to, he could chew on them. His teeth missed the pure pleasure of chomping away on something substantial. It might help to clean his teeth as well. The knife hacked away on the palm leaves, and he salvaged six branches. Fighting a feeling of remiss, Jack sent the barren palm on its way. He had learned to harvest.

PART 4
ONE DOWN!

Chapter 1

Not Everyone Lives

After three days of immobility, judging by the frequency of how often Rose saw the light vanish behind a sheet of gray, the storm relented. Waking from the self-inflicted semi-coma, she floated on the lumbering swell feeling the gentle lift against her spine. She wiggled her fingers and listened for the sound of movement, enclosed as she was, from inside the pod, there was no way of knowing if the others came through unscathed. A rumble in her gut confirmed that hunger and thirst were surging with life too. Inching her arms down, she tugged on a rope and struggled a bottle of water toward her. Ron had thought of everything. Everything it would take to survive.

But storms often had other ideas of just what that entailed. Secondly, the urge to rise and stand overruled even hunger. She hoped everyone else's limbs were intact. Hers seemed to be, but the test would come later. Rose was grateful for one thing. Constipation. It was a matter of input versus output.

She clambered halfway out of her pod. Unbuttoning her shirt, she noticed movement next to her. Mark was alive. Ron still lay motionless, halfway out of his pod, his eyes were shut, his chest was moving. Strapped to her chest was a precious resource. A bag of boiled rice and a Mars bar melted from her body heat. Despite the prolonged abstinence, she still craved the meaty bite of a cheeseburger, a lasagna, or steak, and French fries. She was sick of seafood.

"Roll call." Ron partly raised himself. Then he reached for her fingertips and squeezed; both glad to have survived together.

"Trish?"

"Here."

"Rose?" He winked.

"Here."

"Li Wei?"

"Here, bossman."

After everyone was accounted for, the others slowly un-strapped themselves. The sun decided to help them along by glaring with the precision of an arc welder and dried their clothing, soaked with feces and urine. A prerequisite for these journeys was to embrace humility. Mark strained but couldn't raise his head off the ground.

"I've got whiplash. I swear I broke a rib," he groaned.

Ted mumbled, "me too," Everyone exercised their limbs. While they ate and drank what they had strapped to their bodies, they also took turns bathing in the ocean, tethered to a line while everyone bashfully turned away.

"That was a piece of cake."

Ron climbed aboard naked after his bath. Flotilla, as Ron affectionately called the raft, had done him proud and floated like an iceberg. Because of Ron's ingenuity, it afforded them the capability to store enough supplies for months if they had to. Everyone understood the drill of rationing, finding the container had been an added blessing.

"It's only the first of the season." Rose reached for her toes to stretch her legs.

Rose couldn't always find the positive glimmer Ron saw in everything. She still believed in miracles; she just didn't have the patience to wait for their arrival. She had already scanned the three-sixty view on the horizon for a ship, better yet a sliver of land.

Despite being immobile for three days and seldom lifting a finger, riding out the storm exhausted everyone. Tonight, they'd sleep under the tarp. Everyone would snuggle up and be warm and relatively dry. Trish raked her fingers through her wet hair and spun the long coil onto her head. Something about unlimited amounts of Vitamin D made their hair and nails grow unchecked.

Upside down in her yoga pose, Rose watched Ron's eyes shift as if a foreign object had attacked his peripheral vision. He sprinted toward the edge of the raft, wobbling, shaking the raft side to side, and everyone with it. Falling on his knees, he pulled on the rope dangling limp in the water. It came up empty. Desperate to find what he was searching for, he peered into the depths, then tied himself off. A second later, he vanished into the caldron of cold water.

Rose looked around. She counted heads. Mark, Trish, Ted, and Amanda. Ron surfaced and spat. A second later, filled with more air, he dived under again.

"What the fuck! Where's Li?" Rose ran toward the edge of the raft.

Trapped by disbelief, they waited for a head to pop up in the water. To see bubbles, any sign of life. But only Ron surfaced, he gulped down a fresh batch of air and dived again.

"Why would anyone give up after surviving for so long?" Rose clutched the braided rope; she didn't want to believe what the clues were spelling out. Mark hunkered down next to her, ready to dive too.

"Wait. There's no point in losing both of you." She held Mark back. She'd not let Ron vanish either and looked for signs in the turbulent water. It was bad enough that Lei Wei had done the unthinkable. "Not without tying off."

On her knees and leaning dangerously close over the edge she stared into the steel-gray girders of rifting water, hoping for a glimpse of Li Wei. It happened so fast, yet when Rose realized she'd been holding her breath, she gasped like she was drowning too. Mark groaned when he lifted his arms to adjust the cord around his waist, shielding his chest, and listened to her demand before diving. They were losing precious seconds, Ken, Amanda, and Trish stood still waiting for a command from Rose, from Mark, anyone.

Just as Mark adjusted the cord and prepared to dive, Ron surfaced ten feet away from the raft. He shook his head, signaling for Mark to stay on board. Everyone knew Ron would exhaust himself before he'd surrender, but he was also a realist. Lei Wei prepared for this moment for days knowing if he didn't time his descent to the last intricate detail, Ron would bring him back.

Breathing erratically, Ron coughed and spat water for ten minutes before anyone dared to break the silence. Next to Rose, and in shock, Mark had forgotten about his whiplash. But when he moved, it reminded him again, and he had difficulty moving his head without wincing.

The raft wasn't equipped with a reverse gear. It could only move forward at the mercy of the current. Trish finally broke the ten-minute barrier and sunk next to Ron, sobbing as she went to her knees. Trish didn't cry for Li Wei. She cried for everyone else because Li Wei had taken control of his own destiny. But it was Ron who paid the price for Li Wei's freedom. He shook his head, cradling it in the palms of despair.

"I failed him. I failed all of you." His shoulders slumped; he became silent while dry tears heaved his body. Li Wei played a crucial part in their survival. But the instinct to survive didn't cater to weak hearts. Because of Li Wei's poor language skills, his intuition had been stunted from the moment they found him floating in a giant cooler. He was the runt. Not because of his size, but because of happenstance. A guilt Ron would harvest with consuming greed.

"Sorry for that display. I'm just so devastated that I lost someone on my watch."

"There's nothing you could have done."

"Yeah, well. If it only were that easy. Let's get a move on. The raft needs tending to."

Each person on the raft had a belief, though none chose to call on their complex version of God. This was bigger than any church they had ever prayed in. They no longer needed commandments. Circumstances had stripped away all the pomp, greed, selfishness. On the ocean, surviving didn't imply the greater good. It was the greater good.

Rose communed silently with Li Wei, scanning the surface while retying the netting on the starboard side, clinging to the slim chance he changed his mind. The storm had done its best at hacking away on the raft, but it held together. They worked in silence, on their knees, thinking about moments they shared with the funny little man who had affected their lives in no small way. That he had done what they all fought against wasn't easy to absorb.

Chapter 2

Battening The Hatches

While the storm system granted them a reprieve, everyone busied themselves tying the raft back together. It was an endless project; they were amidst the warehouse of bad weather. Ron and Ted fished to replenish their stock, Trish sliced and dried the meat, Amanda took charge of refilling their water source. Rose's fingers deftly tied knots keeping pace with Mark, who stuffed more plastic into the shifting holes. And no one dared to admit that the thought of giving up hadn't slithered across their mind during those epic moments when all hope seemed lost. Hanging on for one more day wasn't just a saying: it was the recipe to stay alive.

"I wonder what triggered it? I mean, what happened to make Li Wei finally do what we've all thought about?" Rose wound a length of cord around the netting.

"I've no idea. I'm a survivor. I'll go down fighting like a cat in a handbag. Remember, we're born with the instinct to live. Bad weather has nothing to do with it."

"That's you. Obviously, we're not all made of the same fabric as you. I'd like to ask Li Wei a few questions. For starters, Why?"

"Your heart's too big. It's simply a sign of weakness that we overlooked in him. I had no idea he had such dark thoughts."

Rose didn't like Mark's answer. What Li Wei did wasn't an act of weakness. If anything, she thought it was courageous. But Mark saw his world only in shades of black and white. Gray wasn't an option. Being stranded as they were, Rose had learned a valuable lesson about herself. Compassion was a skill she had in spades and being needed wasn't a burden. She thrived under its umbrella.

"Rose. How about you help Trish with lunch. Mark. You've worked hard enough. Take a break."

Ron traded places with them. He had already handed two dorado over to Trish. Although he was still devastated, he fostered something else: a bond with the survivors.

Trish embraced Rose. The scent of fresh fish wafted from her hands.

"How you doing?" Rose rubbed Trish's spine.

"Awful. I had no idea. You?" Trish whispered. Rose shook her head. No, she hadn't seen it coming, and it blindsided her as much as anyone.

"He never let it show. In part, I'm angry that I was never given a chance to help him. And I feel guilty too. That I missed seeing some clue that must have presented itself. He seemed so happy when he discovered the chocolate."

"Me too. Now, I'm worried about Ron. Losing someone to such circumstances is devastating." Trish held up her hand. "Not that I think he would ever. But who knows what triggers depression?"

"Ron's a fighter. His punishment is that he'll carry the guilt with him forever. But you'll see. He'll bounce."

They ate lunch under the tarp stretched to prevent the sun from cooking them. No one spoke, they took turns yawning.

"We can't allow this accident to get us down. I refuse." Ron finally broke the tension. With a long glance, he took everyone into his embrace. Eye to eye, soul to soul, was more potent than words every time. "I regret missing the clues. Li must always have felt like an outsider. It isn't skin color that binds or separates us, but that we can talk about things. Conversation is everything. It's all we have."

"I feel disrespectful for feeling glad to be alive. At least to his memory," Ted said.

"I'm mad as hell. What he did makes me feel that our misery, that my misery, isn't as terrible as his. He took that away from me. I know it sounds selfish, but it's how I feel. I'm not stuffing my resentment down." Amanda brushed the back of her hand across the tears, rolling like wayward emotions across her full cheeks.

"Let it out, Amanda. You're entitled to feel what you feel." Ron reached for her hand.

"I'm okay with it. His choice. Every man has a right to decide about his life. I've always believed that. It doesn't matter that I think what he did was selfish or cowardly. From what I knew of the little guy, he was as tough as nails. But! We all have a breaking point. Sometimes it snaps."

"So none of you think that it might have been accidental? That the cord tore?" Rose had toyed with the idea that somehow one of her braided ropes had failed.

"No way! Li Wei was a fantastic swimmer. He made a choice, and it has no bearing on what we did or didn't do." Mark's jaw tightened.

"I'm gonna ask. Anyone else have doubts?" Ron passed the burden of the question around like a plate.

"I have moments when I think I can't stand another second. Yet I do. My biggest downfall is that I have this undying hope that any minute now, this will be over. Trish? What about you?"

"I worry about dying. All the time. There are a hundred scenarios I envision every day. Shark attack, drowning, starving, run over by Rose's imaginary rescue ship. Some sort of infection and agonizing death. Most days, several of those thoughts cross my mind. But never, never, that."

"Me neither. My biggest fear is to fail you. That I miscalculate something and put you all in harm's way. And that my promises to get you rescued won't come true."

"We wouldn't be alive; if it wasn't for you, Ron. I know I'm grateful, as I'm sure everyone else is for all you do. So please, stop beating yourself up."

"I say, let's do something happier. I'm sorry Li Wei was so unhappy, so worn out from trying to survive, but I'm not giving up." Mark scrambled to stand. He winced, but when Mark made up his mind, there was no stopping him.

"Sing something." Trish put a smile on her face. She meant Ron, who had a resonating soprano voice and a mind to remember the words of popular hits. Or at least popular before the tsunami ripped him away from the coast of Japan seven years earlier.

Inhaling deeply, Ron sang. "Sitting on the dock," he drummed on his thigh to the beat.

When he finished the song, everyone clapped. It suited the mood. And the lyrics captured their feelings, although everyone had their own rendition of life and what inevitably went wrong.

"Requests?" Ron blushed slightly.

"How about Louis? I'd like to dedicate the song to you all. How grateful I am to have you." Rose loved that song. It was her funeral song, she always joked. She still believed life was wonderful. Ron sang a medley of three others. Favorite songs that suited the mood.

"You better be careful, or you'll have to pay royalties if you keep singing those hits and entertaining the crowds."

"I know. Some of those bands keep a tight grip on their music, but if they want to sue me, I say, bring it on."

Ron laughed. Everyone knew he missed his real guitar. To make up for the missing, Ron had constructed one from a square vegetable oil can. One he picked at and strummed on those rare nights when the ocean was quiet and it had a sound reminiscent of a musical instrument. On those nights on the island, Trish played the bongos made of salvaged cans and a seal skin that she stretched and tanned in the sun. Trish never sang, but she hummed along in a haunting timbre.

While drifting along, one member always took the role of barrelman and scouted for treasure and sight of a ship. Or a tanker, yacht, an airplane. Although the raft didn't have a crow's nest, remaining vigilant meant survival. They often joked they would even have taken their chances on a pirate ship.

"Look what I found!"

Ted held up a pristine set of Mares flippers for them to inspect. They were still neatly tied together with a bungee. They were no longer surprised by what floated toward them and used what they could to survive with. Coconuts were a favorite treasure and surprisingly washed up often. Opening one took some skill that thankfully Ted had mastered. The ocean and their island continually shapeshifted, and storms took back what they had gifted earlier. Everyone clapped when Ted handed the flippers around to be examined.

"I want to give these to Mark. So he can use them when he risks his life, time and again."

"Awe. Thanks. Appreciate it, but today I'd prefer a massage with strong fingers."

He massaged his own neck.

"I'll make sure they're tied securely. It'll be weeks before we get back." Rose took the flippers and assessed them.

"Nice. I bet they're expensive. Wouldn't it be great if who-ever lost these came looking?" She handed them to Mark, who was struggling to breathe. He groaned when he lifted his arm and instead curled onto his side. Being brave, he had exerted himself, and the muscles holding his neck up had turned to mush. He closed his eyes and bit down on the pain.

"Well, Mark, it's official. You're on a furlough. The rest of us, it's storm season. We have to remain vigilant. You never know what the next storm will stir up. Mark might get his wish yet. A slick little yacht or a fancy catamaran."

Ron winked. He knew better than to look a gift horse in the mouth. On the day the tsunami hit, Ron had had a wish too. He'd never forgiven himself for grumbling about his demanding job. If anything, he longed for another shot. He hoped his wife got a hefty settlement.

On Ron's insistence, Mark was ordered to relax. While the others worked, he stared at the sky, keeping his body still. He closed his eyes, pretending to sleep.

Rose picked up the flippers again and studied them. De-spite wearing a brave and cheerful armor, Rose didn't wish this punishment on anyone. And yet she understood just how for-tunate she was. One had to nearly lose life to appreciate living.

"You asleep?" She whispered.

Mark blinked. He tolerated the others, but he had feelings for her. If they were inspired by his situation or not, it wasn't a riddle she would bother to solve. Here, life followed a natural rhythm and didn't require fancy footwork.

"How about I work on your shoulders and neck." She sat in lotus and cradled his head on her lap. He winced each time she shifted him, his grimace projected the diagnosis, the pain was getting worse.

Rose had long and nimble fingers. She could be gentle, and she could dig deep like a gravedigger to get at the knots. Even for a man of Mark's strength and endurance, his eyes watered while she manipulated the damaged muscle tissues. For a mere second, he looked into her eyes, but he didn't want her to see that he was vulnerable. Just like the others.

The muscle tissue surrounding his neck was bruised and tense and would take weeks to heal fully. But Rose sensed that it wasn't the only area of his body that hurt. Li Wei's suicide hurt his heart. He had thought they shared a kinship. They worked so well together, and if anyone should have detected a flaw in the little man's armor, it should have been him. Or so he believed.

"When we get back, let's make some plans." He spoke softly.

On the island, Rose had moved in with him, and, under the circumstances, it seemed a natural thing to do. Did he love her? She tried to find the answer reflected in his eyes. Would they have a future if they followed his suggestion and took off on their own looking for land? He was a gambler; Rose wasn't even any good at poker. Deep down Rose knew, she wasn't in love.

Despite the pain, Mark fell asleep in her lap. She massaged the nodules of tension from his shoulders and neck, and his breathing eased to a purr. Did she have a future with Mark? Here, on the island, or in the real world if they ever left? She doubted they could survive either voyage.

Chapter 3

Surfing Toward a Ship Ahoy!

Beneath the tarp, sitting amidst the comfort of shade, the midday heat was bearable. Everyone took turns napping, there wasn't much else to do.

"I need to sit up. Help me." Mark grabbed onto Rose's arm. She propped him against the warm water tank. "I'll keep you company while you watch." Mark wanted to work on gaining stamina, despite the pain shooting through his body. He only complained with his silence.

In the distance, a pod of whales breached. The whales were heading north, splashing, and diving as if being on the Pacific was fun. But Mark and Rose knew better. The Pacific was a monster. Standing on a shore watching its docile waves crash near the countless resorts was one thing, being stuck in the middle of its formidable mouth, another.

"Have a nap. I'll watch for a while." Mark said. He hated relying on others.

He padded his thigh for Rose to use as a pillow. She complied and curled up. While she feigned sleep, Mark played with a strand of her hair. She felt exposed to Mark's scrutiny. Would he notice her large pores? The small hairs she was sure were sprouting from the mole on her upper lip. She didn't want Mark to see her flaws, she wanted the chance to rectify them. Beneath her, the ocean rolled contently for the moment. Sometimes in between hurricanes and tropical storms, the weather gods gave them a week, or two, to recoup. It was a game nature liked to play.

"What are you doing?" Mark whispered to Ron.

"Just making notes on the last storm."

"You never stop, do you?" Mark said.

"True. For me, it's a mental game of chess. I can't allow the situation to win." Ron said.

"I get it." Mark played with the fringes of his cutaway shorts; Rose could feel his hands move next to her ear. "What's the most number of storms you had in one year?"

Ron flipped through his little book and counted.

"Three years ago, we lived through five. Alfred, Barry, Chase, Don, and Eddy. I think meteorologists have a different method for naming storms, last year I used female names."

"Why do you bother? Naming them." Mark didn't care one way or the other. He just wanted to talk since his body betrayed him and left him no other options.

"I found if I named them, I could get my anger out. Kind of like Ahab in Moby Dick."

"Never read it. Too long and too boring."

"True. But I like the therapeutic pleasure of chewing my way through such novels. It makes me feel like I've accomplished something. And I spent long swaths of time on my own. In my job, reading was almost mandatory to keep my sanity. In a way, it prepared me for this."

"Do you think your wife thinks you're dead? What about your mother? Your children."

"I think for a long time, they clung to the hope that I survived. Without a body, acknowledging death is hard. My children probably got over it faster. My wife, well, I hope she cashed in my life insurance. As far as my mother is concerned, I wouldn't doubt it if she didn't still expect to hear my footsteps on the stairs."

"You were close?"

"Absolutely. After my father died, we moved her in with us. It wasn't easy for my wife, but she understood. We renovated the basement, and my mother found her own life, eventually. What about you? Any significant others? Siblings?"

Ron had lowered the tone in his voice. Mark answered without hesitation.

"Not a soul. I have some good friends I chum with. My father was always a no-show, my mother couldn't cope. My older brother took off when he was fourteen, my sister tried to take care of us, but in the end, she met someone, and that was that. I left home when I was sixteen."

"I miss my kids. My wife and I waited. I had tuition bills, and then she took a kick at the education thing too. It was only fair. Stella was thirty-six when we had our first. Tyler and then a year later, Sophie. Having kids changes everything."

"Can't argue that. Maybe one day I'll try it on. It'll be interesting to see if my plumbing business is still afloat. Not glamorous, but I had shops in three towns. Kept me busy."

"Lucrative, I bet. How'd you come by that trade?"

"An old biker took me on when I was a pup. He taught me what I needed to know and paid for my apprenticeship. He died before I could pay him back."

"Deep friendships?"

"The best. Took me in as if I was one of his kids."

"Now that you've been through this, what do you see in your future when we go back?"

"Nice optimism. I'm not sure I can stay stationary. What I think I want, when, as you say, we get out of here, I want it all."

"I see a little cottage for myself. With Trish. I'm not counting on my wife still waiting for me. If anything, I hope she's found love again. It would be so much better for the kids."

"That's generous of you." Mark shifted himself higher without disturbing Rose.

"Or selfish."

Ron untangled himself from Trish and rose. "If I ever make it, I'm gonna find Li Wei's family among the fishing villages in China. No matter how challenging, I vow I'll find them. But I won't tell them how. I'll just say the ocean ended his life."

"I bet there's a thousand Li Wei's fishing for a living, and a thousand villages to sort through. But I'd go with you."

"Thanks, Mark. His wife and family have a right to know."

"For us, there'll only ever be one Li Wei."

"What's that?" Ron suddenly moved as if he heard or saw something. Trish rolled over onto her knees and slowly rose to standing too. Her gaze followed that of Ron's toward the natural curve of the ocean.

"What is it?"

"Look at the waves."

Ron pointed to the long line of waves that lapped against the raft. Not a breath of wind stirred the air. Waves were born from winds and were tumultuous, and this set ran parallel and in a straight line.

"Listen."

Ron cupped his ear to the low hum, apparently only discernible to his ears. Whatever he was listening for, no one was privy to until he said: "Ship!"

Everyone strained to follow the furrow stretching toward the defining horizon in the distance. The glare of the sun blinded them. The ocean was eerily silent, and everyone tuned in their hearing to hear what they hoped was their salvation. A ship or tanker on the horizon signified hope, which just as suddenly switched to devastation when it sailed out of sight. Those were the risks everyone was willing to endure, not unlike betting on winning the lottery. Ron was confident they were within the wake of the ship's path. That they had missed seeing it no longer surprised him. They were the needle in a haystack of needles. If they were ever going to get rescued, all elements had to come out and play. Someone on the ship would have to look up at precisely the right moment to discover them floating on the sea.

Mark took Rose's hand and eased himself to standing.

"Can you see anything?" Everyone kept their breath in check in fear of missing a sound, any sound. If Ron thought there was a vessel, they believed him.

"Whatever you do, don't touch the water. Whatever is on the fishing lines, throw it out!"

"But I have a big one on the line."

"We're floating in blackwater."

Rose took a step closer toward Mark. Ron had explained often enough that blackwater had the power to kill them just as surely as a shark. Ron said he'd rather risk swimming in shark-infested waters than in the poop-soup that cruise ships dumped into the ocean.

"Should we wave some clothes and yell?"

"It's worth a try."

Straining their voices, everyone screamed in unison. Over here! Help! Fire! SOS!

The sound of their voices was deafening, yet utterly futile. If a ship were out there, even on the quiet ocean, their feeble voices wouldn't stand a chance. It had already missed them once, but they had to try. Rose yelled louder than anyone at the ship passing some twenty miles to the south of them; the ship they knew was out there even if they couldn't see its bulk.

No matter how hard they denied it, everyone had dreams that surfaced like a perfect storm when hope dangled a carrot in their face. Like marionettes in a puppet show, they all clamored to be heard and seen. Their screams were annoying, but the silence, as they ran out of steam, reverberated off the ocean with a sickening thud was worse.

One by one, they sank to their knees. Humbled, they tucked away their fantasy rescue. No one spoke, and Rose fell asleep without caring if morning ever rose again.

PART 5
HOPE

Chapter 1

Beached

Kai adjusted the volume of the television; the incoming news became more dismal as the footage flickered on the screen. Transfixed by the unfolding events, his wife reached for his hand and held it within her warm palm. His father's breathing became erratic next to him. Overnight their world had succumbed to a new sort of chaos. Hawaii, the sanctuary they had known, had died. Kai's free hand clapped his mouth shut, tears ran freely over his wife's cheeks and splashed onto the pink flowers printed on her blouse.

"I have the day off. I'm going down there."

"I'll trade shifts. I'm going too."

They sprang into action. His wife went in search of clothing, something old she figured would be ruined. Kai rummaged under the sink for trash bags. He knew they just bought a whole box. His father watched from the chair, shifting his focus from the footage to voice his advice.

"Bring gloves."

While Kai rinsed out the cooler, his wife filled a thermos with cold tap water. Next, she wrapped up the peanut butter sandwiches, meant for Kai's lunch, with wax paper. She added a tub of sliced pineapple and a handful of rambutan she had picked off the tree in the park.

"Pops. Your lunch is in the fridge. I'm sorry, but it'll just be sandwiches."

"Don't worry about me. Just go."

When they arrived on the beach an hour later, a crowd had already gathered. They stood on the edge of the beach. Mesmerized by the churning soup of trash, everyone stared, speechless. The pristine ocean had vomited a soup of tidewrack and produced more litter with each heave. As if pleading: get this shit off me.

Assessing the situation before them, Kai made out a person who seemingly put himself in charge of the mess. With his wife in tow, Kai trudged across the trash and trampled sand.

"We brought bags. Where do you want us?"

"Pick a spot. Any spot. Haul the bags to the muster point. Someone is coming with a dumpster." He pointed to the parking lot next to the tiki hut bar rendered useless by the muck.

"What happened?"

Kai asked, even though he knew the answer. The last storm that sailed through a week ago had unleashed a small batch of hell on the beach and did the unpardonable. Return to sender. Apparently, the storm was even busier out at sea. Kai had heard of the Patch, but he doubted it could be as dire as inconsistent news briefs predicted. If those news briefs were accurate, wouldn't every conscientious government on the planet do something to rectify the problem? And radicals on rafts weren't always reasonable. But witnessing what radicals had predicted and warned everyone about, shifted him over to their point of view. Something had to be done. Kai doubted it could leave the last of the naysayers untouched.

Kai unfolded his bag and stuffed a handful into the deep pockets of his cargo shorts. The sheer volume of churning plastic trash seemed insurmountable. He stooped to pick up a basket. The sort the dollar stores sold by the millions. It was nearly in pristine condition except for the greenish-brown sludge stuck to the weave. An assortment of bottles and cans mingled on the beach, and he was torn between wanting to recycle as many of the beverage containers as he could, but as he scanned the vast volumes gathering around his feet, it was too daunting. Now wasn't the time. His wife held up a brand-new sneaker; a famous brand he couldn't afford.

"Look. Someone has made a home of it already." She dumped the small ghost crab on the sand. It scurried and took cover.

Kai hoped no one would find Jack's body parts. No one deserved to die among all this trash. Yet a feeling in his gut wouldn't let go that the possibility existed. That a person could end up dead among the waste, if not dead from the trash.

By mid-morning, Kai and his wife emptied their carton and had filled a mountain of bags. The soup churned out more. A tractor complete with a front-loading bucket came to their rescue and ladled scoop after scoop and dumped the contents into the back of a dump truck. Seawater sluiced out through the gaps. A hundred or so people walked with their heads down. They scooped: bottles, tubs, fishing nets, tangled lines, baskets, buckets, shoes, flip-flops, balls, plastic toys, lighters, sunglasses, hats, umbrellas, dolls, toothbrushes, shampoo bottles, razors, cutlery, and endless plastic bags. Somehow their ugliness diminished the beauty of the conch shells, the mother of pearl oyster shells, the driftwood pieces Kai had collected as a child and made into gifts for his family. He sifted through countless fish carcasses, and starfish, jellyfish, sea sponges. He made a mental list to repeat everything he saw to his father. If it weren't so sad, Kai thought he'd make up a gameshow to entertain his father by having him guess the origin of the blue, white, pink, and orange plastic laundry aids. Kai had already counted five combs, four broken surfboards, three flippers, and nineteen mismatched flip-flops.

Kai straightened his back and watched his wife stoop to pick up a blue piece of Styrofoam. It squeaked when she stuffed it into the flapping trash bag. Of course, Kai kept an eye out for Kilo. Fragments of a canoe. Each day he got more frustrated that nothing turned up. Not from the cops, not from his friends or cousins. Where the fuck was his canoe. He sure hoped it wasn't among the trash. Someone found a beautiful wooden paddle amidst the trash, something worth salvaging. Finders keepers. And it seemed implausible that his canoe should end up on this beach, which lay in the complete opposite direction of the hotel.

"Are you crying?"

Kai had been so absorbed in his own misery he had failed to see tears fall like rain from his wife's eyes. She simply nodded, sniffled, and kept going.

"This is the saddest thing I've ever seen in my life. Our beautiful island drowned in this garbage. You know how I feel about all this."

She extended her palm as if she were introducing Kai to her world of misery. She hated that their government incinerated garbage, but this was infinitely worse, in her opinion. Their solution had been to take the easy route. Out of sight, out of mind, seemed the lesser of two evils. Kai nodded. His wife cried over a few things: hurt animals and children, and her beloved islands.

"We used to have such a good time on this beach. Remember?"

Kai tried to remind her of the many times they came for Sunday picnics. Their sons had learned to swim in the low tidewaters.

"Yes, we did. Don't remind me. It makes it even harder. You don't think that Jack Spencer could be washed up among all this junk?"

"No. First, that would be assuming he was dead. Second, that he ended up in the water. We just don't have any evidence."

"Always the wannabe cop."

"Do keep an eye out for needles."

"You've already thought it through then that he couldn't have ended up out here. You still think he's alive somewhere?"

Kai picked up a handful of trash: straws, limp bags, odds bits of debris. He believed in many things. That no one had the right to give up on Jack Spencer being alive; unless they found something conclusive was one of them. He also believed hope had the final say, until that devastating moment when truth leveled a person. If a person didn't yield to hope, the big game show of life wasn't worth a thing.

"I do. People believe in stranger things, and his mother deserves all the support I can lend her. You'd do the same."

"You're right. As bad as things sometimes get, the Spencers are proving we have nothing to complain about. Even this stinking heap of trash is small in comparison. I feel sad for their entire family. At least with this trash, I feel like I'm doing something. That it's within my power to do something."

"It's all we got. But you're right."

Kai straightened and arched his back. Although they stuffed more than forty bags, the sight remained unchanged. Other than the wall they built, and the trash kept on rolling in.

"So, no one has found even a small clue yet?"

"Nope. Last we have is of Jack stumbling near the beach. That's where the cameras stop."

"What a mystery. And the girl? Did you find her?"

"No. I have my suspicions that she is hiding in plain sight."

"Often are. But you think she had something to do with his disappearance?"

"I know I would come forward just for peace of mind. Something is fishy. Maybe Jack Spencer isn't the saint everyone paints him as?"

The thought occurred to Kai before too, but who was he to judge? Everyone kept a closet full of secrets, pride and ego were in charge of the key and lock.

Chapter 2

Knees

Myra noticed that her mouth was agape. She could feel the cold air from the air conditioner, set on full blast, caressing the skin on her teeth while she watched the epic news coverage for the second time. Without taking her eyes off the television, she picked up the telephone and canceled her hair appointment. She slipped into her tracksuit and set out her indoor trainers. Under the kitchen sink, she rummaged and found a set of vinyl gloves. There was nothing to do but go and help. Of course, she also hoped that, by some miracle, clues of her son had washed ashore as well. Clues she desperately wanted to find.

When Michael saw what she was watching, he snapped his laptop shut.

"You should go. But be careful. You never know what's in that quagmire of crap. And you've always been such a people person. Do you good. I'd come too if it weren't for transitioning Brody into his new job."

Michael had a teleconference he couldn't miss. It was the nature of the business. She kissed him on the temple and smiled, and she had to admit, the thought of being active was just what she needed. Waiting for news was the torture of its own weaving.

Myra sensed that with each passing day, John and Michael's resolve softened toward conceding the victory to the unfathomable. With each passing day, Myra told herself: today I'll find you, Jack. There were moments when she was confident that Jack, in that exact moment, was reaching out to her too. She felt the tug, and with all her heart, she always answered. Jack, I'm coming for you.

The police, that boorish captain, the Coast Guard, the hotel staff, and the reporter all thought of Jack Spencer as a missing person. They spoke of Jack in the past tense, an innocent slip of the tongue. Often, they used language meant to impress her. They threw words at her: drift trajectory, wind, currents stats, leeway calculations. Each meeting invariably led back to the whispers she wasn't meant to overhear. Presumably dead. But to Myra, Jack was still too alive in her memory. She'd not allow her son to become a statistic.

In a few days, the doctors would go and get their granddaughter out, whether she or Stacy was ready. Myra desperately longed to be part of Stacy's joy, but a large piece of her refused to leave. She was marooned to her grief of missing Jack. And her daughter would soon understand what it meant to be a mother. Nothing would ever be the same for Stacy again. Giving birth had the power to change a woman. Forever.

Myra stuffed a protein bar into her pocket and reached for a water bottle. Who knew how long it would take to fix the travesty on the beach. She also brought the handful of large trash bags she found while rummaging under the sink. She'd get more at the corner store.

"You got the GPS and know where you're going? "Michael met her at the door.

"I do. This island isn't that big."

Half an hour later, she wedged the Land Rover onto a piece of rugged lawn. There was no mistake, she had found the right place. The scene on the beach sank Myra's heart. Dire wasn't dire enough to use as a word to describe the carnage floating on the ocean. Nothing, in her spoiled life, had prepared Myra for the truth floating on the shoreline.

"What can I do?" She asked the first person she saw.

"Doesn't really matter. Pick a spot. Stay out of the way of the tractor."

It was a conflicting sight. On the beach facing the condominium, Myra watched as people rotated themselves under the morning sun. Basking to take home the ultimate souvenir: a golden tan. She was just as confused about the benefits of vitamin D and the risks of sun exposure as anyone else. But if the populace didn't come to some sort of agreement on the prevalent plastic issue, they'd not have to worry about the effects of skin cancer for much longer.

Myra looked for an open spot and stooped. She quickly filled the bag with a plethora of throwaways. Cups from everyone's favorite coffee shop, she recognized the logo in her hand. A wrapper from a drive-through chain that populated the world like an invasive species.

"Mrs. Spencer?"

Myra looked up. Who would know her on this beach in Hawaii? The sun's glare momentarily blinded her. But through the dark lens of her Serengeti glasses, she made out a familiar shape.

"Kai."

She snapped her glove off and extended it to shake his hand. Of course, Kai'd be here. She sensed from the few conversations they shared; Kai loved his island. How proud he'd been when he spoke of the pristine beach and gardens at the hotel.

"I hadn't expected you on this side of the island?"

"Couldn't help myself. I saw the news. There was just one thing to do."

"Awful. May I introduce my wife?"

Kai pointed to the woman who had slunk closer. Her eyes cast sideways to the path recently cleared by her husband.

"Cindy. My wife."

Cindy must have overheard the dreadful name: Mrs. Spencer. A shy glance gave away the aching sadness creeping in Cindy's brown eyes.

"Nice to meet you. Kai keeps me abreast about your son's disappearance. I wish we could do more to help."

"Thank you. Please, both of you, call me Myra. And thank you. Your husband has been most helpful."

"Have you had any news from the captain?"

"Nothing conclusive. It's as if Jack simply vanished. But I won't give up."

"You're absolutely right. And if your son's on Kilo, then he stands a chance."

"Kilo?"

"Sorry. The canoe. It has a name. Kilo."

"Oh? That's nice. What does it mean?"

"Stargazer."

"Do you have any photographs? It may help."

"My wife is right. If your son is on Kilo, he stands a chance. I'll get you some photos. It might help you to know that if on the odd chance Jack floated away on the canoe, he has the means to survive. I always kept bottles of water, a few snacks, fishing lines and lures, a flag."

The news startled Myra. If. Such a small word for such auspicious tidings. Suddenly, she wanted nothing more than to believe her son did. If—Jack had taken the canoe. Which he'd never do. Jack wasn't the sort who would do something so un-characteristic. But a new surge of hope flashed through her. She pictured Jack afloat on something solid. A lifesaving water bottle in his hand. But there was simply no way of confirming the fact.

"Mrs. Spencer. He's out there someplace. Or on the island. Don't give up."

"Thank you."

Myra swallowed. That Jack might have the means of sur-viving on the ocean spurred a new thought. The police had checked with every hospital, looking for someone who matched Jack Spencer's description. They didn't want to rule out amnesia. Foul play. Ill health of any sort. Mumbling, Officer Malone said they ran a check with every morgue. Dead bodies turned up unannounced and unclaimed all the time. He told her as if such information would reassure her.

"Have you had lunch?"

Kai interrupted the thoughts spinning into a weave, un-derstanding that she was shifting sideways with the new bits of information.

"I brought a protein bar and some water."

"We'll share ours if you don't mind peanut butter and jelly."

"I shouldn't, but I'm hungrier than I thought."

Myra followed them to the parking lot. Kai asked her to hold out her hands while he squirted sanitizer and then rinsed with water from a jug. Cindy spread a tattered towel under a palm and patted a seat for Myra to take.

"Don't ever sit under a coconut palm. They can kill you."

Myra glanced up but saw no coconuts. Only the sound of the wind as it whistled through the fronds of the round palm leaves issued any sort of warning. Cindy unwrapped the sandwiches and set out the slices of pineapple.

"Help yourself."

The pasty sandwich was undoubtedly the best she had ever eaten. Since Jack vanished, she hadn't eaten enough. Her ribs were already poking out. At least tonight, she'd not have to lie to John when he'd ask her what she had eaten for lunch.

"What are those?" Myra pointed to the furry red balls on the blanket.

"Rambutan."

"Do you eat them?"

Cindy smiled at Myra's ignorance and dumped the balls on her palm. She held one up.

"They're yummy. Supposedly good for controlling blood sugar. The latest in superfoods."

Myra reached for one of the balls. The fur was hard and prickly.

"With your manicure, I don't suggest it. Here, allow me." Cindy dug her nail into the skin and peeled away just enough for the white fruit to peek out. She handed it to Myra. "Don't be afraid. It's delicious."

It took some digging, but Myra unearthed the white flesh and plopped it into her mouth. Slithery and sweet, the fruit rolled around in her mouth while her teeth tore into the slippery flesh. Cindy had shown her to spit the large seed into her palm.

"Amazing. Where do you buy these?"

"Some local markets, but we have a tree in the park. Season's almost done."

"I'd like to get some for Michael. He'd get a kick out of them. He loves anything exotic."

After lunch, they split up and collected another three hours' worth of trash. Slowly they were making headway, but the beach was not out of danger yet.

Before saying goodbye at the car, Kai extended an invitation. "How about dinner?"

"I'd love to come, but I'm..." Myra lied and said, "a call from Stacy. My daughter." What she kept from the Hales was that she had a meeting with Officer Malone, Rockport, and the captain. They were to converge and rehash the search plan. As far as Myra was concerned, they weren't doing enough. But she was learning that flattery worked better to soothe contempt.

"How about lunch on Sunday? Myra couldn't refuse Cindy's invitation. "Your son is invited too."

"That sounds lovely."

"It's Kai's birthday. But no gifts." Cindy whispered while Kai loaded their truck.

The drive back was serene. A thousand shades of green fluttered in her periphery, and she instinctively knew, Jack wasn't hidden among the lush vegetation. It wasn't a feeling she could explain. Although Myra longed for a hot shower, she caught herself smiling in the rearview mirror. It felt good to accomplish something, and the Hales were lovely people.

Back at the condo, Myra took a long shower and then cooked dinner for Michael, who beamed with pride when she showed him the photographs of the beach. The before and after.

"I'm proud of you."

He swung her into his embrace and kissed the side of her head. Of her three children, Michael was the least squeamish and most adventuresome. His size might have bestowed him with extra confidence. And ever since as a child, he'd put anything into his mouth. He had no aversion to food from any culture. Before dinner, he devoured the rambutans she had saved for him on Cindy's insistence.

"Peanut butter and jelly? You?"

He teased her. She had explained the rambutan and was surprised when he said he'd eaten lychee nuts. He was thrilled at being invited to an authentic luau.

"Can't remember the last time I ate peanut butter, but I loved it."

"Such nice people inviting us to a family function."

"I know. They said something that startled me." Myra couldn't stop her mind from producing realistic images of Jack drifting on a canoe. As if he belonged to one. "If Jack, for any reason, is out on Kai's canoe, he has a chance of surviving. There's food and water on the canoe."

"Really? Wow! Now I almost wish he did." The idea of Jack on the canoe infected Michael as well. Myra could see it reflected in his eyes. But the rations on the canoe weren't enough to sustain anyone for long, but each hour mattered. Every sip of water drew a line between surviving and not.

"That would be something. But I'm still of the opinion that Jack would never go for a joy ride. That's not our Jack.".

Despite not wanting to admit it, Myra wished Jack to be the sort who took other people's canoe. If that meant he was alive. She nodded. She didn't tell Michael what else Cindy allowed to slip. "I don't think people can survive for more than a week without..." She cut her words off then. A burst of red exploded on Cindy's tawny skin. But Kai jumped in with both feet and corrected his wife. "There's that Mexican who survived over four-hundred days. I say, never give up unless you have proof otherwise." Kai had reached for her arm to convey his sincere belief.

Myra set a plate heaped with pasta and muscles in front of Michael. On her way back, Kai had shown her the best seafood supplier on the island. It belonged to his cousin.

"I know. Mentally, I want to increase Jack's chances any way I can. It's already been thirteen days."

"Thirteen and counting. By the way, dinner looks and smells delicious."

"Let's eat. Then we can phone Dad and Stacy. They'll want all the details of how our meeting went. I say we should keep a positive tone. Did you hear that long silence when I mentioned the canoe to Malone? I hope it inspires a new search."

Michael braced his arms on the edge of the table, "we must remember the police, the Coast Guard, to them, Jack is just a body. He's everything to us."

Alone after dinner, Myra poured herself a glass of wine. She was done relying on others. With a notebook open on her lap, she made a list. Tessa. Brody. Mermaid. Jack. One of them was responsible for Jack's vanishing act. She also made another column with the heading suspect X. There was a chance another stranger might have been involved. But who? And she hadn't mentioned her fears regarding Brody to anyone. But Brody had distanced himself too quickly. It wasn't the sort of behavior she expected from Jack's best friend. And since Jack vanished, Brody hadn't once looked her in the eyes.

Fluffing the cushion behind her back, she scrolled through her phone. Kai had sent her the footage of Jack arguing with Tessa. Although he had handed over the surveillance tapes to the police, none thought the incident looked suspicious enough to investigate. Kai, however, said, "something about the anger just doesn't sit right with me. Whatever the argument is about, Tessa crossed a border. I don't know her, and I'm looking at this as a stranger with impartial eyes. You know her best. I wanted you to know."

Tessa. Myra underscored the name. She rewound the small clip and tried to read the onslaught of Tessa's words escalating from her angry mouth. But they came out too fast. Too bitter and swollen with contempt. The word *you* was the one clearly formed on Tessa's mouth. Her stabbing finger on Jack's chest confirmed the threat. Tessa was accusing Jack of something.

So what? Office Malone had suggested, based on Tessa's own testimony when she was interrogated, over the phone, that it had to do with Jack's inappropriate behavior. That she feared Jack would ruin the ceremony. That she was a nervous bride. Nothing more.

Myra hit replay a fourth time: One word wasn't enough to make anyone into a suspect.

Chapter 3

Afflicted

Bruce handed Wayne the pack of cigarettes he bought with his last ten-dollar bill. The gig at the hotel had been slim pickings since the Jack Spencer incident. It seemed there was a set of eyes continually on them. Them—meaning all of the hotel staff.

"Thinking of quitting?"

He knew Wayne meant the hotel job and not cigarettes. He had been through that hell before and vowed never to try again.

"Shit. If I wasn't so broke, I would. You got anything left to fence?"

"Nope. I'm dry."

"Me too."

That was a lie. Bruce had the shoes he had come to love. And although some of his buddies had offered him a hundred bucks, he wasn't going to let them go. He'd never owned anything as comfortable, and the shoes changed something within him. He stood taller. People noticed him and gave him the respect he deserved. He regretted not swiping the navy blue blazer Jack Spencer left carelessly at the foot of the bed. An intrusion overruled opportunity on the morning of the search. When the maid knocked, unexpectedly, he ducked behind the heavy drapes until he heard the water splash in the ensuite. In his business, timing was elemental, and luckily, thinking on his feet was a gift he'd been born with.

"See all the trash wash up on the shore."

"Fuck. Damn tourists. They ruin everything."

Wayne was about to add something but changed his mind. Bruce recognized that slight flinch in Wayne that indicated that he didn't fully agree with his view of the world. But what did Wayne know? He was just a pup in a world of wolves.

"If I had gas money, I'd head down there and help."

"Looks like they got enough volunteers. Bet not one tourist-fuck is down there helping."

Wayne nodded his agreement and took a deep drag sucking the last of the cigarette down to the filter. White plumes, tinged with yellow, escaped his mouth and rose up his nostrils. Wayne never got the hang of inhaling and still mouth-smoked, a sure way to get tongue and mouth cancer.

"I could hit my mom up for a loan. At least enough for a case of beer. Or something."

Bruce didn't care. He had already swiped a twenty-dollar bill from his own mother.

"Sure. I could use a cold one."

While Wayne argued with his mother over money, Bruce inhaled deeply and blew a series of smoke circles toward the yellowing ceiling. Old surf magazines, bottle caps, coasters, and sweat rings littered the table. Wayne's mother wasn't much of a cleaner either. Bruce reached for the Ronson Wayne left on the table next to a small button. The button shimmered in the sunlight; it might have been made from a conch. He picked it up and studied the rainbow in the light streaming in through the broken slats of the blinds. Pretty. As if someone had carved it from a shell. He had never owned a button-down shirt, and he knew Wayne didn't either. A small pool of iridescent light shimmered in the sunbeam. He'd have to ask Wayne about the button. Had Wayne stolen something and was holding out on him? He leaned onto his knees and listened. Wayne's voice rose over that of his mother's in the argument.

Bruce switched on the local news station to drown out their voices. All the stations zoomed in on the beach travesty. The camera panned the entire beach and captured the hundred or so stooped volunteers who filled bag after bag with trash. Dismal. Bruce ground the cigarette butt into the ashtray heaped with yellow filters. Stepping ahead of the camera, the reporter summarized the scene. "It's thanks to the generosity of these volunteers that this once iconic beach has a chance to survive." He gestured, and the camera panned wider, then zoomed in.

Just like that, she was there, trying to avoid the lens. The prettiest local girl he knew. Kelani was hiding in plain sight. Brilliant.

"Now that's funny. Right next to that dickwad."

Bruce spotted the figure of Kai wading in the trash. Only Kai had no idea Kelani was the woman Jack Spencer stole the night he vanished—into the deep beyond.

Chapter 4

Water

Jack crushed the empty plastic water bottle. The annoying noise would have driven him nuts under other circumstances, but, out on the ocean, it was a welcome diversion. He was sick of the endless rush of water, which rarely fused with silence.

"Someone! Anyone!" His voice was bearded too, and coarse. Wherever he was at the moment, the water was no longer blue. Instead, it was like liquid glass and bottle green.

"Help! Over here!"

It was hopeless. He contemplated cutting one of the bottles in half, attempting to make a functional, desalination still. If only he knew how to begin. He saved the other bottles, pacing his greed and calling on his deepest resources from overriding the temptation to guzzle all of them in one go. Inexhaustible thirst made him toy with the idea of making water.

He bounced the bottle off his head, thinking. If he cut the bottom off the bottle...then what? He had seen a survivalist make as simple still on one of those reality shows, and he remembered thinking how dumb that was. All that work for a mouthful of water. He swallowed. A mouthful sounded wonderful.

Before hacking away with the rusted blade, he thought it through and settled on sacrificing one bottle. He cut the bottom off but left it big enough to serve as a cup. Then he folded the cut edge up and forced it into the body of the other.

During the day, it might work. The sun was as relentless as the waves. But he'd have to rig it so that it didn't fall over. No easy feat with no tools and a base that rocked like a cradle.

By his count, he had been at sea for thirteen days. He was out of food, and he hadn't come across any large fish dumb enough to bite on his lure, but the silver ones were nosy and often explored the undies he dangled as a net. *Three a day keeps the doctor at bay.* And the palm fronds made a good bed despite being razor-sharp and kept him more comfortable. The flag shielded him from the cold and sun, if only the damn thing remained dry during the night. As dangerous as the last one had been, Jack wished for another storm. A storm so that he could cup rainwater and drink until his belly exploded.

He propped the water bottle in the vest, but an empty bottle was flimsy and prone to falling over. "Stay." He commanded, slowly moving his hand away.

Jack finished his daily swim. At the height of the sun, when he couldn't stand the laser beam any longer, he checked the waves, and when he deemed it safe, heaved himself over the side of the canoe. As a reward, he allowed himself a dollop of sunscreen after swimming for fifteen minutes. Savoring the scent of coconut and the soothing feel of oil, he smacked his lips.

This voyage came with lessons. Weather, Jack learned, came out of nowhere. The sky and the sun worked in unison while the wind conducted the clouds that sat on the horizon. If the shapes of faces, animals, landscapes, and mythical creatures had any meaning, Jack couldn't decipher their warning. Next to him, the ocean lumbered on with a plan to whisk him away to some foreign destination. Only it never shared the itinerary of just where that mythical location was. Jack believed that eventually, he'd land on an island. Fiji, Tahiti, Easter Island, Tonga. He had heard of Samoa, the French Polynesian Islands, the Marshall Islands, and could vaguely pinpoint them on the map ingrained in his mind. There was a chance he was drifting in the opposite direction toward Canada, toward California or Mexico. Jack pictured himself kissing the solid ground of any strip of land. He heard Canadians were friendly.

But booking the wedding on the Big Island might have been part of Tessa's plan. If he was set adrift and caught a current, he might cycle back to the chain of islands in the north, or. The big or, and to nowhere in the south. Tessa was a born gambler. It had taken Jack days to realize, his best option lay in swimming east. Dead or alive, he'd make landfall.

Over the long and tedious days, his list of priorities was evolving. His mother still charted the list in number one place. He wasn't going to break her heart. Water became his second and food third. While he loved his father, brother, and sister, and his friends, Jack wanted nothing more than to reach a hut on a beach. Any beach. He dreamed of an endless supply of coconut and sushi. Roaming with his tongue, he searched for saliva and came up dry.

"What the fuck! This isn't funny anymore." Jack rose and looked for the ship he was so sure was searching for him. He believed they were on their way, he just had to hold on for another minute, hour, day.

But instead, only a new truth faced him: he'd trade the people he loved in the blink of an eye. Being stranded confirmed what he would have denied a few weeks ago.

Chapter 5

Aftermath

Kai rolled over and watched his wife sleep. Her chest fell in even heaves, and whistling exhales escaped through the partly opened mouth. He loved everything about his wife. Her dark chocolate hair, her smile, and the slightly pointed eyetooth she shyly hid behind her full lips. He loved the curves that filled out her hips and breasts and that she danced the luau for him. There wasn't another woman at the party more graceful or beautiful than his wife.

Echoes of the Pahu drums still rang in his ear. He was glad Cindy had thought to include the Spencers. The luau gave them a break from the monotony of waiting for news. News that when they hit would drown out everything else, either way. But it did nothing to ease his worry about finding his canoe. And more accurately, his worrying over the bills burning a hole in his gut. He didn't show Cindy the mail. A second notice on an overdue bill he had promised to take care of last month lit the match. If she found out, she'd be disappointed. But his truck needed a new alternator. And just like that, three-hundred dollars were gone. Financially, it was a game of playing Whac-a-mole. It was rigged from the start.

They couldn't really afford the lavish party, but in the end, the expense had been worth seeing the sparkle in his father's eyes. A joy that was contagious and spread since Michael sat down and played dominoes. The honor of having such a distinguished person, as Michael Spencer, bestow his time with such humble grace meant everything to the family.

At first, his sons were taken aback when they were informed of the special addition to the party. They heard of the missing man, but not his brother. When they googled Michael Spencer, an all-star college hero, their attitude changed. There wasn't a record Michael didn't break or set. He had all the charms of a hero and none of the assumed ego. Michael was easy to like and bonded when the family football flew across the lawn and straight into Michael's arms. Game on.

Kai grinned. Because of Michael's charm, the walls of financial differences became imaginary lines. For a few hours that evening, they were simply people who needed one another and had a reason to celebrate. Michael even extended an invitation to his youngest son to contact him after he finished school. Implying that his company was always on the lookout for new talent, and Michael said he knew people who knew people.

Cindy had shown Mrs. Spencer the mechanics of dancing the hula. Everyone encouraged the unexpected guest, and whatever lines people thought existed: vanished. Myra had a sultry rhythm of her own. Not quite luau worthy, but one just as ethnic. She laughed so hard, tears spilled out her eyes. And his family did him proud; without needing any urging. To be kind and hospitable came naturally as they drifted together. He could have sworn they stemmed from the same offshoot.

Kai gently caressed Cindy's hair. Lush strands fanned over the pillow and the faint scent of frangipani lingered in her hair. She had worn a crown of the blossoms tucked in her hair. Myra had nearly cried at the generosity when Cindy slipped the handbound lei over her head and welcomed her into the family as a distinguished guest. And as a welcome friend.

Cindy shifted on the bed and slowly blinked. A smile winked on her mouth. Usually, their roles were reversed, and she watched Kai sleep. The intimacy of the moment made her blush. Sometimes, Cindy fretted that she was no longer attractive, and it worried her. He smiled and stroked her cheek. He didn't have the words to convince her how wrong she was.

"Thank you for a great party."

"You're welcome."

Cindy reached and cupped his cheek, shy of her morning breath she brought his hand to her mouth and kissed it.

"Give me a minute."

She slunk from the bed and quietly traipsed to the bath-room, careful not to disturb the overnight guests sprawled on every soft surface of the house. But it was a tradition to make love in the morning after Kai's birthday, and nothing ever intervened. Even if they suspected that some of their guests overhead the soft rocking on the mattress.

Before Cindy returned, Kai shot one wish out to the universe. Please, send Jack Spencer home. Wherever he may be, keep him safe and end his mother's agony. She deserves to know that her son is alive.

When Cindy returned, she slowly allowed the plush robe to slip over her shoulders and down her arms. She hadn't bought Kai a present. She was wearing the sheer lace negligee he had pointed out to her on a Sunday stroll a few months ago. Cindy oozed sensuality even if she was completely unaware of it. He wanted to drink from her fountain of beauty and drown. And to kiss every inch of her lovely brown skin.

Chapter 6

Butcher

Jack woke to the slow thudding knock against the canoe. He had fallen asleep with his hand dragging in the water, and he should have known better. In the darkness that still seemed incomprehensible to Jack, he only saw the backs of the silver waves when the moon dictated light from above. The thud had been gentle at first, but each consecutive knock came at the canoe harder. Jack rolled and peered over the hull. The water was as jet black as the night. Whatever bumped him was merely testing. After a few harrowing minutes, the canoe rocked on the tranquil waves, and only his heart thundered in his ear, loud and fast. The silence frightened him nearly as much as assuming what knocked in the first place.

During the day, he saw many varieties of fish in the water. Little ones, and beautiful big ones with the faces of bulldogs. As of yet, he had only caught a handful of small ones. Again, God, if there was such a thing, must have been on his side. The thought of eating another one didn't assault his palate with want, but his body and stomach had other ideas. They craved anything chewable his teeth could grind. He had eaten some of the palm fronds. Anything to starve that gnawing in his gut and to still his pestering mind. He'd been lucky to have hit several minor storms. Although they were bitter to endure, they always left him with the gift of rainwater. His tongue no longer felt three feet thick.

He had also seen inexplicable things. Yesterday the most bizarre thing floated up to the canoe. The translucent bubble, shimmering in a rainbow of colors, sailed along on the waves. He mistook it at first for a balloon, a half-deflated sack, a bladder with the wings of an angel attached. How it sailed across the waves indicated it had a purpose, and when Jack peered into the depths of the clear water, he saw long strings attached to its body. Whatever it was, it became apparent it was a living being. His instinct had been to touch it, yet a small voice said: don't! At the very last moment, he snatched his fingers back. It was both: hideous and beautiful. And then he remembered the episode on National Geographic, Man O War.

Jack curled under the flag again and closed his eyes. At night, when the stars blinked above, he often saw lights travel across the sky. He had a brilliant vantage point to watch the giant movie screen.

"Look at that!" He said to himself as if to share the memory of seeing the graceful tail of a shooting star with an audience. Talking to himself helped to preserve his sanity, or he often joked that maybe he had already crossed over. The joke was on him, and no one had bothered to send him a text, to inform him of his leaving sanity.

He imagined his sister giving birth. He regretted not being there to hold the baby and kissing the little girl into the world. He regretted not being there to share the moment with his mother and father when the nurse laid their first grandchild into their arms. He was missing out on a family milestone. He hoped they were missing him too.

Like clockwork, the slow trickle of a sunray woke Jack at first dawn. Minutes later, the sun rose. It was a breathtaking spectacle, yet Jack despised the moment. It meant another long day without food and water. He regretted being alive, yet he had a thirst for living. Jack was learning that life was a repeating cycle. A tug of war of giving and taking. Jack assumed he was done with the taking cycle and entering the extended giving program.

He sat up and readied his fishing tackle. To appease his rumbling gut and time.

With an eye on his lure, he urinated over the hull and stared as far as the horizon would allow him to see. Endless water and waves. Green and blue waves calmly went about their business as if selling waves adorned in little tiny white caps was a booming business and had a greedy public clamoring for their share. Next to the canoe, he saw a school of fish. Ugly ones and silver slicers darted in unison; big ones that shone in iridescent shades of blues, gold, and green. He had reached in once and tried to catch one, but their fins cut into his hand. For lunch that day, he sucked on his own blood; again. But today he'd be smart about it and use the flag as a net.

Kneeling he waited patiently while the fish darted, going merrily about their way. He extended himself as far over the hull as he thought was safe and sunk the flag into the water. Learning from failure, he tied the flag to lengths of string from the belt of his pants. Saltwater was slowly corroding everything, and he learned to salvage what he could. Including the barnacles that formed on the canoe faster than he could scrape them off.

"Here, little fishes. Come to papa."

Jack learned that fish were smarter than people. People could be herded en masse with slogans and the right advertising jingle. Fish had a keen sense of survival: trust no one, no matter what they are waving. He waited until his knees begged him to rise, and he did. He had sores on his legs and back from being soaked with saltwater. He ate the scabs when he could.

Before entering the water for his ritualistic morning constitutional, Jack always scanned the water for telltale fins. He had seen a pod of massive whales breach in the distance, though he could not identify the type. He had only his useless television experience to guide him. For several days he'd seen fins slice the water in the distance. Dolphins launched themselves out of the water like rockets, and there seemed to be a correlation between traveling small fish and groups of large ones. As if they depended on one another. He'd seen flocks of gulls or frigates dive into the ocean and seen shoals fly across the water. Breathtaking twinkling streaks of silver.

Jack dipped his toes, cautiously approaching the water. Swimming each day did wonders for his body and gave him a sense of accomplishment. He still swam into the arms of the rising sun, hoping to hit land. What surprised him, whenever he immersed himself, was how clear the water was. A shiver always went through him when the bits of seaweed and plastic trash that floated toward him touched his skin. The soft and limp plastic bags puzzled him. How far had they come, and where were they headed? In recent days, the ocean gave up more surprises. He had scooped up a soda can, a small basket, a dental pick, and a straw. Were they signs that he was drifting closer toward civilization? Without feeding his dreams, Jack always stuffed the fantasy down that he was close to shore. Hoping for rescue was one thing, surviving was another.

Sometimes when he swam, fish nibbled on his body. The first time it happened, he had bolted from the water; his heart ready to explode from fright. His adversary always swam after him with an astonished look on its face: as if asking what the hell?

Cushioning his knees on the extra life vest, he dunked the flag again. He had fastened the two coconut halves, which had deteriorated quickly and split, as weights to sink the flag. He looked forward to any fish nuzzling him. Anything to touch, even if he planned on eating them, should he be so fortunate as to catch one. He waited patiently and waved the water-soaked flag as if he were a matador in the ring. A big bulldog faced fish took the challenge and swam toward the flag. Jack slowed his breath to the speed of hope. His heart rate pounded from excitement. The fish enjoyed the game and swam through the flag without anticipating any danger. For fun, the fish returned and plunged again. This time Jack pulled the flag over its head, and with a quick tug, he yanked the heavy flag into the canoe. Just like that, he had done it. The big fish flopped on the floor, trapped under the cloth.

Jack shoved the knife into the big body and carved it. Tears ran down his face.

"I'm sorry, buddy. I didn't mean to."

Jack had never killed his own food. His food came cooked and served on a platter. He never gave a thought to the cows, or chickens, or fish, and wild game. Killing his own lunch was an emotional bargain he hadn't counted on. The rusty blade carved into the belly of the fish and a basket of guts spilled out. He had no idea which parts were safe to eat and which to toss. The fish stared at him with one eye.

Chapter 7

Swap One Life For Another

Myra watched the footage of her granddaughter's birth repeatedly. Each momentous moment triggered another memory. Tears spilled from her eyes, and she regretted not having been there. Jack would have wanted her to have the experience. But Jack wasn't here to dictate. Yesterday, the captain had called in to say that he had not discovered any trace of Jack. Asking if the Spencers wanted him to continue to troll. But the endeavor, in his opinion, was futile.

Myra reached for a tissue. She was crying for joy and that other immutable thing recognized by its ugly face: grief. The ringing phone startled her.

"Hi, Grandma!"

"Stacy. How are you and Antonia this morning? I hadn't expected another call. You've got your hands full."

"I just wanted you to know I understand better now."

"Understand what, my dear?"

"About Jack. What it means to be a mother and not giving up."

"It's remarkably powerful, isn't it."

"Honestly, it slapped me very hard when the nurse took little Antonia. I felt as if a limb had been severed. I can't imagine what it's like for you. I just wanted you to know that I get it."

"Thank you. It might sound crazy, but in my heart of hearts, I know Jack's alive. I feel it."

"Mom. I feel it too."

"Have I told you yet she's beautiful. She looks just like you did when you were born. Same soulful eyes. That mouth. The spitting image of you."

"Well, I hope she's not a hellion like I was. At least that's what Dad said."

"You were. I hope it's payback time. And Stacy, I'm sorry I couldn't be there for you."

"I know you were in spirit. Love you."

"Me too."

Myra cradled the phone to her heart. Watching Stacy give birth unearthed so many memories of Jack. That singular and momentous moment when the nurse laid Jack on her chest. Everything changed. She rose and went to the window. John agreed and hired the captain to head out for another week with instructions to head in the other direction toward California. The captain hadn't liked the suggestion and mentioned something about the garbage patch being out there. He didn't like having trash bags sucked into the propeller of the boat. But the money was too good to pass up. John made a promise to fix any damages in case the ship ran into floating debris. John had said afterward that the captain was exaggerating.

"I'm off."

Michael said from the hallway. She was losing her second son this morning, and he was loath to leave his mother. No one had told Stacy about the next chapter in the saga. John had insisted she be allowed a few hours of bliss, snug in the sanctuary of motherhood.

"What a mess."

Myra exhaled and walked toward the open arms of her son. Michael nodded. But it was John's turn to need his son.

"I'm still in shock." Michael blindly adjusted his tie.

"I'm not going to say I told you so, but I knew from the moment I met Tessa." Myra snapped her mouth shut.

"Well. I didn't see this freight train coming."

"I can't say I suspected a child in Tessa's past. But she always had an agenda."

Myra looked into the handsome face of her son for reassurance.

"That Jack knew all along is what's blowing me away. Do you think she's the reason he moved across the country?" Michael was just as confused as she was.

"Absolutely. Jack touched on something he shouldn't. Seems we've underestimated Tessa."

"Yet, Brody puzzles me the most."

"Love leaves many people blind." Myra reached and tugged on his tie. He had left it hanging sideways. The news of Brody's resignation came at the worst time.

"But that Brody would jump ship like that and leave us hanging. I find that even worse than what Tessa did, or might have done."

"I agree. His timing to quit is almost unforgivable. We've always treated him like family."

"It's a low blow to hand in his resignation when we need him the most. I saw it in Dad's eyes. He's devastated."

Myra wanted to add something else. That she suspected Jack had unearthed something else. And then her mouth betrayed her.

"You don't think Tessa or even Brody had anything to do with Jack's disappearance?"

Michael shook his head, that sort of thinking hadn't really crossed his mind yet. His heart wasn't ready to allow that sort of trickery. Jack had trespassed on dangerous territory when he hired a man to investigate Tessa. But Tessa didn't strike him as the sort of person who would resort to malice. And Brody, no. He was a victim of circumstance.

"Well, your father needs you. He hasn't the time to deal with the soap opera Tessa and Brody are starring in. And with you at his side, maybe you two can settle the merger."

"I love you, Mom. Phone me day or night. Promise."

"I will.

While holding onto Michael in a long embrace, Myra continued speculating.

"Let me know if Kai finds any older surveillance footage on Jack and Tessa. Or anyone else suspicious for that matter. I still believe his disappearance is unrelated."

"People have done worse for less, but I'll let you know as soon as I hear anything."

"Good."

Michael picked up his luggage. He kissed her again.

"I'm sorry you've cut your Hawaiian romance short. Vonnie seems like a special lady."

"She is. We'll see. Right now, Dad needs me."

"I'll walk you down."

Myra picked up Michael's briefcase while he maneuvered his luggage down the corridor.

"Keep your chin up. Kai promised he'd help you any way possible. He's a good man."

"I know. I'm meeting Cindy for lunch."

"That's great. They've engulfed us like family."

"I know. I feel blessed."

In the lobby, Myra reached her arms around her son and allowed her heartbeat to reach his through osmosis.

"Take care of your father."

Within seconds the car whisked Michael out of sight. At least she knew where he was going. She decided to go for a short walk along the beach before the heat became too much. Her skin could handle the rays, but her hormones had lost control over body temperature. Something she shared with Cindy. How soothing it was to have someone to laugh about the symptoms of a broken thermostat with.

At the boardwalk, Myra turned right and walked away from the protruding rock formation separating the beach from the hotel on the other side. Myra watched the docile tide trick people into playing in the sea. She no longer doubted Jack was in the water. She never said it aloud, but she believed Jack had taken the canoe. It wasn't as illogical as they all first suggested. The coincidence was too great, and the storm must have sent Jack farther adrift than he intended to go that night. Watching the last bit of video footage clearly implicated how drunk her son was. That Tessa was the motivation behind the copious amounts of alcohol were seconded by the entire wedding party. Jack's friends knew Jack liked his liquor. But the amounts he indulged in since their arrival on the island had silently alarmed everyone. Slowly, one by one, the truth trickled in, and that they were concerned. Some even admitted approaching him, but he brushed them off. No one mentioned it because they wanted to keep things light. For the wedding, for Jack's sake. For the Spencers. Until one of the bride's maids casually confessed her concern to John, on the flight back home. The conviction that something was amiss with Jack snowballed from there.

"Jack. Damn it! Where are you?"

Myra watched the sand measure and print the soles of her sneakers while she walked along the wet shore. It was fascinating to watch how precisely the sand cast them down to the logo in the tread. The ocean emitted an infallible truth: that in the big scale of life, people were mere ants on its back, and meaningless. Only people's egos inflated them to believe otherwise; their own importance only fed ignorance.

She was looking forward to having lunch with Cindy. It surprised Myra how easy it had been to pick up a conversation and run alongside a virtual stranger and shape a bond. Woman to woman. Mother to mother. Michael had suggested buying Kai a replacement canoe to fish from. He overheard fragments of conversation through the grapevine that the outrigger was the Hales' empire and that two or three hundred dollars had the power to sink or float a family. And on his one date with Vonnie, Kai's niece, Michael poked the hive to harvest the indisputable truth.

PART 6
SOLID GROUND

Chapter 1

Stuff it!

A sound woke Rose from her slumber. She never knew if it was imagined or real. The others were curled around the misery of their disappointing dreams. Mark had shut down, and although Ron tried, he could not rile anyone after their last ship of hope sailed out of sight. They were a miserable bunch.

She unfolded herself from the plastic sheet and made her way toward the edge of the raft. The clear water sloshed next to her. Its color reminded her of the green Depression glassware that her grandmother kept in the credenza. A tear splashed into the water, then another. A feeling of desperation, inspired by bouts of homesickness, made her think the unthinkable. But she wasn't the sort of person who could or would.

The raft limped along on the waves. She assumed they had floated away from the sewage that the cruise ship dumped. A streak of silver minnows darted in the water. Small agile swimmers that were good to eat raw. Herring or Sardines. She couldn't tell the difference. While everyone slept on, nestled into the vestiges of their dreams or fighting elements of their nightmares, Rose envisioned being rescued. It was an ongoing fantasy and an escape from the nightmare. On the island and the raft, she was entangled in the chores of surviving. Wishful thinking took a backseat, but like a bitter aftertaste, always present. While scanning the water and horizon, she wondered if touching solid ground would feel like having wobbly legs. Would it feel similar to a person newly released from prison? Would the world have changed, or would she have changed so much that she could no longer find her place among the freedom of being free? Would that feeling seal the bond between her and Mark? That common thread. She dreaded the thought, yet it was a strong possibility.

Behind her, someone shifted the raft with movement. She heard Ron cough, and then his shadow nestled up to hers.

"You okay?"

Ron always put everyone's needs ahead of his own. Rose nodded then padded the seat next to her. Ron had a gift for making her see the light. He was the father figure sadly missing, even if she had nurtured an imposter in her previous life claiming that title.

"I'm fine. You?" Rose grinned, despite.

"Seen better days. But I'll never give in. You know that don't you?"

"I do. I just thought about what it would be like to fit in with society once we get rescued. For some stupid reason, I still think that ship we missed is going to turn around and save us."

"Kiddo, you're an optimist like me. And if you survived this," he gestured grandly toward the vast ocean and sky, "then you can survive anything. I'm pretty sure I will write that book and kindly explain to my audience that we can't carry on as we have."

"I'm sure it would be a bestseller. Hope you're open to harsh criticism."

"Like I said, surviving on the Patch for seven years, I can handle just about anything. Sticks and stones, my dear."

"Do you think you and Trish will get married?"

"Hard to say. But we've talked about it as a possibility. Her husband is gone, she hopes her family has come to terms. If they've moved on, then there's a good chance Trish and I will stay together. What about you?"

"Mark and I? I was just trying to decipher that riddle. Mark is a good person, but I've always held on to that fantasy that I'd meet that one person. You know love at first sight."

"I do know. And I hope you find it. I'm sure it is out there waiting for you. Despite what your father did to scar you emotionally, you're an amazing woman. Any man would be lucky to love you."

Rose reached for Ron's hand. He'd been the person who rescued her physically and emotionally. If her father had been different, not that she believed he could have been, she might not have been so desperate to get on that cruise ship. Not that she blamed the ship, it was entirely her fault that she fell. She sat with Ron in the silence. She wanted her own version of a Ron, a man blessed with kindness and graced with the gift of gab.

"I miss my children. I had such plans for them. My wife and I always kept a secret bank account set aside for their education. And I hope my wife remarried. We had a friend whom I'd like to see her with. Not that I ever suspected that they had feelings other than friendship for one another, but they'd be a good match."

"That's kind of you to think that, but you know the heart plays tricks. Often we don't see what is right in front of our noses."

"True. You're wise, my young friend."

Ron leaned away from Rose and reached for the pole behind him. Within a minute, he fished out a trash bag and a plastic six-pack holder. A sign that they were nearing home. Rose pulled out her blade and cut the plastic rings and started to braid the strands into rope. Ron fished for more trash. Under the tarp, the others were slowly waking from their nap. Mark took a seat next to Rose and rubbed her shoulder.

"Your fingers did wonders on my back. Thanks." He plunged his legs in the water, dangling them.

"So. Looks like we're almost back to where we started."

Mark played with the rope Rose had braided from the plastic and Ron pulled a yogurt container covered in barnacles aboard.

"Why? This trash looks familiar."

"Just the quantity. Let me grab a pole, I'll help. Who knows? Maybe we'll find our ticket out of here.

Ron looked at Rose. The truth that they were all stuck in this miserable rut always sounded worse when implied by someone else. It seemed nearly unreasonable even when it confirmed precisely what everyone else wished for.

"Maybe he's right."

"Maybe he's right, and we're right back where we started. The shithole island that I sometimes can't bear thinking about. Then I remember, lucky fucking me, and resign myself to my destiny."

"Look!" Mark startled them. Everyone rose and followed his gaze. The truth rocked on the waves as if it had awaited them.

"We're a few days out. I don't see any other storms brewing. Must be another El Niño year. Which is good and bad."

Rose saw the wide circle floating like cream on the ocean. But by the trick of the waves, it vanished randomly into the trough and then resurfaced like a shimmering mirage. She was glad and sad at the same time. The island meant home and jail, and more importantly, her dream of being rescued died with the sight.

Mark hooked his fingers over hers. She had promised to make plans with him and leave. He tried to convince her that trying to reach Mexico or California was the only way out of this misery. She was unsure and thought life on the island could be worse. They could have perished at sea. With Ron's plan, they survived to allow an unexpecting rescue team to find them. Or not.

All afternoon they fished for trash. Not that they put a dent in the amount that floated on the current, but it gave them a sense of purpose. With their heads tucked in and their hands busy, they wove what they found into rope or mats. Ron assessed the solid pieces and decided what could be salvaged into something usable.

"There! I see something."

Mark had everyone's attention. He'd been teased before that he had eagle eyes, and it was true that his distance vision measured off the Snellen chart. He pointed toward something only he could see floating on the water.

"What is it?"

"Not sure yet. But it's something. There, it's gone again."

"It's too far out. It'll take us a week to get there on this thing."

"There's no wind. And chances are whatever is out there is floating at the same rate or faster than us. Too bad we don't have a canoe or kayak."

"No point in wishing." Mark suddenly stomped off. He often joked that if they ever found an even remotely seaworthy canoe or boat, he'd take his chances despite Ron's gentle persuading that it couldn't be done. Mark had sworn Rose to secrecy about their escape plan.

"I can't advise it," Ron said as an apology to no one in particular as if he had read Mark's secret. Of course, anyone could paddle straight east and pray to hit land. Eventually. But during Ron's seven years trapped on the island, no one ever made it. There had been several who had found just such a vessel as Mark dreamed of and set off into the sun's rising face. They all promised to send someone, and, sadly, they all failed to keep their promise.

Ron put his fishing rod down and plodded toward Mark. "Look, Mark, let's talk about it."

Mark owed Ron that much respect and slowly turned to face him.

"What's there to say?"

"If we ever find a ship or raft that can take us home, I'll gladly risk my life to get everyone there. I promise. If that thing out there is that thing, I'll take the chance. Promise."

"What do I care?"

Mark picked up the pole and stabbed at a tangled mess of cords floating nearest to him. Anything to avoid dealing with the rising resentment that afflicted everyone from time to time.

"What's that orange thing?"

Rose pointed. Several orange lumps floated on the water. If there was a godsend to the trash, it always had a surprise in store for them.

"What the ...?" Ron formed his hands into binoculars.

"Mark. Use your eagle eyes."

Everyone waited for Mark's guess. They knew that's all it could be at the moment: a guess. As if it made a difference, they held their breath in unison to keep the raft steady.

"Damn. I think those are sacks of oranges. Or tennis balls. Could it be? I'm going in."

"Not without tying up."

Mark consented to have a thick and sturdy cord tied around his waist. He suggested they give him a second cord to haul the loot back. Mark's arms made short work of the water and the distance. Soon he was just a head and arms climbing the small waves as if they were miniature mountains exploding from below. He was gone for a good ten minutes when he signaled.

"That's the good thing about plastic bags, we have enough to make miles and miles of cording," Ted said while feeding foot after foot of cording into the water. Up in the distance, Mark was surrounded by floating lumps of orange. Ron didn't take his eyes off Mark during the entire expedition. If anything went awry, he was ready to dive in. He wasn't willing to lose another one on his shift. Sure, Mark was sullen some of the time, but he also served as a beneficial cog in their survival. He was strong, brilliant, and could solve problems almost better than Ron. Mark's shortcoming was that he lacked any diplomatic skill. It was what made Li Wei such a critical friend. Li Wei's poor English saved him from being stung by Mark's sharp words. And Mark appreciated Li Wei for being a doer. A risk-taker.

Chapter 2

Fiber

Rose could still taste and smell oranges. Canker sores blistered on the inside of her mouth and she couldn't resist the urge to probe them with her tongue. It had been another feast; she knew it was always an epic war of feast and famine. She untangled herself from Mark's arms and kissed his nose. Even he smelled of citrus. They had hauled in ten bags of oranges, three crates of green bananas, and two cartons of semi-ripe pineapples that had miraculously floated on top of a wooden door toward them. The storm must have torn their latest harvest off a ship heading toward the mainland. The fruits were clearly marked as Hawaiian. Everyone had feasted despite knowing the dangers of too much fiber.

They had celebrated the bounty Mark hauled home. And the simple act of being useful fueled Mark's happiness. There was a truth to the provider theory and men. He was completely changed when he finally swam home with the last batch. Men needed to provide and have a sense of purpose, just as women needed to nurture. On the raft and in survival mode, those facts were not convoluted by what he said, or she said. They just were.

Next to them, the floating assortment of trash thickened. Some clung to the raft, and Rose recognized the logo of a store she used to frequent. They sold anything coverable in chocolate. Marshmallow, Jujubes, raisins, pretzels, nuts of every imaginable type, and once a month, they sold delectable chocolate-covered strawberries and bananas by special order. Rose was a preferred customer.

Although they had found the cases of chocolates, the lure of candy had already lost its appeal. Only by deprivation had she overcome her addiction. Abstinence by force had been her cure. If there was one thing she really missed: it was bread. Especially the European bakery sort of bread with a chewy crust. But now was not the time to crave; it was the time to appreciate what they had. Something that applied to the people she was surrounded by.

At times, always being near someone was difficult and tested her nerves. It's what she loved about running the make-shift store on the island. It gave her something to do, and it was her own space.

"Full?"

"Yes. You still thinking about that thing you saw floating on the horizon? You were talking in your sleep."

Rose watched as a shadow clouded Mark's eye. He hated admitting something so personal as hope, even if it escaped as mumbled words in his sleep. But this morning, he used it to his advantage. He took a seat next to Rose at the edge of the raft and took her hand.

"If that is a canoe or boat or anything even remotely sea-worthy, will you come with me?"

She knew the question was coming. Rose had never considered risking her life by setting off as the others had. Her trust lay entirely with Ron, and the thought of surrendering her life into Mark's proposal made her uncomfortable.

"I …" Rose stammered.

"What's there to think about? If we can get out of here, I doubt Mexico or California are that far. If we're smart, we can do this."

"Honestly, I never thought of leaving. I always laid my hope on some ship or plane coming to find us."

"That's Ron's stupid idea, and you've been brainwashed. I agree we can't make it on a raft made out of soda bottles and floating shit. But if we had a boat of sorts, we could do it. Other people have survived it."

"You know this how?"

"I read."

Rose nodded. Yes, Mark read. Or so he rubbed into their faces whenever he had a chance. But did reading make anyone an expert on anything? If it were true, she would be a princess in a foreign land, and dukes and princes would be clamoring to climb up her tower. That all men were smitten by her at a glance. No. She wasn't an expert on romance, or love, despite having read hundreds of novels.

What surprised Rose was the underlying resentment that surfaced in Mark's accusation. Without the soda bottle raft and island, they'd all be dead. Everyone owed being alive to Ron.

"I'll think about it. I promise. But don't say a word."

She hushed her mouth with her finger just as Ron and Trish rose behind them. Rose didn't think she could betray Ron by leaving and giving up on his dream of rescue. But she couldn't bear to see Mark sulk either. They had time. Without wind, the raft didn't go far on any given day and instead lumbered away on the current. Besides, the odds of a canoe or boat miraculously showing up were next to nil.

"Thanks again, Mark. Your contributions to our survival are monumental. I mean, we can't thank you enough."

"Don't mention it."

Ron never forgot to give thanks for the blessings, big or small, that floated into their lives. And he gave Mark credit for being an essential cog in their survival.

"I mean it, Mark. You're a treasure, and I'm honored to have you on my team."

Ron also had a knack for landing compliments that made everyone keenly aware that the team's survival depended on every facet. And that he could read their thoughts. Rose quickly looked at what was in her hands, she didn't want Ron to see the guilt she felt rising in her eyes and that her loyalty was divided. That she hated this place, despite the display she put on for all to see.

PART 7
ALOHA

Chapter 1

Puzzle Pieces Fall

Kai paced the lobby. He had swallowed his nerves for breakfast, and instead of his usual meal, he chewed on a handful of antacid tablets. Remnants of the chalky tablet came off his teeth and foamed. He was keen to see the formidable PI off his island. The young woman whom the PI attacked on the street had filed a complaint, and Kai had been questioned to verify her side of things. Kai could not lie.

"So, you're glad to be getting rid of me then?"

It wasn't a question but an accusation. The scent of hot chocolate rushed from the man's mouth and clothing. A glare directed at Kai suggested that he was still the prime suspect in his investigation. But despite their differences, they both wanted Jack Spencer, one way or the other, recovered. If not to appease their own egos, then the minds of the Spencers.

"No. I'm not glad. I hoped one of us would find Jack. That has been my wish all along. I'm sorry we got off on bad footing." Kai extended his hand to the PI, and, to safeguard his feelings, took the rebuff in stride.

"Spare me. Not sure how you managed to wrap Mrs. Spencer around your little finger."

"No such thing. I simply promised I would do whatever to help find Jack."

"Including hoodwinking Mrs. Spencer?"

Kai abruptly turned. He had never hoodwinked anyone, and especially not Mrs. Spencer. He'd never admit to the PI that he'd been asked to call her Myra. She also let it slip that she didn't fully distrust the PI as well. Uncouth, she had implied. Kai saluted over his shoulder and never looked at the leaving PI again. Besides, he had a meeting with one of the bartenders. A man who'd been away on vacation since the whole saga unfolded. Kai took the stairs two at a time and met the young man in the locker room.

"Sheldon?"

"Yes. I'm sorry I didn't come sooner, but I've been camping in the bay. I had no idea."

"You saw the poster?"

Sheldon nodded.

"And the poster of the girl. She's a regular or was a regular. She's not exactly the sort you can ever get out of your mind. And she knows her way around the hotel."

"You left when?"

"I'd say the morning after. But she's been at many events. Like I said, she's not a newbie.

"Know her name at all?"

"My business is loud. The music drowns out most of the conversations, and I rely on gestures and drink names. But my mind vaguely remembers something like Kesley or Delani."

"Ask around, will you?"

"Sure. They still have nothing on the missing person?"

"Nothing."

Kai couldn't wait to share the news with Myra. Ever since his birthday party, they included her in the family. Cindy and Myra bonded over something he wasn't privy to, but it hardly mattered and they planned meeting for lunch. He might just surprise them.

He found himself whistling at his desk. His cousin was still fishing for him and reassured him that the way the fish were biting the three or four extras he hauled in for Kai didn't intrude on his day at all. "Besides," he had teased Kai at the party, "what is family for?" They were watching Michael flirt with their niece.

Kai had also asked the shuttle driver to make sure the PI got on the plane. He didn't want that creep spying on him any longer. Not that he had anything to hide but having someone invade your privacy was uncomfortable. They had had that incident at the party when a drone hovered above them. No one in his neighborhood could afford such a camera-equipped model. Michael had launched a series of pebbles at the invasive creature, and the drone took a direct hit before vanishing. Everyone congratulated Michael on his throwing arm.

Kai rewound the tape of the night of Jack's disappearance again. There wasn't a day when he didn't watch the footage looking for a new clue. The bartender had given them new hope that they'd track the beautiful woman down.

He busied himself doing the menial chore of adding new staff statistics and adding security access to their badges. Next, he'd delete the ones on their way out. It was a tedious but necessary job and they had fallen behind. When he finished with the new hires, he took the tangled bunch of swipe-cards from their lanyards and nearly fell from his chair. He brought the distorted photograph closer to his eyes. Not Chelsea or Kelsey. Shit. Kelani. Hiding in plain sight. She had quit two weeks ago. With a quick search, he pulled up her employment file. The photograph on file was purposely distorted, and she hid behind ghastly plastic glasses, her hair pulled into a severe bun. The reason listed on her resignation stated family concerns. But there it was: her address.

Bingo. Kelani. To validate his hunch, he plopped her name into a Google search, and images of her populated the screen on Instagram, Facebook, and Twitter. The stunning girl on the arm of Jack Spencer.

Kai glanced at the clock. He was certain Cindy and Myra were meeting at noon. He tapped his pen impatiently to the count of the seconds on the clock. Cindy was famously late, and he wasn't sure about Myra. But this was the best news in three weeks. Had it really been that long since Jack vanished? He couldn't fathom how long three weeks measured in Myra's sense of time. In an instant, he decided and swung his chair away from his desk.

"I might be late."

Kai said to his partner while he struggled his arms into the blazer he was forced to wear on hotel property while on duty. On second thought, he wanted to bring the identification card with him. He untangled Kelani's badge from the others cluttering his desk. He stuffed the Post-it note with her address into his pocket.

He arrived at the restaurant just as Myra came sauntering down the street. She seemed lost in her thoughts while window shopping the colorful souvenir displays rolled out onto the sidewalk. She spotted him and waved, then walked briskly toward him.

"What a surprise! I thought it was just Cindy and me."

She no longer shrunk back when he bowed slightly and then lightly kissed her right cheek. At his party, she had to endure the unfamiliar greeting a hundred times. Her smile, however, was always genuine. When Cindy surprised them on the sidewalk, it was Myra who performed the customary greeting ritual.

"I'm sorry to intrude on your ladies' lunch, but I have some news. If you want, we can order take-out and eat on the way."

"On the way?"

Cindy stalled him; a puzzled look demanded that he explain himself. Kai dug into his pocket, retrieved the card, and dangled it.

"This is her! Kelani. The last person seen with Jack."

"You're joking?"

The color drained from Myra's face, and she reached for Cindy's arm to steady herself.

"I have her address."

Cindy tugged Myra along behind her. Kai led the way to his truck.

"Let's go. We can eat later."

"Her address?"

"We were right. Hiding in plain sight. Something only a professional would dare."

Kai unlocked the passenger door, and Cindy hopped in first. He closed the door gently on Myra, who couldn't resist staring at the blurred photo.

"I've seen her at the hotel. Oh, my God."

Kai drove the speed limit though today wasn't a great day to be a model citizen. Once they confirmed Kelani, they'd have to call the police. But Jack had never been a priority for them as he had been for Kai, and the woman sitting next to him with her mouth slightly agape, her hand on the dashboard.

Kai plugged the address into his GPS, and the truck nearly rolled up on her street as if by magic. Kai was as eager as Myra to face the woman who held the magic key to the mystery.

"Let me," Myra said, getting out of the truck the instant he parked.

Kai killed the engine, nodded, and gripped the steering wheel as he watched Myra mount the decrepit cement steps leading to the screened front door. Then, he eased himself from the truck and followed at a close distance without invading the space Myra needed to take care of business. He waited beneath the shadow of a palm. While Myra knocked, he sauntered along the fence, never taking his eyes off the house. Cindy leaned on the fender of his truck and waited. If they could sort this for Myra, it would be a miracle. Within a minute, a form appeared in the doorframe, and then the screen door pushed open. Myra looked over her shoulder and pointed toward them. A second later, she entered the house.

It was the right thing to do and the wrong thing. Kai knew they were messing with a crucial witness. But people under duress did stupid things. Kai kept his eye on the door, the dark windows, and listened for raised voices. Ten agonizing minutes passed, and Myra reappeared. She was dabbing something from her eyes.

"It's her. She admitted being with Jack and that she stole his gold chain."

Myra held the chain in the palm of her hand. "I gave it to him for his twenty-first birthday."

"Did she say anything else?"

Myra shook her head. "Only that she is sorry. You can ask her. She said she needed a minute to get dressed, and she's willing to go to the police."

"Okay. Did she take the key to Jack's room?"

"She didn't say."

They waited on the sidewalk for what seemed an eternity for Kelani to join them. Kai checked his watch and allowed her another minute. While waiting, he scanned the windows for her silhouette but saw nothing. When a dog barked behind the house, Kai bolted. He took the length of the sidewalk in a few short strides leaving Cindy to console Myra on her own.

He rapped his knuckles on the screen door and waited. The absence of footsteps, he knew were the tidings of an ill omen. He backtracked to the back garden and instantly saw their mistake. The garage door was ajar, the spot was empty. The tethered dog barked again to confirm Kai's suspicions. Kelani had escaped. Kai took a running leap over the fence and saw the rear bumper of a red Honda round the corner.

"Get in the car!" Kai yelled as he came flying around the corner of the house.

Cindy heaved Myra into the truck and climbed into the seat before Kai wrenched his side open. He backed out narrowly missing the street's community mailboxes.

He slammed his foot on the accelerator, eyes on the road. "She's fled.

Chapter 2

Perfume

Bruce could smell the faint lingering of her perfume. She was here, in his house. He closed the door quietly and walked down the carpeted hallway toward his room. His mother was out, he knew that. But what on earth was she doing here? They hadn't talked since that night when she ended up in bed with that missing tourist. Bitch had never handed over the loot she absconded with and had ignored his attempts to reach her. Bruce slowly pushed on the door, leaving enough of a gap to peer inside. Like Goldilocks, she had found the bed best suited to her needs in times of trouble.

"Kel! Get up."

He still hadn't forgiven her for betraying him and never would. She blinked and then yawned into her palm.

"Where you been?" Kelani moaned like a kitten.

"Out."

"You should know that woman, his mother, came to my house. She brought that security dude. They know who I am."

"Not my problem."

When Kelani swung her bare legs over the side of the bed, her shorts didn't leave any room for speculation. She was beautiful, but now was not the time to go soft.

"Trust me. It's your problem."

Bruce had to think, which was impossible, while staring at her beautiful body. He could see right through her sheer blouse.

"Put something decent on."

"Like what? I had to run."

Bruce left the room and returned with a robe that he took from his mother's room and flung it on the bed. When he did, and Kelani reached for it, she hesitated.

"Are those his shoes?"

"No! Can't a man have decent shoes?"

"Those are his shoes. Oh, my God! Those are Jack's shoes."

"I found them on the beach."

"I'm gonna be sick."

Kelani cupped her long fingers over her mouth. Her exotic eyes widened with panic as the ramifications dawned and blossomed on her cheeks. Bruce kicked the door shut. He read Kelani's fear imprinted in her eyes. She could try escaping, but he'd prevent her route the only way possible.

Chapter 3

Ringlets

Kai followed Officer Malone into the house. Curtains blew in the draft entering the house from the open back door. An uneaten slice of pizza sat abandoned on the kitchen table, and the can of soda had gone flat. Kelani had fled with just the clothes on her back. Although Kai knew the streets from years of delivering take-out, Kelani had had too much of a head start. All he saw of her was the rear bumper of her red Honda, and then she meshed into the dozens of vehicles on the busy road and vanished.

"Looks like she lives here with someone else. There's three bedrooms in use."

"We'll wait."

Kai didn't touch anything, and he knew that Officer Malone was breaking some of the rules by allowing him to tag along.

"If she's smart, she'll turn herself in. The law might take a softer approach if she confesses." Malone scanned each room with a snapshot gaze.

"Confesses what?"

Kai didn't believe Kelani harmed Jack Spencer or was a party to his disappearance. She was a thief who used her looks to get into the pants and rooms of hapless victims. But Kai guessed that Kelani was the link that might bring them face to face with whoever knew what happened to Jack. Thank God, Cindy had taken the afternoon off to be with Myra, who hadn't stopped trembling since.

The gold chain proved to be a warranted link that Jack and the girl had a connection. It was the last tether that Jack had been a victim of foul play. Whatever it cost, they had to find Kelani. Whatever she knew about Jack's disappearance had to be crucial.

Kai followed Malone from room to room like a puppy. He had promised John Spencer over the phone he wouldn't lose sight of any clue. John Spencer also mentioned that Myra thought the world of him. That compliment enforced Kai's mission. He'd not let them down. The good news was that Myra's daughter had booked a flight and, even at this moment, was en route with the newborn to be with Myra.

"You want to stake out the house with me?" Malone asked over his shoulder.

Horses couldn't drag Kai away from the opportunity to capture Kelani, or whomever else lived in the house. Despite having had plans to search for his canoe that evening, he gulped before answering, his mouth changed his plans indefinitely.

"Absolutely."

His canoe had to take the back seat again because of circumstances, because of Jack Spencer. But what was he to say, "no, I can't I have more important shit to take care of?"

They let themselves out, and Malone stuffed his notepad and latex gloves into his pocket. He had already rehearsed his probable cause theory on Kai.

They parked Malone's car within a bird's eye view of the house and waited. Malone wasn't a bad cop. His downfall lay in being inundated and overworked by petty crime. Which was a good thing if you looked at it from the other side of the perspective.

Kai flinched with boredom in the car. Stakeouts were a tedious business, and Malone used his downtime to catch up on sleep. Kai wanted to be part of this mission, but he also wanted to be with Myra and Cindy. This was the biggest scoop in nearly three weeks, and he had unearthed it. Kai never lost that feeling that somehow Jack's disappearance was at least partly his fault. Although no one blamed him, he blamed himself. The PI's words still rang loudly in his ears, and if he hadn't fallen asleep, he might have acted. He had already rewritten protocol for the security team that if any guest should ever end up as inebriated as Jack, they were to walk that guest or guests to their room. Too little too late.

His oldest son casually walked past the car and dropped off some coffee and dinner. Kai hadn't eaten since breakfast. The house remained dark, but for many locals, quitting time wasn't for another hour.

Malone found a string of fake blond ringlets in one of the bedrooms. The sort girls clipped on for effect. There was a selection of wigs, in an array of colors, even blue, and pink. When Malone slid the closet door aside, they both gasped at the sheer number of garments squeezed into the small space. Stiletto heels in a perfect size six lined the floor. Kai didn't know a single woman in his circle of family or friends who could afford such a collection on the wages of a domestic maid. He doubted his boss could afford such items. But now they knew Kelani supplemented her wages the only way she knew how. But a thief typically had connections to a fence who would trade what she stole.

And there were portfolios. Professional photographs. Kelani used her looks to get what she wanted. But that she'd risk the life of someone didn't fit her m.o., although Malone argued criminals operated by an entirely different set of standards. He implied that just because Kelani looked the part of an angel, didn't mean she had wings.

Chapter 4

Damn Fish

Jack's body trembled from exhaustion. The canoe reeked of vomit and excrement. He hadn't washed his clothing and body for days. Every few minutes, he opened his mouth and suckled on the light rain shower. Despite the canoe slowly filling with water, Jack hadn't the strength to bail.

Every bite of fish he ate three days ago had taken revenge and come out of every orifice of his body. Including his nose. He shouldn't have eaten the fish on the third day, but he thought it safe, and that it had dried enough in the sun. It didn't smell bad when he put it into his mouth. Coming out told another story.

This was the end of his journey. The ocean won. But why? For fuck's sake, why was it keeping him alive for another day or even another excruciating hour? Covered in vomit and poop, he didn't give a fuck if anyone came to rescue him now.

Blinking under the intense glare of the midday sun, he saw his name scratched into the side of the canoe. *Jack Spencer was here in 2018.* He had planned to add a small message to his mom, his father, to Michael and Stacy. He'd been waiting for the right words to formulate in his mind to say how much he loved them. As if, I love you, didn't say it clearly enough.

Another soft moan escaped his mouth when he adjusted his long limbs in the canoe. While floating aimlessly, he noticed that small bits of trash floating next to the canoe increased in frequency. A gift that allowed him to rescue a plastic tub that might have been a margarine container at one time in its long life on earth. The least he could do was repurpose it into storing some precious rainwater. He took a small sip and ran his tongue over his coarse lips. In his feverish state, Jack could have sworn he saw bags of oranges float on the water.

"Please, God. If you exist, show me some mercy. Anything."

There it was again. That bargaining chip called anything that he had offered to God a hundred times since he found himself adrift. He'd been foolish to believe God would distinguish him with an epic message, a heroic survival. After all, he, Jack Spencer, was just an ordinary man who didn't mean squat to someone who could choose from billions of willing devotees.

"It's not for me, but for my mom. My family."

Jack tried that bargaining tool as well. By his calculations, he had had three weeks to think over his life, and the best he had come up with was that he had wronged Brody. He tried to forgive Tessa and said it aloud to add validity. That she had a kid, well, it took two to tango. And who was he to criticize anyone? He had forsaken friendship for a quick romp and his own satisfaction.

"Brody. I'm so sorry. And I know, you think I'm just saying that to get out of this predicament. But if you can hear me, I owe you that apology. But what I do hope is that you'll never have to find out that I betrayed your trust and friendship. I was never worthy of it."

The shame of having wronged his best friend seemed un-forgivable even while floating on the fringes of death on the ocean. There was no use in explaining that he had conceded to moving across the country because Tessa demanded it and that it really was the only solution. At the hotel, when he asked Tessa if there was any chance she'd allow him to move back, to be near his family, her forked tongue answered. "I'm gonna hold this over your fucking head for the rest of your fucking life," she promised him.

Sometimes, when Jack woke in the middle of his feverish delirium, he saw a bird squawking on the stern of the canoe. It flapped its wings and chatted away in a language he didn't understand. He wasn't even sure the gull existed in real life. If it did, was he close to land? Wasn't that some old seafaring trick sailors used? Did they symbolize freedom? Jack was unable to finish any thought. Should he try to eat it? His brain was on fire, yet he shivered. The purity of the bird's white and gray feathers seemed to suggest to Jack he had crossed over. Only the pain ransacking his guts, and flaming bowels confirmed otherwise.

Jack stretched his limbs, but he was too tired to hold up his arms for long. Even the slightest movement exhausted his deadweight body. With what little strength he had left, he tugged the soiled flag closer around him. Anything to keep heat in and keep heat out.

Jack closed his eyes and prayed. *Let it be over.* There was no point in saying please.

Chapter 5

Tiny Fingers of Hope

Myra kissed the soft palm of her granddaughter. The scent of the baby unleashed a million memories and helped to seal the terrible truth. Life didn't come to a standstill. When Jack was little, as little as Antonia was now, she used to wake him with her kisses. She wanted to stare into his never-ending blue eyes, which over time, changed into a soft amber brown. His tiny fingers and toes used to mesmerize her. They were so perfect and kissable.

"I'm so glad you came. Thanks for bringing me this miracle."

"You're welcome. I would have been here sooner, but this little bundle takes all my time."

"Isn't it wonderful that it does?"

"Wouldn't trade it."

"She's so beautiful. Just like you were."

Myra reached for her daughter's hand and squeezed. She loved her children, but lately, she felt twinges of guilt for devoting her time to waiting on Jack. There were no further developments on Kelani or even a glimmer of hope. From the police investigation, they knew she hadn't boarded a plane, but had vanished just like Jack. Still, it rekindled the embers of hope.

"So, what happened with Brody? Tell me everything."

"He quit. You heard, I'm sure, that Tessa and Brody reconciled. But bitch that she is, she implicated Jack in some sort of scheme to sabotage her marriage to Brody."

"Let's not call her names. I don't like her either, but let's not. I just can't believe Jack would stoop to that. It does explain the reason why Jack moved away from us. Tessa's devious, but I guess so is Jack. I'm surprised to find myself admitting that aloud."

"I had no idea he hated her as much."

"I bet he's got his reasons, and I hope to hear them one day. But it seems so unlike Jack."

"Well, Tessa should have been upfront about her past. I'm fairly certain Brody could have handled the truth. Or deserved the truth."

"A lie spun out of control. There are so many layers to Tessa's life I still can't fathom."

"And that Brody has chosen her over us. We've been like a second family to him for as long as I can remember. He was like a brother."

"Love. We'll never understand what motivates a person in love."

"Or hate."

Myra kissed the tender violet eyelids of the sleeping baby. The revelation that Jack hired a professional to trick Tessa into some sort of tryst came as a shock. Could Jack have been capable of something else underhanded they didn't know about? Did it have any bearing on him vanishing like that? Myra didn't allow those thoughts to fester for long. If Jack did what he did to separate Brody from Tessa, he had to have had a valid reason.

"Thanks for these adorable outfits."

Stacy folded the gifts Myra picked up. She had already vowed to spoil her granddaughter with love and gifts. And by the looks of the baby contently sleeping in her arms, it wouldn't be difficult to uphold.

"So, want to know more gossip?"

Stacy had a way of making her eyes tease, and from the looks of her playful grin, the gossip involved her other brother.

"Tell."

"Apparently, my little brother has a crush on some un-named beauty from an island in the Pacific."

"That I can believe. Wait until you meet her. She's a beauty. But what is the rumor mill churning?"

"Only that he has a guest flying out next weekend. He's keeping it quiet because he feels a bit guilty. You know."

"Ooh. Can't wait to tell Cindy and Kai what their niece is up to. But good for them. I've never seen Michael so smitten with one glance."

"Love at first sight. It happens to the best of us. I mean, look at you and the little critter in your arms. One look and you were a goner."

"True. Grandmas have a soft spot and are easily persuaded by tiny fingers and toes."

"Moms too! Despite the hell of being pregnant, and all its horrible side effects, I wouldn't give her away for a million bucks."

"If you change your mind, I'm always free. I couldn't have done it without my mother."

"Mom? We'll find Jack. I just wanted to tell you again that I understand what unconditional love means. Though it isn't strictly unconditional, there are many conditions involved."

"I can't explain it, but I know Jack is alive. Just as I know you are, and Michael. I feel his heartbeat, and I get some of his messages."

Stacy nodded. She slipped a sheer cover-up over her already slimming body, but the scar smiling up from the bikini line was still too raw for pool water. But Stacy intended to make the best of her time in Hawaii with her mother. She smiled.

"Let's go and find Jack. He's out there."

Stacy assumed that clues to Jack's disappearance were clearly spelled out like an enormous SOS for anyone to see. She had a hunch that they lay in the open expanse of the beach, that she could just harvest them. Myra snuggled the baby into the body sling and kissed her tender head. Stacy wasn't present when they scoured the hotel grounds from top to bottom. The long stretch of beach. But it was refreshing that Stacy had her mind focused on finding her brother as if it were a game of hide-and-seek.

Kai arranged for them to have armbands and that they were allowed access to the hotel. That anything was available to them. In the shuttle Kai sent over, Myra watched her daughter's profile. Same nose and chin as Jack's, but the rest of the resemblance belonged to the lineage of Spencers. Stacy's face was oval, not heart-shaped like Jack's. Stacy wanted to investigate the scene, to get a better feel of the hopeless situation. She was confident the clues were in abundance. When the shuttle turned under the hotel portico, Myra's heart stopped.

In the parking lot, she saw the man with the shoes. He was boarding the bus employees used. He stood out. It wasn't his unattractive facial features that made her gasp, but the shoes.

Before she could get the driver to come for a full stop, the full bus merged with traffic.

"That bus!"

"Madam? What bus?"

Myra pointed frantically while staring at the backside of the bus. She zeroed in on the number 0020, marking the yellow stripe.

"Where does it go?"

"Not sure what you mean. It goes to the bus terminal eventually, but probably makes ten or more stops along the way. But I can drive you wherever you need to go."

He smiled at Myra, proud of his job to chauffeur her and her handsome daughter around. He heard they were good tippers.

"Can you follow the bus?"

Myra couldn't contain the urgency in her voice. She couldn't keep the panic from trembling in her hands. She was drowning below the surface of an irrefutable clue.

"Sure. I just need to call it in."

"Fuck calling it in. Follow the damn fucking bus!"

Myra leaned back. The bus was slowly weaving in and out of traffic and out of sight. While the driver swung back out onto the road, she heard the crackling of the radio come on.

"Mom? What is it? You look like you just saw a ghost. It wasn't Jack, was it?"

Jack. No, it wasn't Jack. But the forces of nature had timed her passing the same man with the unmistakable shoes twice. Jack's shoes. She'd stake her life on it that they were and that the despicable man knew something about Jack she needed to know.

"I just saw a man that might know something about our Jack. I have to track him down."

"That's amazing. We have something to go on. Drive faster!" Stacy tapped the driver on the shoulder. "We're gonna find Jack."

Myra exhaled and forced a smile on her lips, she didn't say that lately the messages from Jack were getting fainter, but an unequivocal code kept her motivated. She still received the signal: Jack was alive. She didn't dare think Jack was running out of time. The man with the shoes, he was a vital link.

PART 8

HOMECOMING

Chapter 1

Careful What You Wish For

They all lay on their backs and looked up at the night sky. A million stars winked down on them. Next to them, the ocean heaved softly on the current. Once in a while, something large bumped the raft. They had seen a pod of whales a day ago, and the sight always revived their spirits, even if they were dangerous.

Mark hadn't mentioned leaving again and seemed more jovial. Trish worked her wonders in her makeshift kitchen, and everyone gorged on mahi-mahi ceviche with pineapple and orange chutney. She really did know her way around food. Trish had a dream of one day opening a small and intimate restaurant. Not the sort that listed a hundred items on their menu but more like Mama's Kitchen Table that offered two or three dishes. A meal always finished with coffee, dessert, and conversation.

"That is the tenth plane or satellite tonight."

"Seven shooting stars. Those alone should have the magic to get us home."

"You seen that thing again, Mark?"

"What thing?"

"You know that thing you thought was a canoe or a boat or something big?"

"No. Must have been an optical illusion."

"Well, if we ever get out of here, I want us all to promise to stay in touch."

"Promise."

Rose knew promises were easy to make. Back in the real world, although their world certainly had an authentic feel to it, they'd have difficulty finding common ground with others. It wasn't unlike a prisoner being released back into a society that had moved on. A man returning from the moon.

"I'm buying a house right next to yours. So that you can fix whatever I need fixing."

Rose teased Ron. She twisted her face to see him laugh.

"Anytime, dear. But just so you know, I'll probably drop off whatever critters I'll rescue."

"We'll make a good team then."

While they thought everyone was asleep, Rose had over-heard Trish and Ron talk at low volume while everyone napped or pretended to nap. Trish spoke of buying a small house, a Cape Cod decked out with a mansard roofline and winking windows. She had dreams of filling it with refurbished antiques she'd scour the small-town markets for. Ron said he wanted a dog. Trish said she wanted one too. Ron said he wanted a Labrador, and Trish added she'd like a medium-sized mutt.

"I think my wife won't mind. I believe she'll be happy that I'm alive and found someone."

"You still worry about the children?" Trish turned her face sideways to catch his answer.

"Always. Part of being a parent."

"I hope they'll like me. No matter how our lives turn out."

"They will."

"Regardless, it will be strange."

"I can't wait to see my gravestone. Not too many people get the chance to read the inscription. Unless they pre-ordered it."

"That's just morbid." Trish teased but couldn't stop herself from smiling.

"Of course, not providing them with a body must have made it harder to move on. No closure. You'd think that it would ultimately be better to still cling to hope?" Ron laced his fingers into Trish's after he wiped a tear from his eyes.

Rose found it touching that their dreams were so simple and that they still, after all they had endured, found the strength to put others before their own needs. They also went through the list of what they'd eat first, what they wanted to do first.

"I crave Shepherd's pie and a cold crisp lager." Ron's only wish.

"Pizza and glass of red wine. Malbec or Merlot. A day at the spa is in order, I should think. A haircut, manicure and trimming the unmentionables, a walk in the park with mother."

"I can't wait to hear Mozart, Beethoven. Anything but the rushing noise of the waves."

"Something to dance to. Like a sultry salsa with the man of my dreams in my arms."

"He has two left feet."

"He can stand still. I'll do the dancing."

Rose felt no shame in listening in on their dreams. Living in such close proximity, they forfeited their claims to any privacy. It wasn't something anyone could argue. Rose liked their dreams, and she could picture Trish with a cute bob, just long enough to brush a strand behind her ears while she walked among oaks, maples, and evergreens in the park holding on to the arm of her mother whom Rose imagined as slightly frail and stooped. She didn't dare consider that Trish's mother had died. Thoughts like that were simply too cruel. Rose also pictured Ron up on a ladder, hanging Christmas lights from the eaves and Trish bringing him a cup of hot cocoa. They'd be the sort of couple who did things for each other. She pictured Trish writing little notes to put in Ron's stocking. Sexy hints at what racy outfit she'd wear for him on what day. Ron would scour the local markets for dainty tables and cubby hole desks and refurbish them for Trish. He'd find vintage jewelry, ornaments, and trinkets. There'd be a fire glowing in the potbelly stove, their dogs would sprawl out on the old carpet while chasing rabbits in their sleep.

But Rose needed to construct her own version. She substituted Mark in for Ron and herself in Trish's role, but she couldn't get past the image of Mark being in the fantasy with her. There was always another figure walking toward her in the fantasy. A character who would send Mark on his way. A figure who would change her life forever.

They floated on the lazy current for five days. Gradually the trash around them took on a familiarity signifying they were nearly back to where they started.

"If the yacht is still afloat, I'll look at her in earnest and see what we can salvage." Ron turned to face Mark; he knew the question always simmered on Mark's mind.

"I'm afraid we'll have to think beyond the yacht and this raft. I'm not sounding ungrateful, Ron. But this raft we're floating on is too cumbersome. We need something more aerodynamic."

"I'm open to suggestions. I know this is important to you. It is to all of us," Ron hauled a fish aboard.

"I know you think this is crazy, but if we had something small, but reliable, I think I could make it to Mexico. California.

I'm thinking of building something agile and making a trailer for it to haul supplies."

"Maybe it would work. But how would you ever find us again?"

"Come hell or high water, I swear I would. But you'd have to promise to stay on the island until I come for you."

"I'll think it through. How's that? I know one man I would trust, it's you, Mark."

Rose listened in on their conversation and she knew, Ron did what he could to ensure that those goals that were even remotely within reach of his power, he'd see them through. Honest to a fault. But Mark never mentioned that he intended on bringing her. Had he changed his mind? Or was it that he knew Ron would talk them out of it.

"What's that?"

Rose stood and pointed. They were within several hundred yards of the first island. Ron raised himself to his knees, then stood too. He shielded his eyes from the glare and followed Rose's pointing finger. Mark came closer too. They all saw the same thing.

Chapter 2

Heaven or Hell: You Choose.

Was that a bare foot poking him? Were those voices asking him to wake up? Jack tried. But his eyes refused to open, they were sealed shut with the goop of feverish nightmares. And speaking, well, he didn't have the energy to answer his own questions. He hadn't moved in days and his limbs were cemented into a fixed position. There had been so many moments when he wished for death to come swiftly despite that annoying pipsqueak voice driving him to fight back.

"You think he's alive?"

"God, he stinks."

"Looks like his bowels went on him."

"I don't think he's gonna make it."

The canoe rocked with a jolt under the pressure of someone else boarding the narrow space behind him. Jack's eyes fluttered open enough to see the familiar glint of the sun. He despised the sun and hated the ocean. He hated fish and hated the night. He'd rather go blind than see the never-ending blue again. Did he already say he hated fish? But he loved the light touch of the gentle fingers caressing his brow and peeling his eyelid open.

"He wrote his last testament. Jack Spencer, 2018."

"If he survives, then he's one lucky man."

"I'm not going to give up on you, Jack Spencer. Or whatever your name is."

A soft voice, warm breath, caressed his ear. He smelled oranges and sweat, and he tried to focus on the glimpses of her chocolate skin. He loved hearing a voice whisper his name. Jack. If he could have, he would have risen from his canoe grave and shouted his name to the world. "I'm Jack Spencer! I'm alive!"

"Rose. He's too far gone. He might carry disease."

"Get me some drinking water."

"How do you think he got here in his catatonic state? That canoe looks Hawaiian."

"What's left of the flag is."

"Drink."

Jack partly opened his mouth but didn't have the strength to suckle and swallow. Delicious water trickled out the side of his mouth.

"Get me something to prop him up."

That same gentle hand lifted his heavy head. In the last few days, it gained a ton of weight. All muscle tissue supporting it had dissolved, and his head wobbled uncontrollably from side to side. As if hunger had massacred his body and feasted on what little fat and muscle remained on his frame.

The scent of sweat, oranges, and pineapple wafted all around him and mingled with something not as pleasant. His own stink. If he weren't so weak, he'd be embarrassed by his condition. Whenever his eyes fluttered open enough, he saw her smile; surely that of an angel. He tried to speak, nothing but a groan escaped from his parched throat.

"Don't talk. Just rest and try to drink."

Jack wanted to drink. If he had the energy, thirst would have driven him the rest of the way, and he'd have crossed over to madness. His tongue moved with the agility of a slug. While she nursed him, Jack wanted to see her again, but his eyes denied him the pleasure. Whenever he glimpsed something of her, he noticed the familiar glow on her skin, just like his mother's. Like someone who bathed in tubs of amber.

"Trish. Get me a sponge. I'll try getting water into him that way."

"We've got to get him off this canoe. He's sitting in his own poop."

It was comforting that the person didn't demean him and say shit. His own shit.

"Get that door we found the other day. We'll use it as a stretcher to get him off the canoe."

A chorus of voices. Drifting in and out, he heard a melody he had missed so much. The boat rocked again. Hands gripped him firmly and the worst pain since he smashed his fingers while opening the coconut ripped through his body as if savages were tearing him from limb to limb. He passed out.

Once the agony subsided, he woke and found himself on something more comfortable than the cramped floor of the canoe. Gentle hands tugged him out of his trousers and wrestled him from his shirt. Warm water bathed him, yet he shivered uncontrollably.

The scent of citrus was everywhere. He must have made it back to one of the Hawaiian Islands. Any moment they'd call his mother. She would send a boat, an ambulance to whisk him away. All those voices, maybe the Coast Guard was already here. Fragments of conversation concerning him tuned in and out on a frequency he couldn't dial in. *The likelihood of someone surviving …* and *true but look at us …* and *if that canoe got him from Hawaii to here …* the tone suggested concern over the condition he was in; as if he'd done something wrong. Jack didn't want to disappoint anyone least of all the voice telling him over and over, *hang on, Jack. Don't give up on me now … just fight a little bit longer. Okay, Jack.*

He sensed rather than saw the two women hovering next to him. Nurses. He could feel the tenderness of their touch while they washed him, and sponge-fed him water mixed with bitter orange.

Although he was no longer on the canoe, Jack was drifting on the fragile currents of consciousness. Each time he woke, confusion misplaced him again. Was this a bad dream or a good dream? The excruciating pain invading every fiber of his body decided for him and made him suspicious of being alive. One minute he was feverish and then—snap, freezing to death. His lips burned like the coals of hell, and his open sores stung like an angry nest of hornets. Yet, he hadn't felt so good in days.

"Hang on, dear." A warm hand was cupping his. "Can you say your name, Jack?"

He tried to nod, but his neck was permanently fused into a crook. He lost count how often he passed out, but each time he woke, they were still there. He felt dry and clean and relieved that he hadn't dreamed of their voices. He could hear them and feel them move around him.

"I can't believe we found those crates of oranges and pineapple. Like this Jack here, they must have drifted away from Hawaii."

"Might just save his life." The soft voice of the woman said. "If I can get him to swallow."

"He might still die. Don't get too attached."

"Attached? You think you can take care of a person and not get attached?"

"Don't get bent out of shape, Rose. You know nothing about him. He could be a criminal."

"Based on what? Mark, you're an ass. How can I not care about a man on the brink of death and do everything to save him?"

"Well, just because he's the same skin color as you doesn't make him a saint."

"You're insane. Just because he's black has nothing to do with it. He's a person. Someone probably loves him and is worried sick."

"Yeah. I thought so. And I guess it answers my question about you coming with me."

Jack felt movement, someone was walking away from him, but the warm and gentle hand remained on his. He could feel himself smiling. She had a name—Rose.

When he woke later, Jack remembered segments from his dream state and that they told him he was in the patch. The voices must have confused the words patch and Pacific. They said someplace south of Hawaii and west of California. The voices went further and said he had landed on their island. Not a real island, a deeper voice corrected, but a place they made from the trash trapped within the endless circle of the gyre. "Do you understand English? What we're telling you?"

Jack nodded. He could feel his face go through the motion of nodding. Yet what they were suggesting seemed surreal as if he had landed on the pages of a fictional novel.

"We, and you, are lucky to be alive."

"Did you come from Hawaii?"

Jack nodded, pretending to understand what the man with the bad cut-off shorts was trying so hard to extract from him.

"Just keep talking to him. I can tell he's listening."

"Do you remember when you went into the water? Anything at all? Like what island?"

"If you drifted here from Hawaii, then you're a lucky son of a bitch to be alive."

"Do you remember anything at all?"

Jack watched the footage of his voyage. He saw himself as if he were the star of the show. There was a cast of others in the background continually taking the stage: his mother, a beautiful woman on the stairway, Tessa. And then his body spasmed violently. He found himself gripping something solid and warm. An arm perhaps leading him deeper into the thickening fog. A coconut on the beach. Laughter. Darkness. Who was laughing? Cigarette smoke. And them.

"Brody! Brody! Get away from them. They're bad! They're the guys who shoved me into the canoe and sent me off. Brody? Why are you talking to them, and why are you pointing at me? Brody!" His words came back to him as if in his waking reality they were perpetually suspended.

"He's having another nightmare. Should we wake him?"

"Yes. Do it gently. He's already been to the gates of hell. Bring him back."

"Jack. Time to wake up." A soft voice said. Gentle hands shifted his body upward.

"Drink. You need to build up your strength."

He forced his eyes open and gazed into the beautiful, almond-shaped eyes of his mother. Only it wasn't his mother. This woman hid beneath volumes of wild corkscrew hair, which tumbled in giant clumps over her shoulders. He saw her halo through the sunshine of curls, and she cast a protective shadow over him. Her soft hands stroked his face tenderly.

Yet, it was all a blur. Nothing seemed real, yet Jack hoped it was. What seemed like hours later, Jack catapulted up and then fell back again. In his continuing nightmare, the ocean swallowed his canoe, and he couldn't save Brody. The image of Brody standing in the garden and handing something to the two goons was clearly framed in his mind. Although he tried,

Jack had no way of proving if it was an accurate portrait or an abstract created in his feverish state.

"Mark. Thanks for cleaning the canoe. It's a sturdy little unit. "I've come to tell you lunch is ready. Trish cooked rice and mahi. We got to get some meat on that guy."

"Tough guy, whoever this Jack Spencer is."

"Looks like he's one of us now."

"Did you see this? It has a secret compartment. It's where Jack kept all his survival gear."

"Kilo. What a weird name for a canoe."

Jack listened to the voices with his eyes closed while they discussed his beloved Kilo. Until now, he wasn't sure it had survived. Kilo wasn't a weird name. It meant friend and savior, at least to Jack. Whatever happened next, he'd never give up the canoe. If he were rescued, he'd have it restored and mounted on a wall as a monument to his survival. Or was that fair? Maybe Kilo loved being on the ocean. That being a canoe was its purpose. Of course, Jack debated, Kilo had an owner. Someone who probably appreciated it for its agility.

On his good days out on the ocean, he made himself a promise to track down the person who owned Kilo. He wanted to thank them, but he'd never have the heart to return it. The canoe signified what was truly important in life: a place to belong to.

To pass the afternoons and nights, he often visualized the person he imagined would own a canoe like Kilo. Probably a local who knew the ins and outs of being on the open waters. Someone who could read the surf and the sky. A man who could navigate by the stars and survive just about anything. Jack wasn't the sort of person who could perform any of the most basic survival skills. He had failed, miserably, yet he clung to life even when he begged God, the sky guy, and the universe for mercy. He wanted his suffering to end not extended.

While he tried to make sense of the dreams, and where he was, that gentle hand reached for his and stroked his fingers. The soft sound of humming soothed Jack's nightmares away. He became aware he was comfortable for the first time in weeks and warm, and miraculously dry. The hand holding his soothed his agitation and was smaller. To feel the touch of another human felt alien; yet so welcome. More importantly, the voice called him Jack. He heard it whispered a hundred times: Jack-Jack-Jack. Just like he had carved onto the canoe. He was alive.

In the darkness, he couldn't see a face, but he knew someone was always watching him and keeping him safe. Even though it wasn't his mother, he knew she had something to do with his survival. Hers had been the voice that begged him to hang on. Her voice had been the loudest. Jack allowed the spell of the humming to comfort him when he felt secure enough, he dozed.

A dream that days or weeks ago had been a devastating reality rekindled itself while he slept. Jack couldn't say with any certainty that he had seen what he thought he had seen. But an enormous white blur had taken shape on the horizon. A recognizable mass. At first, he assumed his eyes were playing tricks, a cloud formation, but there it was. A giant cruise ship plodding along on her pleasure voyage and not a phantom. Balancing carefully, he had raised himself to stand, his frantic waving rocked the canoe beneath him. He grabbed for the flag and unfurled it in the wind. If anyone was looking, Jack was so sure they'd see him fly the flag.

"Over here!" He hollered.

Jack waited for a sign that someone heard or saw him. He could make out a million of its winking portals, and a plume of faint smoke puffed along the blue sky. Jack envisioned a thousand people staring out at the ocean at him.

"Help! I'm Jack Spencer!" He strained his vocal cords and raised himself on tiptoes. It hurt just to stand. "Over here! Someone!"

Jack pictured a person leaning on the railing of the white lumbering beast. They'd just had brunch and were contemplating life and how awful it would be to be adrift. The ocean's power humbled them and its beauty mesmerized them for a moment.

With a little luck, they'd spot him. Whoever was staring at the waves was probably hoping to catch a glimpse of an elusive whale, dolphin, turtle, or porpoise. Wouldn't they be surprised to see him? The brochure in their hand spelled out their options, and they'd plan their next adventure on the ship. Jack knew he was competing with the lure of the buffet dining hall, the thrill of the casino, the deck chairs by the aquamarine pool. No one on board gave a rat's ass about Jack Spencer. They had never heard of him. They had no idea that his mother was desperate to find him. They had no idea that Jack Spencer was desperate to survive.

He waved the unfurled the Hawaiian flag into the breeze, straining to stand taller. Slowly, and yet surprisingly quick, the giant white ship vanished from his field of vision. Disappointment buckled his knees, and he cried soul-wrenching sobs into the flag.

Hope was a strange companion, a relentless one and encouraged Jack to imagine the ship tooting its horn to signal it would come back for him. But the waves stole his message, they weren't in the delivery business. Devastated, Jack had considered his options. He wasn't the sort of person who could pack it in and give up without a fight. If he were going to go down, he'd fight with all his might. He'd even barter his soul to the devil if only the devil offered him a trade. It didn't have to be fair either. He had to survive for his mother.

And then he ate the last of the fish.

Epilogue

Brody set the empty crystal tumbler on his glass desk. His smeared lip and fingerprints diminished the intricate Heritage Waterford design but not the sunlight playing in the pinwheels. There were six, but one had fallen from his clasp a week ago and smashed into a million glittering pieces, not unlike his life. They were a lavish wedding shower gift from the Spencers before everything went sideways.

At eight o'clock in the morning, he was refueling on his second shot of whiskey—the breakfast of champions. But nothing had been the same since the impossible news of a man surviving in the Pacific made his heart, nearly, come out his throat. Only whiskey had the power to pass the obstruction in this throat without returning on the bitter taste of bile. So much for *fake news*, Brody joked with himself. Anything to make light of the inevitable.

With the click of his remote, he clicked through the news channels one by one. The headlines were the same; the footage shot from various angles depicted the same scenario. Not even the president could compete.

A close-up of the gaunt man, his Hawaiian canoe, and the endless waiting for vital information had consumed Brody for a week when his nightmare landed and crawled ashore. There was footage of that too, shot with the camera phone by a man walking his dog.

A man, miraculously, drifted ashore in Mexico, just north of Ensenada. Relief that it wasn't Jack kick-started his heart again. Was it possible that Jack had survived his ordeal too? Experts randomly interviewed on the topic reassured him: it wasn't possible.

Of course, an enthusiastic team of journalists dug deeper and fought back with the conflicting opinions that it was possible. It was a matter of elements and circumstances. They came up with an extensive list of the Who's Who of drifters that sucker-punched Brody in the gut. That damned Mexican, who set a record for being adrift the longest, and, depending on whose version a person chose to believe, survived for 438 days — drinking urine and blood. And Steven Callahan, who made a career as an expert after surviving for 76 God-forsaken days on a raft that wasn't built to stay intact but did, and lived to tell the harrowing tale of what it took, with considerable effort, to stay alive and afloat.

Brody contemplated filling his glass a third time. It was becoming a ritual. What Brody detested more than anything: there were no definitive answers. News media had the enviable power of producing doubters in the same breath as believers, using nothing but a regurgitated piece of news to ensnare them either way.

Jack Spencer was still missing. His best friend since kindergarten and betrayer of the ultimate trust. All for a quick fuck! If Jack had been honest and confessed, Brody was sure they could have survived the infraction and laughed about it. Tessa was dispensable. And Brody knew Jack better than anyone. Twenty-eight years of friendship gave him an insight into Jack that his mother would be envious of. And like Myra, he had loved Jack despite his flaws too. But, there it was—one glaring flaw. Jack had made a fool out of him. And their friendship didn't have an escape clause. In the end, Jack's weakness brought him down. His adulterous affair with Tessa was proof that he didn't have an ounce of decency or discipline. It was the latter that served as a nail in Jack's water coffin.

Brody muted the volume of the television despite the images that continued to haunt him. He had watched repeatedly and could recite the banter verbatim and fake the monologue if he had to. Despite the odds, Brody clung to one quote. *"All elements have to come into play for someone to survive as a castaway as long as ..."* Of course, the expert didn't name Jack Spencer.

For a week, the piecemeal footage of Mark Spelling's harrowing experience consumed every fiber in Brody's thoughts, and his mind substituted Jack into Mark's predicament, and he didn't like the odds.

"It's been confirmed, five more survivors are expected to be alive and floating in a nest of garbage in the Pacific."

"Confirmed my ass," Brody's dry Adam's apple bobbed. It was becoming more difficult to breathe and swallow. The anchor pointed to a map on the screen—a mark someplace off the Mexican Baja. Pictures of the five possible survivors cruelly fed the greedy news banner ticking along the bottom of the screen. Categorized as possible but not confirmed.

"This area, known as the Pacific Garbage Patch, experts predict, is the size of Texas and is holding them hostage. Some argue the area is even more extensive and growing daily. Evidence suggests, such gyres are collecting monumental amounts of trash." A prompter pointed to the Pacific, the Atlantic, and the Indian Ocean with the thud of a high school geography lesson.

After a three-minute commercial, a fresh-faced reporter held up an intricately carved oar. Filmed while standing on the shore, he spoke to the camera. *"Mark Spelling suggests that this oar, which experts have traced to California, was among the trash he and his shipwreck mates sorted through daily. The good news in this tragedy, however, is a double-edged sword. The garbage that is killing the ocean and marine life is also what saved Mark and his mates."*

"La-de-fucking-da! Five fucking people in trade for a gazillion dead fish and millions of harmed whales." Brody grunted. That was another thing he loved about the media. It no longer mattered if the facts aligned if they were first to broadcast.

"If, and it is a big if, Mr. Spellings' remarkable tale is accurate, then five lives might have been spared because of the excess trash."

Footage of Mark's gaunt body took up residence in the corner of the screen again. As if there was still a person on the planet that hadn't seen it ten times over.

"A massive recovery expedition is en route."

A flotilla of rescue ships leaving ports along the West Coast dotted the blue Pacific, their sails set and engines gunned. Brody mentally yelled at the television. "A million kids are starving in Africa! What about them?"

"Although the Coast Guard is skeptical of a successful mission, they won't endorse private vessels attempting a risky rescue op." An inserted picture of a Coast Guard vessel reminded the audience that they had the latest equipment at their disposal, but emotionally, this was bigger than anything they'd ever attempted. The anchor drove the point home. *"We've interviewed a dozen sea captains who unanimously claim, "we've no other choice. Lives depend on it."*

Brody knew the list of names off by heart, Ron, Rose, Ted, Amanda, and Trish. Missing Person's hotlines couldn't cope with the increased demands of finding loved ones presumed missing on the ocean. Families overlooked that one detail, that Mark survived his ordeal on the Pacific; and not in the Atlantic.

But Mark Spelling changed the rules of the game and became a spokesperson for hope's revival.

The anchor went to a shot of the endless blue ocean and a trajectory map of currents. Leeway. Improbability. *A person can survive three days without water.* Brody feared that it was a myth already dispelled by an Austrian. *Surviving for 30 hours or longer after exposure to hypothermia,* Brody scoffed at the idea that fat people stood a better chance. "Too bad for you, Jack. Skinny bugger." *Thirty days without food,* a contested average. The endless stats both mesmerized Brody and made him nauseous. Yet Mark didn't claim any of those numbers. He stood tall as the poster boy—anything is possible. Brody had watched interview after interview, in which Mark explained, *"I set out on the canoe alone because I believed my chances of reaching land were better."*

So, Mark was a gambler. A screenshot of Mark, propped up on a hospital bed hooked to hydrating IV fluids, subbed in for the screenshot of the endless ocean.

"How is it possible you survived? What was your darkest moment?" A microphone, shoved into Mark's emaciated face, waited to record the answer for all eternity.

"A miracle. The will to live. I just kept paddling, knowing that sooner or later I would hit land. I had water, I fished, and I don't mind saying, I'm relentless. It's why I had to risk it."

In an interview with 60 Minutes, Mark hinted that life on the plastic island had become as routine as walking down the street. Only their street was a woven trail of plastic. *"But I owe my life to Ron. I should say we survived because of him."*

Then an uncouth question lobbed as a bomb exposed all the possibilities again. Brody's breath came in faster than he thought was healthy. He broke out in a sweat when he heard the answer to the question, *"Where did you say the canoe you used came from?"*

"Are you still watching that horrible footage?" Tessa asked.

Brody nodded. When he heard Tessa come out of the ensuite, he slid his glass behind the stack of documents on his desk. She didn't need to know everything. Reconciling with Tessa had been a hard bargain he made with himself, but the need to bury his motive overruled hate. What Tessa had done to him was many things: disgusting, predictable, selfish, slutish. What Jack did to him was unforgivable. But, he had paid to have the evidence on film. Besides, there was enough time to deal with Tessa and make her suffer. Revenge was a game he was good at playing. His winning strategy was patience.

"Did you hear about Myra?" Tessa swung her elegant leg over the other when she sat on the corner of the sofa in the den. The short hem of her skirt rode up her shapely thigh.

"No. I'm obviously out of the loop. And you forget, I don't follow gossip."

Brody felt the resurgence of doubts regarding the Spencers, and despite massaging his chest muscles, it burned. They had always treated him like a son, and John Spencer had been his role model. There was a time when he even had a house key and a Christmas to remember when he walked in on Jack and Tessa, two days after he had proposed to Tessa. Too bad, Jack Spencer didn't have the same rudimentary ethics as his parents.

"I was on Stacy's Facebook. She's still in Hawaii with Myra. They arrested some guy who stole Jack's shoes. Myra recognized them on the guy wearing them. You know the Gucci shoes I insisted you all wear for the wedding?"

"What? When?" Brody composed himself. "Might be a coincidence."

"I doubt that. But look. Stacy posted this late last night. There's an up-close photo of the creep." Tessa held up her phone, open to her Facebook page.

Brody hired Bruce on the recommendation of his PI. The man said Bruce came highly recommended and wouldn't have reservations about the job Brody needed to be carried out.

"Can you believe it? He worked at the hotel. What a creep!"

"What about real news? Something not fabricated by social media?"

"Here. I've not confirmed it, but there's a quote from that awful officer, Malone what's his face, *"We've confirmed that the suspect in custody is tied to the disappearance of John Spencer Junior. On a search of his house, we discovered another missing person. Kelani ... missing for a week. Sequestered against her will by Mr. Bruce Meyers, Ms. Kelani was the last known person to see Jack Spencer alive."*

"Not sure what all the fuss is about? She's not that pretty." Tessa quickly swiped sideways with her manicured finger. And there she was. Kelani, wearing an elegant evening gown, not unlike the mermaid dress Brody remembered charged to his credit card. It said she was an aspiring part-time model and professional dancer. Kelani was reported missing by her brother a week ago.

"Look, babe. I gotta run, or I'll be late. I assume you're still working from home?"

"Yeah. The office is still being painted. Bye." Brody couldn't wait for Tessa to leave, and as soon as she did, he refilled his glass.

He googled the latest news from Hawaii and, at a glance, sorted through the headlines: surf's up, homicides, on trial, 100-year old Marathoner dies, and there was a picture of Myra Spencer standing next to Officer Malone. Myra was wearing something he hadn't seen for some time, a brilliant and hopeful smile. Brody didn't recognize the man standing at her elbow, nor the woman holding Stacy's baby. At a glance, they looked like a family coming together by a binding force. Maybe he should have worked harder on his relationship with Stacy; only then, he wasn't ready to commit. Brody weeded through website after website and found one explanation. Kai Hale and his wife Cindy had become intimate friends of Myra. Kai owned the canoe presumed Jack sailed into the sunrise on, and it looked remarkably like the canoe Mark had used. When he looked up, the news feed wrapped up Brody's biggest fear and gift wrapped the bundle of news. Mark omitted crucial information. There was a sixth person on the island. On the big screen, Brody came face to face with Jack Spencer.

"He was half-dead when we found him. Yes, that could be him." Mark nodded when an extended hand shoved a photograph under his nose.

Brody swiveled in the chair and stared out the window; there wasn't much to see but a row of bricks and a shuttered window. In the distance, a siren wailed. A dime a dozen, but how long before they came for him?

Brody loosened his tie, rose and shut the door of the den, and tested the door handle. Would it hold his weight?

Acknowledgments

I'm grateful to Stevan V. Nikolic at Adelaide Books for choosing to publish my novel, *The Lucky Man, An Act of Malice*, for his spring 2021 collection. Venues like Adelaide Books are a rare and kind retreat for authors. Thanks to Heidi Philips and Georgina Kolm for reading the rough draft. Dr. Sylvia Earle and her relentless dedication to the marine world and sharing her discoveries.

About the Author

Monika R. Martyn immigrated from Austria to Canada as a teen. Determined to succeed in the cosmetic industry, she attended Seneca College in Toronto, then enjoyed a successful career with Loblaw Ltd, rising from cosmetician to Category Manager under the Westfair banner, managing the cosmetic buying department for western Canada. Since retiring young, she has lived in Panama, Colombia, and Mexico, as well as Europe. She enjoys a nomadic and minimalist lifestyle with her husband. Her greatest influences are her parents, notably her mother. In college, she discovered a love for classic literature and remains an ardent Jane Austen reader. If asked to provide a list of modern authors she'd like to aspire to, that list would include Anita Shreve, Carol Shields, Judy Blunt, Bryce Courtenay, John Irving, and Henning Mankell.

She is passionate about animals, the oceans, displaced people, women's rights and issues, the environment, and truth if there is any left to discover. When she is not writing, she must be sleeping.

Made in the USA
Monee, IL
17 May 2021